What People Are Saying
About *Ravenous* . . .

"As the sequel to the masterpiece *Insatiable, Ravenous* is an invaluable gift to any teenager, adult or parent who may be struggling with an eating disorder. The novel is an exemplary addition to the literature currently available portraying the trials and tribulations of young adults dealing with eating disorders. The stories depicted in this book are compassionate, honest and extremely reflective, fascinating and engaging. *Ravenous* is an unusually well-written, extraordinary achievement. One of the best eating-disorder novels I have ever had the privilege of reading. Bravo!"

—Johanna S. Kandel
founder, The Alliance for Eating Disorders Awareness

"*Ravenous* is a wonderful book!!! Eve Eliot did an excellent job of showing what life is like as you are on the path of recovery from an eating disorder. As someone who suffered from an eating disorder as a young teen, I am glad to see books out there that show the truth on how recovery is more than just eating or not bingeing and purging. It also showed how life for a teen is when it comes to love and losing the one love you so truly want. The book was awesome."

—K. M. Patzman
founder, *www.palebluetears.com*

"*Ravenous* offers information that every boy and girl in their teenage years should have. Fortunately, Eve Eliot's compelling novel makes it likely that teens will absorb that information. My work with teenagers and the long-perceived lack of information on topics such as eating disorders, body image and other pressing problems suggest to me that *Ravenous* will be a winner. The real winners, though, will be teenagers themselves—they need a book like this!"

—**Robin Shepard**
learning specialist, New York City

Ravenous

The Stirring Tale of Teen Love, Loss and Courage

EVE ELIOT

The Sequel to *Insatiable*

Health Communications, Inc.
Deerfield Beach, Florida

www.bcibooks.com

Library of Congress Cataloging-in-Publication Data

Eliot, Eve, date.
    Ravenous : the stirring tale of teen love, loss, and courage / Eve Eliot.
      p. cm.
    Sequel to: Insatiable.
    ISBN-13: 978-0-7573-0005-9 (trade paper)
    ISBN-10: 0-7573-0005-7 (trade paper)
    1. Eating disorders in adolescence.   2. Eating disorders—Patients.
3. Teenagers—Mental health.   4. Body image.   I. Eliot, Eve, date.
Insatiable.   II. Title.

RJ506.E18 E446 2002
616.85'26'00835—dc21

                                             2002022105

Publisher: Health Communications, Inc.
             3201 S.W. 15th Street
             Deerfield Beach, FL 33442-8190

R-04-07

Cover and inside book design by Lawna Patterson Oldfield
Front cover photo ©PhotoDisc
Author photo by James Del Grosso

Dedicated,
with love and thanks,
to all my clients, past and present.

RAVENOUS

When Daryl phoned Phoebe she was standing on her head, waiting for his call. She had been practicing yoga ever since Hannah had taken her to a class, and she loved it. She could easily resist cookies when she was standing on her head. Upside-down, time was suspended, and she felt weightless, or in outer space, and even gingersnaps lost their gravitational pull.

"Hey, Morgenstern! How are you?" the now-upright Phoebe said when she heard Daryl's voice, the voice she entirely loved, the voice she hardly ever stopped hearing in her head, the voice that belonged to the boy who still belonged to the adorable, chubby Gabriella. Gabby. That lucky girl.

"Good," replied Daryl, unconvincingly. Since his mother's death a year earlier, he had gone away to college as a premed major, seen his twin sisters move in with their aunt, and maintained a long-distance relationship with Gabby, his high-school girlfriend. Phoebe had urged him to get some therapy, but Daryl saw himself as a cowboy, alone on his horse, braving the wilderness, riding the range.

Phoebe's therapist, Gale Holland, said most men thought of themselves this way, that cowboys didn't get therapy, they got drunk. Phoebe knew Daryl didn't ever get drunk, not even to quiet the pain of his recent losses. Phoebe herself preferred food to drinking or drugs. She had once gotten extremely drunk and vowed, when she found her cheek pressing against the tile floor of a bathroom in a bistro in Paris, that she would never drink again. And she hadn't. She had tried marijuana (one of the models at her father's photo studio had pulled her into the darkroom and offered her a drag on a joint) and felt giggly, but weird, and she'd had to eat two bagels with lots of cream cheese to get her equilibrium back.

"I'm good," repeated Daryl, as though to convince Phoebe of the truth of it, or to convince himself.

"Oh yeah?" replied Phoebe playfully. "What's so good about you?"

Daryl didn't laugh, as he usually would have when

Phoebe flirted. He didn't say anything. Phoebe waited and then said, "Daryl?"

Still there was silence. It was not that relaxed sort of silence that happens when you are just hanging out. It was a tense silence. Stiff. It made Phoebe's muscles ache.

"Daryl? Are you there? What's wrong?"

"It's—it's—Gabby," answered Daryl. "Gabby and me."

"What? What about her?" asked Phoebe impatiently.

"Me and Gabby," said Daryl softly. "We're—engaged. I mean, we're going to be. I mean—it's too hard long distance. She says we need commitment. We need structure. We—she said we need to be engaged, otherwise . . ."

"Otherwise?" prompted Phoebe.

"Otherwise she says we can't . . ."

"Can't WHAT?" demanded Phoebe, horrified and interrupting Daryl again. But she knew what Daryl was about to say.

Before Daryl had phoned, Phoebe had been feeling incredibly good. That was how she described how she felt to herself. She even felt that she looked incredibly good. Her thick, springy, long brown curls shone. Her creamy skin radiated a rosy glow. Her body felt strong. It was not the tall slender body of a fashion model. It was the curvy, size-sixteen body of a girl of five-foot-three who had, in the past year, lost over forty-five pounds.

Phoebe sat on the floor of her room in a numbed condition, holding the phone so tightly against her head that her EAR was actually sweating. Her ear was sweating. Daryl and Gabby were going to be engaged. Engaged to be MARRIED. Phoebe felt simultaneously protective of Daryl's feelings and hopeful that Gabby WOULD break up with him, since she knew that Daryl—kind, strong, loyal Daryl, gallant cowboy Daryl—would NEVER break up with her.

"Can't go on," continued Daryl. "Gabby said she can't go on with this long-distance thing."

"*Ugh!*" exclaimed Phoebe disgustedly. "What is she thinking? Manipulation?"

"Maybe she's right," said Daryl.

"What is she afraid of?" asked Phoebe.

"She's afraid if I don't commit to her, somebody else will sweep me off my feet."

Phoebe pictured Daryl on a big, chestnut horse, bridle gleaming, tooled saddle glowing dully in the sunset, a cowgirl clip-clopping along on a shiny black pony, lassoing him.

"Well, girls ARE always chasing you around. But she isn't giving you much credit for having the ability to say 'no' to them. Is she." It was not really a question. Phoebe sighed. Girls and women, females of all ages, could not keep their eyes or their hands off Daryl.

Phoebe glanced at the time: 6:25.

"Oh no! I have to go!" she said. She would have to dash if she was going to make it to Gale's 7:00 group on time. She stepped over several copies of *The Star* and *The Enquirer* as she crossed the room, glimpsing a headline proclaiming that a sheep had given birth to a human baby, and, on another front page, a picture of Michael Jackson, whose nose looked even smaller than in the last photo she'd seen of him. Grabbing the keys to the dark-green Toyota Land Cruiser her parents had given her for graduation, she headed for the driveway. Her little apricot-colored poodles, Tom and Nicole, jumped up and down around her legs. Cookies spoke to her from the inside of the cookie jar shaped like a giant frosted chocolate cupcake.

* * *

Hannah put the finishing touches on her first wedding cake, placing candied violets around the iced perimeter of the cake's three white tiers. It gave her a wonderful feeling of accomplishment to view her handiwork at the end of this day at the bakery. She'd also written some good fortunes to place inside the little pink and white and yellow meringues she'd made.

Only the spoon knows what's in the soup.

You can't fix it if you don't admit it's broken.

Hannah's employer, Devie (her full name was Devon Poole), was impressed with her creativity and willingness to work hard. Botticelli Bakery had an excellent reputation in the community, and people from surrounding Long Island towns went out of their way for their raspberry cheese pie, chocolate pound cake and crusty herb bread.

Hannah had a bit of a headache, and her neck felt stiff. She wondered if she had meningitis, encephalitis or mad cow disease, if she'd soon begin to have convulsions, followed by coma. Hannah was terrified of being sick, while always suspecting she was. Her mother, after a lifetime of anorexia, had died at the age of thirty-six after having been diagnosed with breast cancer. It was the anorexia, though, the doctors said, that had prematurely ended her life.

Hannah was proud that she had not purged in several months. She had finally gone to see a doctor about the blood she had noticed when she threw up. Gale had been firm when she'd told Hannah last spring that she would not see her again until she'd seen a doctor, and Hannah had reluctantly but quickly made the appointment at a clinic during the next week, when she knew her father would be away on business.

Gale had also asked that Hannah sign a release giving

Gale permission to speak with the doctor about his findings and had Hannah ask the doctor to sign a similar release giving him permission to do the same. This was necessary because often clients would see the doctor and say it was for a general checkup, never mentioning the bulimia or the bleeding, therefore complying with the requirement to see a doctor but not addressing the life-threatening symptoms. If untreated, bleeding from the esophagus, the tube connecting the mouth to the stomach, was fatal more than 50 percent of the time. Gale had been worried about Hannah, and she had communicated this to Hannah so emphatically that Hannah had been worried, too—worried enough to tell the doctor the truth.

Hannah knew Gale found it amazing that, given Hannah's proclivity for attributing dire causes to every symptom, she could nonetheless continue to purge without fear of the consequences. Denial, Gale had told Hannah about a thousand times, was a baffling, treacherous thing.

The doctor had examined Hannah with an endoscope, a tube with a tiny camera on the end of it, and had taken some blood for a complete blood count. He'd explained that vigorous vomiting could easily tear the small blood vessels of the esophagus, which would account for her bleeding. After he'd performed the endoscopy, he'd admitted her to the hospital for two days of intravenous feeding. Since the source of

Hannah's bleeding was in the neck region, the upper part of her esophagus, and the tears looked tiny, the doctor told her she could go home after the two days of I.V. feeding if she finished the course of antibiotics he prescribed—and stopped purging. She would have to return for weekly follow-up visits for at least a month, he'd told her, and she had.

Hannah was relieved that when the statement from the insurance company came, it said she'd been treated in the hospital for esophageal bleeding. When her father, who'd still been away on business when Hannah was in the hospital, questioned her about it, she said she'd had food poisoning and had thrown up a lot. She told Gale she'd felt bad about lying, but not as bad as she would have felt if she'd had to tell her father the truth. Anyway, food, she reasoned, WAS a sort of poison for her.

She'd developed an interest in esophageal bleeding after her discharge from the hospital and found references to it on many Internet sites. When she'd read about it, and about how the dehydration from purging could cause kidney failure and heart irregularities that could lead to her death, Hannah had been terrified of hurting herself further and had stopped purging right away.

Hannah was looking for a way not to go home. For today, at least, she had escaped the magnetic force of cinnamon raisin loaf, olive bread and pound cake. Her need to produce dozens of these, and make each one perfect, captured her imagination.

It was aimlessness, unstructured time, which made her vulnerable to bingeing. When her hands and mind were occupied by something challenging that required her to stretch her creative capabilities, Hannah felt practically normal. Time disappeared, and so did her fear and self-doubt, and she floated through her tasks in a velvety soft internal silence.

Without that sanctuary, she was apprehensive about the thoughts that could come, about what those thoughts could make her feel, and about what the feelings might make her do. The thought, the realization, that she was gay plagued her daily, hourly if she was not productively occupied.

Why did "it" have to be called that, Hannah reflected irritably as she wiped flour off the counters in the bakery's big kitchen. Were all homosexuals all over the planet, at this moment, whistling, smiling or humming? What was so "gay" about being gay, she wondered angrily. What could be cheery about identifying oneself as a member of a third gender, which was in the minority?

Hannah had a crush on her boss. That her boss was married, and the mother of two boys, did not seem to have any dampening effect on Hannah's ardor. It wasn't only the motherly way Devie took pride in Hannah's dedication to her baking that pleased Hannah so much. Hannah thrived on the nurturing provided by her appreciative employer, especially without a mother of her own. It was the longing for Devie's touch that terrified Hannah, her craving to be held by this small, dark woman, to have her stroke her hair.

Devie came into the bakery on her way home from picking up one of her boys. She came in through the bakery's back entrance, and a gust of wind lifted puffs of flour and powdered sugar out of the big drums in which they were stored. Hannah's face was smudged with flour, her hands sticky from icing, which she was licking off her fingers when Devie came in. She loved icing best when she could eat it with her hands. When Hannah was little and her mother had made icing, she would let Hannah lick some off her fingers.

"Make sure you clean up really well before you close up," said Devie, looking at the crowded counters covered with bowls that had been full of batter and dough and buttercream.

Devie had never said anything like that to Hannah. In fact, she usually said how pleased she was with how clean and orderly everything was since Hannah had come to work for her.

When Devie left, Hannah felt extremely angry and confused. Until now, she'd thought of Devie as gentle, as someone who admired and appreciated her. Until now, she'd felt safe with Devie, had enjoyed imagining herself as part of

Devie's family. She was glad it was almost time for her to go to her Tuesday night group.

* * *

Samantha looked at herself in the bathroom mirror and noticed the dark circles beneath her eyes, the slight puffiness there, too. Other than these small departures from total perfection, her heart-shaped face, framed by straight blonde hair that fell to her shoulders with a fringe of long bangs, was unmarked by the exhaustion she felt. She was grateful that the scar on her left shoulder from where she'd cut herself last year was healing. She had not cut herself by accident. She was ashamed of what she used to do.

She was ashamed of the amount of time she spent looking into mirrors, didn't want to admit to herself that if she didn't look at herself as often as she possibly could, she'd feel as though she had disappeared, so urgent was her need to reassure herself of her solidity.

She remembered one of Hannah's cookie fortunes:

Do not look into mirrors to find yourself.
Look into your heart.

There were many things Samantha knew but did not want to know. She didn't want to know that Len's feelings for her had shifted, which she assumed they had since his e-mails had recently taken on a distant, polite tone.

"Hope your exams went well and that you are taking care of yourself," instead of, "Hey, Sam—I hope you're eating enough because I'm crazy about you."

He might as well have sent her a greeting card saying, "Wishing you all the best for the coming year." She didn't want to consider that he was probably dating someone else or that he had his eye on someone. Certainly someone— probably several someones—had their eyes on him. Aside from being cuter than average—with thick, dark hair he wore long so that it curled handsomely around his ears and brushed the tip of his jaw, strong features with pleasingly full lips, and a lean, strong body—he knew how to listen. He trained his hazel eyes on Samantha and they stayed fixed there, which made her feel as though she existed more emphatically than she did when she was alone or with any-one else. His gaze made her feel important, beautiful, pro-tected and thin—though she was already underweight. Now, without the constancy of his attention, she did not feel safe any longer from the unpredictable horrors that befell, she believed, people who were alone.

She also didn't want to know that her father was dating

one of his students at the college. He had separated from her mom a year ago, and Samantha had heard the rumors. She'd dismissed them at first. But it was as though she didn't know this man the girls spoke about. The discomfort penetrated deep. She didn't want to know who the girl was, but knew that this news, too, would inevitably reach her. The community was small, hungry for news. What could her father be thinking?

Samantha came out of the bathroom and into her large bedroom, to her collection of stuffed and carved zebras, trophies for high school track, and to the expanse of carpet which she was proud that she no longer felt compelled to vacuum several times a day. She was gratified, too, that she had not cut herself since her father and mother had separated, though she had certainly come close when Len left for college in Rhode Island and she had visited her father in his new house for the first time, all in the same day.

She noticed that her zebra wall clock, its tail a pendulum, said 6:44—time to leave for group. She had begun to attend therapy sessions with Gale Holland the previous year after an ultimatum from her mom: either Samantha got therapy, or she would have to get residential treatment for her anorexia. Samantha hated therapy at first, but after joining Gale's Tuesday evening group, she felt differently about it. She worried, though, that she was not making progress as quickly as the other group members. Except for Faye Thomas, an older woman who had been anorexic for over twenty years and seemed not to care to change, the other members of the group had been making progress.

Samantha felt a sudden surge of shame when she thought of how lame it was that everyone else could get better except her. She had eaten nothing except lettuce and an apple that day. And she felt humiliated by Len's sudden formal way of communicating with her. Her high-school boyfriend, Brian, had broken up with her in the middle of her senior year. Now Len was distancing himself as well. And her dad! She didn't want to go to group and have to talk about all this.

Samantha didn't want to let herself think that in her dressing table, crowded into the very back of its little drawer behind the plastic bag of cotton balls, tubes of lipstick and tiny pots of eye shadow, was a double-edged razor blade, waiting.

✳ ✳ ✳

"Where's Hannah?" asked Billy as the group trooped into the spacious office Gale rented on the second floor of a big, white clapboard house. It was a cool mid-September evening and Gale had made a fire in the fireplace around which the group's chairs were arranged.

"Yeah, where's Hannah?" echoed Faye. "She's never been late, not once."

"She's always early," reflected Scott.

Phoebe and Samantha exchanged worried looks. The last time Hannah had been late she'd actually never shown up at all because she'd taken too many aspirins and antihistamines and wound up in the hospital.

"Don't jump to conclusions," cautioned Gale, seating herself in one of the upholstered armchairs in front of the fireplace. "Let's start," said Gale, looking at her Timex. "When Hannah comes, we'll fill her in. How are you all doing with feelings and food?"

"I want to eat all those logs right now," said Phoebe, indicating the wood stacked on the left side of the fireplace with a nod of her head.

"What happened?" asked Faye.

"Daryl's getting engaged!" Phoebe moaned.

"To who?" asked Scott. "Or is it 'to whom'?"

"I think it's 'to whom,'" said Billy.

"Oh, never mind the grammar!" said Samantha impatiently. "What's going on, Phoebe?"

"To Gabby, of course!" answered Phoebe sadly, looking down at the pink tissue she was shredding into her lap.

"She's putting pressure on him because of the long-distance thing. She's afraid of drift. But Daryl doesn't wander. He is not a wanderer. He is steadfast. That's what's so wonderful about him. Among other things. Daryl's heart doesn't drift. It stays put. The more wonderful he seems, the more I want him, and the more I want him, the less I can ever hope."

"You can ALWAYS hope," said Billy. "It springs eternal, and it's not fattening."

A soft knock preceded the appearance of Hannah, her face pale and puffy, her shoulders slumped in an attitude of defeat.

"I'm a mess," she announced without preamble as she hauled herself over to the vacant armchair. "I'm such a loser. I'm sorry I interrupted all of you. What did I interrupt?"

"Phoebe was telling us that Daryl's getting engaged to Gabby," answered Billy.

"Oh God!" exclaimed Hannah, looking at Phoebe sympathetically.

"What's up with you, Han?" asked Samantha. "Why were you late?"

"I don't want to steer all the attention in my direction. It makes me feel large. Anyway, I barged in here in the middle. I hate being late. I'll just wait for Phoebe to finish."

"I finished," Phoebe reassured her. "I'm just glad I'm here right now. There's nothing to eat here. What's happening with you, Han?"

"I binged and purged just now. Big surprise."

Hannah had not purged in the almost four months she'd been working at the bakery. She had not binged there either. She had not purged when her father told her there was a woman he had become close with. She had not purged when her grandmother had a stroke and had spent over two weeks in the hospital. She had not purged when her face had ballooned up after having had all of her wisdom teeth pulled. But when she realized that what Devie said to her about keeping the bakery clean—not so much what she'd said but the context and the WAY she'd said it— reminded her of how her mother had treated her, Hannah had eaten six chocolate cupcakes and a quart of rum raisin ice cream and then purged. She had not eaten the cupcakes at the bakery but had bought them at a convenience store.

"Forgive yourself now," said Scott solemnly.

"I can't!" wailed Hannah. "Devie was so mean to me. Just like my mom used to be. It wasn't anything big, it was just . . . attitude. When my mom was mean, it WAS big, it was AWFUL. She'd tell me I was stupid and selfish. It's like my mother has come back to life. And I want to KILL her. How can I forgive myself?"

"You must!" insisted Phoebe. "Don't beat yourself up! You're already beat up from the cupcakes and the rum raisin and the purging!"

"You got that right," said Hannah from a place of bottomless despair. Then she added softly, "And I'm afraid of bleeding again."

"Did you bleed again?" asked Gale.

"No," said Hannah. "But my mother was right. I AM stupid. I COULD have made myself bleed again."

"Well, you'd want me to forgive myself if it was me," said Scott, who, though he'd never thrown up blood, was no stranger to bingeing and purging.

"That's true," said Hannah. "But you're not a complete loser. You're not bulimic PLUS being gay. I don't know HOW to be gay. It's not TAUGHT anywhere. I can't take a COURSE. And the way I feel right now, if I could take a course in how to be gay, I'd fail it. I'm a complete failure at everything."

"Why do you feel you'd fail it? Tell us," prodded Gale.

"I failed therapy! I purged! How stupid is that—to do something I could DIE from?"

"You're a bulimic!" said Gale. "That's what bulimics DO. They purge."

"Oh, so does that mean I'll never get over this?" Hannah asked, her eyes closed, her head tilted back.

"You will get better. You HAVE gotten better. You ARE getting better," said Gale firmly. "It's all right, Hannah. YOU'RE all right. You have a destructive illness. It makes you vulnerable to doing dangerous things."

Hannah sighed. "At least I didn't binge at the bakery," she said, brightening a little. Then she thought for a minute, dispirited. "I binged in the car. I said I wasn't going to binge in the car anymore. Then I purged in the bathroom at the diner, and I'll bet everyone heard me. I didn't bleed," she assured Gale, then added, "I didn't want to be late! I'm sorry!"

"Hannah, you're doing fine," said Gale reassuringly. She admitted to herself that she sounded more confident about Hannah than she felt.

"You're working on yourself," said Scott. "You're not going to get perfect in like a year."

"You're taking responsibility for yourself," said Billy. "What else can you do?"

"I could stick myself into a rehab," said Hannah. "I don't want to die. That WOULD be stupid."

"Well, a rehab might be necessary," said Gale. "It might come to that. Being hospitalized would keep you safe. Is it what you want to do? I could do some research tonight for you and . . ."

"I don't think I need that just yet," said Hannah. "I'm not going to let this happen again anytime soon."

"How can you trust yourself to keep your word?" asked Scott.

"I don't know," said Hannah. "I don't know if I can. But I need to at least try."

After group, Phoebe flopped onto her bed, with Tom and Nicole racing back and forth on the bed, and wrote in her journal.

> All colors come flying in and out of my head, mixing themselves up behind my eyes, turn into lies, and then come out half-baked anyway, unfit to eat and I'm on a diet anyway. Nothing is happening and everything is happening and nothing is the same and nothing is different and I don't recognize who I just saw in the mirror, the face is blurred or maybe just fat. A girl by any other name would still be glad to be in one piece but not me. Daryl is getting engaged to Gabby. I'm happy for him. I want him to be happy. I'm lying! I am furious at him. I'm hurt. I feel like I've been kicked in the stomach. I want him to be happy but not without me!!!

Tom and Nicole, poodlishly playful as ever, suddenly stopped racing back and forth across the bed, and flopped at Phoebe's feet, panting. Tom draped one paw over one of Nicole's.

Why can't that be Daryl and me? thought Phoebe, as she looked at her companionable pets.

"It can't be that I'm still fat. Gabby is fat! It must be ME, something about the me of me that grosses the him out of him. What could it be? My clothes? What's wrong with them? They're normal clothes. They're regular Gap clothes, sewn by women in Honduras or somewhere who make fifty cents an hour while the CEO of Gap makes about $4,585 an hour. Daryl's girlfriend wears Gap clothes, too, though. I once asked him about how she dresses. Everybody's clothes are sewn or knitted or beaded or whatever by people who are disgustingly paid who live in Central America or Taiwan. I don't know how to sew. I can't make my own clothes. I have to wear clothes made by the downtrodden, someone Hispanic or Indonesian or Mexican or who has no self-confidence even though they sew great. It can't be my clothes.

"Maybe it's my chin. My Dad thinks it's too small. He said it recedes. I don't see it really, I think it's just a normal type of chin. I could change that though. There's surgery for that.

"Maybe it's my breasts. Are they too big for Daryl? Gabby is flatter. Don't guys LIKE that though, when your breasts are big? I always thought there WERE no breasts that were too big for guys. Anyway, there's surgery for that, too.

"Maybe it's my disgusting toes. I don't think even models get toe transplants. I don't think even Joan Rivers or Cher have had their TOES worked on. Anyway, aren't everybody's toes gross?

"My hair! Maybe it's my hair! I have fat hair, frizzy, but I can use hair products. I just have a hair-product deficit right now.

"Maybe it's my teeth. Actually, I LIKE my teeth. The better to bite into a doughnut with, my dear. The ones on the side—the little fangy, pointy ones—they're a little too pointy, but I LIKE them. They make my smile interesting. But if it's my teeth, I could go to a dentist for that.

"Maybe I'm too smart. *Cosmo* said girls shouldn't be too smart. *The Rules* said girls shouldn't seem too smart or happy or enthusiastic when a guy they like calls them. They can be as smart and happy and enthusiastic as they want when a guy they don't care about calls them. But when the guy is someone they like, the guy who is the fulfillment of all their dreams, when he calls them, they should be aloof. *The Rules* say the girl should end the conversation first if she is talking to the guy of her dreams. Otherwise, she can blab all night long with some guy she isn't in love with.

"It's too late to play dumb or disinterested with Daryl. Why would a guy want a girl who was dumb or disinterested, though?"

Phoebe petted the poodles.

She wrote:

> # Misfit Mourns As Hunky Heartthrob Finds Romance with Glamorous Galpal Gabriella!

* * *

Samantha looked at the page covered in circles the sizes of quarters with the word "GENOGRAM" printed across the top. Today, the young, cute psych professor was talking about the way traits and patterns repeat in families.

"It is extremely helpful to see your family history in a visual way, to see where you came from, who made you," said Dr. Aguillado in his Spanish accent, so that when he said "visual" it sounded like "vishual."

Samantha filled in the circles without much interest or enthusiasm. She didn't want to know any more about herself than she already knew. She wanted to know LESS about herself. She had already learned too much, in her opinion, from Brian and Len. She'd learned she wasn't good enough to keep a boyfriend. Even though Len hadn't actually broken up with her, he WAS acting strange, and it hurt her to think about it.

She'd recently learned that she was too much of a baby to go away to college without going crazy. She'd started freshman year at the University of Vermont, but less than two weeks after having started classes, she wanted to cut herself again, wanted that feeling of being grounded and soothed that the cutting used to provide. She already had scars from cuts she'd made on her body during high school. Though she hadn't cut herself, she'd stopped eating altogether, in spite of the fact that she weighed too little when she'd arrived in Vermont in late August. Her English teacher, who had once suffered with anorexia, had noticed Samantha's low weight and observed how withdrawn she was, not talking with other students, keeping to herself.

Her parents had been alerted. Marge Rosen came to Burlington and took her home less than two weeks after she'd arrived, and Samantha, too humiliated to let her friends know she'd come back home, had spent the weekend

vacuuming her spotless room, watching videos, and prom-
ising her mother she'd go back to therapy twice a week if
only she wouldn't have to go away to a hospital to have a
feeding tube put in her throat.

She hated the individual therapy sessions. There was too
much attention placed on her, and this exclusive focus
made her feel fat, too large and important. She didn't
mind going to group, because most of the people she'd
met when she'd started group at the end of her senior year
were still coming. Phoebe and Hannah had not gone away
to school.

Hannah was working at a bakery and had become quite
the expert at decorating cakes and making breads, and she
was making fortune cookies, too, and writing the little messages that went inside. Samantha couldn't fathom why
someone who wanted to work on her bulimia would be
working in a bakery. Neither could their therapist, Gale
Holland. But Hannah insisted that she was doing well—so
far. And she seemed happy not to be in school full-time.
She was taking one three-credit class. She kept saying she
was in "Earth school."

Phoebe was struggling with her weight. She'd lost almost
fifty pounds. The news that Daryl was getting engaged to
Gabby had really gotten Phoebe flustered, and Phoebe said
being flustered made visions of cake form in her mind,

pictures of chocolate cake in extreme close-up, the frosting sticking to her teeth.

Phoebe had decided to attend the state university in nearby Brookdale, so that she could work at her father's photo studio. Even though the McIntyres could well afford to send Phoebe to any school in the world, and even though she'd been valedictorian and winner of every academic honor the high school awarded, she wanted to be able to work at the studio. She'd told the group it was important to be near her father, but that she didn't understand why she felt that way since he alternated so exasperatingly from being supportive to being cruel to her about her weight. Samantha couldn't understand how her chubby friend could endure being around all those broomstick-thin models. Phoebe explained this by saying she suspected she had a tinge of masochism in her personality. Or was it grandiosity? Samantha couldn't remember.

As Samantha filled in her genogram, it once again amazed her that her great-grandfather on her mother's side had the same first and last names. His parents had named him Sidney L. Sydney. His middle name was Lewis and people called him Lew Sydney. But why had his parents done such a strange thing as give the same first and last names to their baby boy? Perhaps, speculated Samantha, they thought it would lend him distinction. But what a curse with which to go through life. And the two names were spelled differently, so he constantly would have had to be spelling each one. Were her great-grandparents sadists, or what?

Samantha wondered if her entire screwed-up life had developed in this warped direction because of her great-great-grandparents having given her great-grandfather the same first and last names. Didn't the weird naming reveal something about the psyches of her great-great-grandparents? And didn't the psyches of her maternal great-great-grandparents reflect on the psyche of her maternal great-grandparents, and reflect on the psyche of her maternal grandparents, and ultimately upon the psyche of her mother, Marge Sydney Rosen? And didn't the psyche of her mother reflect upon her own? She was getting the hang of this genogram thing.

Samantha sighed and looked anxiously at her watch. She had only a few minutes to get to her job working in the kitchen of Little Pisa. Len, who would be home for the weekend, had not e-mailed or called her for the past two days. Since he'd left for Rhode Island to study art, they'd fallen into the pattern of connecting with each other daily either by e-mail, phone, snail mail or all three. In the snail mail, he'd send her drawings, elaborate designs, copies of assignments. Samantha always felt reassured after hearing from Len and she had come to depend on contact, on the continuity of their connection, to feel okay.

Now it had been two whole days without contact. Well, not two WHOLE days—one whole day and two-thirds of this day. Today—tonight—there was still a chance she would get home from work and find an e-mail or a letter. She had been checking her cell phone's voice mail every ten minutes throughout the day.

His e-mails were usually personal, not the sorts of forwarded messages not written by the person who sent them. From her cousin Steven she had received a series of actual classified ads, such as "Nice parachute, never opened, used once." But lately, though Len was not forwarding her things, his e-mails had become less and less personal.

When Samantha got home, she glanced through the mail on the hall table. Nothing for her. Then she ran past her mother and sister, who were in the living room watching *Oprah,* and raced upstairs to her computer, her instrument of connection, of salvation.

* * *

Phoebe wrote:

Dear Journal Exclusive!!!!!!!!!! Phoebe McIntyre in Love with College Hunk, and He Couldn't Care Less!!!!!!!

Fat, funny Phoebe McIntyre's not-so-secret heartthrob was seen at a college coffeehouse with the glamorous Gabriella, fiancée and galpal of his dreams, while the hapless, heartsick Phoebe pines away for him!

"Her feelings for Daryl have really escalated," said a source close to the beleaguered freshwoman.

"We're worried that she will regain all her lost weight!" said one of her coworkers at the photo studio of her famous dad, Michael McIntyre.

❊ ❊ ❊

Hannah thought of Devie with an anxious tightening in her belly. She felt suddenly panicky in the presence of a huge bowl of vanilla frosting. She moved away from the bowl, staring at it, feeling as though a horror movie monster was approaching.

She wanted Devie to love her in a way she could trust. She wanted to be able to expect Devie to be kind, her moods even and predictable. Hannah knew this would be impossible, just as it had been with her mother. Gale had told her not to assume Devie's remark was really about the cleanliness of the bakery or about Hannah's competence. Gale had said that Hannah's mother's behavior was more about her mother—her fears, her illness, her undereating which made her irritable, her envy of Hannah's youth, of Hannah's life, full of potential, of triumphs as yet unclaimed. Perhaps, Gale had suggested, the same had been true for Devie, a thirty-nine-year-old mother of two envying her beautiful young employee. Hannah considered this.

A sort of vagueness came over her as she stood in the bakery, something behind her eyes going out of focus, her attention sliding sideways, up and to her left somewhere, and she didn't know where she was, only that wherever it was, it was less painful than staying in the center of herself.

She stood in the bakery kitchen amidst the stainless steel counters and wire shelving that held dozens of pies, and bowls of buttercream, and trays of cookies. The fragrance of sugar and butter and herb bread filled the air. She moved toward the opposite counter where a big gleaming stainless steel bowl held some recently mixed chocolate-chip cookie batter. The bowl of batter seemed to be glowing, as though

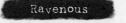

the light falling on it was brighter than on anything else in the large kitchen. Moving toward the bowl of cookie batter did not feel good. Her heartbeat accelerated. She stopped and stood, remembering.

In the last few group sessions, Gale had talked about how helpful it was to breathe when panic comes. Not understanding how breathing could feel as good as eating chocolate-chip cookie batter, she nonetheless decided to try it out. If she still wanted the batter after, she would let herself have it without beating herself up about it.

That was one of the things she was becoming good at: letting herself stay soothed by the eating that scared her so much, rather than canceling out its soothing effects by hating herself afterwards. Gale called this "plusing and minusing." She said if you were trying to "plus" yourself with food (meaning trying to soothe yourself), there was absolutely no point in "minusing" yourself afterward (subtracting the soothed feeling). She suggested letting the "plus" stay in place. After a while, she said, the "plus" times would add up to feeling nurtured and you wouldn't have such a strong need to feed yourself so much in the first place.

Hannah closed her eyes. She breathed. How the breathing could help defend her against the need to eat chocolate-chip cookie batter she had not a clue. She breathed in the cloying sweet aroma of the bakery and was immediately reminded of her mother and grandmother, on the days she would sit in the kitchen with them while they removed cookies from aluminum baking sheets with spatulas. The just-baked cookies seemed so big and inviting, like large warm pillows she could sink into and rest on.

Hannah breathed in the memory of her mother stroking her head while they sat in the big cream-colored bedroom on the satin bedspread. She breathed in images of her mother gazing at her, being held by her mother's eyes. She breathed in and out and could picture her mother's face in extreme close-up, so close she could see the fine downy hairs on it, her familiar earlobe with its pearl earring.

She felt herself getting dizzy and opened her eyes. Holding onto the edge of the countertop, she took another long, deep breath and looked around. The big bowl of cookie batter no longer held her interest. It had blended into the many other objects in the kitchen.

❋ ❋ ❋

At 1:11 A.M. on Thursday night—actually Friday morning—Samantha sat on her bed surrounded by her stuffed, ceramic and carved wooden zebras and the trophies for track she'd received in earlier, pre-anorexia times.

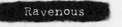

Where was he? Why hadn't he called or e-mailed her by now? Len was an on-time kind of person; that was one of the things about him that Samantha loved.

I'm not going to drive myself crazy, Samantha thought. *And I'm not going to call him. I call him too much. That's what Lacey said. I'm going to—I'm going to—I don't know WHAT I'm going to do!*

She forced herself to relax and tried the breathing technique Gale had taught the group: inhaling to the count of four, holding the breath for four counts, and exhaling to the count of four. But when she held her breath, her chest ached.

She picked a long blonde hair off her black leggings. She checked her e-mails again. There was another one from her cousin Steven, this time with a series of Jewish haikus.

"After the warm rain, the sweet scent of camellias.
Did you wipe your feet?"

"Today I am a man, tomorrow I return
To the seventh grade."

Samantha, gazing around her room from her position on the bed, noticed the vacuum cleaner just inside the opened closet door. She had not been compelled to vacuum her room more than once every couple of weeks, she realized.

All this time she had been complaining to Gale and to the members of the Tuesday group that she had not changed at all, completely neglecting to acknowledge herself for the disappearance of her need to clean her room several times a day.

At 2:10 A.M., Samantha called Len's dorm room, got his answering machine and hung up without leaving a message. She called his cell phone, got no answer and didn't leave her recorded voice for him there, either.

At 2:18 A.M., a sensation of cold gathered inside her, in the center of her body, a straight, hard column of fear. Her hands and feet felt weighted with stones. Her neck felt like a huge rubber band stretched tight enough to snap. Her throat was dry. Her phone rang.

"Sam?" said Len, his familiar voice immediately soothing Samantha, instantly dissolving the sensation of coldness.

"Hey!" said Samantha warmly, suddenly relieved, and forgetting entirely how upset she'd been while waiting. Normalcy had been restored. Everything would be all right.

"Sam—we have to talk," said Len, and the coldness came back, and expanded within her, turning her hands to ice.

✳　✳　✳

On Sunday night, Hannah wrapped herself in yellow police tape and went to the "Come as You See Yourself in Your Imagination to Celebrate Lacey's Birthday" party as a crime scene. A piece of tape diagonally spanned her upper torso, from her left shoulder to her right hip, exactly where the "Miss America" ribbon would be. The yellow plastic tape said "CAUTION" and "DO NOT CROSS."

Her friend, Kaneesha, said, "Fantastic!" when Hannah slid into the Sebring's passenger seat. Hannah was saving for her own car; she'd calculated that she'd be in her own vehicle by Christmas.

When they arrived at Lacey's house, the music reminded Hannah suddenly of her mother, who used to love old Frank Sinatra records. She didn't want to be at a party, even one in which people didn't have to be themselves because they were in disguise. Billy was dressed as Batman, and Phoebe was in a cheerleader outfit. Samantha hadn't come yet, but Hannah guessed she'd be dressed as a bride. People were "disguised" as the very parts of themselves they were keeping secret. So they were actually less disguised than usual.

Hannah could feel herself sinking, sliding into the stillness in the center of herself. She remembered this place. Her arms and hands felt warm, and something in her hummed like a hundred purring cats leaning against her, and time stopped. She would go there when she'd sit with her mother on the cream-colored satin bedspread.

When Hannah pictured her mother dead now, she imagined the wonderful surrender of it. Her own experience of surrender centered exclusively upon bingeing. She couldn't even surrender in yoga class. Somehow, bingeing had become her only way to lose control, her way of being like her mother, of being *with* her.

❋ ❋ ❋

Gale Holland's clock said 3:38 A.M. She was completely alert, her heart racing. She took immediate stock. Nothing, she concluded, was wrong. There was nothing she had forgotten to worry about. She had not left the split pea soup bubbling in a pot on the stove. She had unplugged the iron, and the coffee pot was waiting in the dark to turn itself on at seven. She wondered if she could turn HERSELF on at seven. No—nothing was the matter. She was just excited about starting the day.

I am distilling myself, she thought as she squinted at her face in the bathroom mirror through sleep-deprived eyes. *I feel myself becoming more intensely me. It's thrilling. I am*

either on the right track or a total lunatic. Either way, though,
I'm exhausted!

As she poured coffee on Wednesday morning, Gale
found herself reflecting on what was going on during the
meetings of her Tuesday night group.

Hannah, she noted, had blossomed into quite a
hypochondriac. It was as though the fear and guilt she used
to discharge by throwing up had turned against her. If a
mark appeared on her body, she immediately concluded it
was Kaposi's sarcoma and she was dying of AIDS. If she had
a stiff neck or numb fingertips from sleeping all scrunched
up or baking all day, she believed she had multiple sclerosis.
At the same time, Gale reflected, Hannah's belief that she
was dying was a way to be like her mother, to be with her.
Gale had a sense that this was true about Hannah's bingeing as well.

Gale stepped into a pair of gray sweatpants and, still
thinking of Hannah, slipped a white cotton sweater over
her head. Hannah would need extra support when her dad
introduced her to the woman he was interested in. That
would be hard for Hannah. Her relationship with her boss,
Devie, bore watching. Hannah was getting better at asking
for help, though, getting more accepting of having that
scary "N" word—needs. She had become close with
Samantha and Phoebe and Scott.

Samantha was extra stressed, too, thought Gale as she sipped her coffee in the big wicker chair in her kitchen. Len was infatuated with a girl at school. He told Samantha he was drawing her, and that was all—just drawing her. He said he was infatuated with DRAWING her, not with HER, that he only imagined what she was actually like since he had never spoken to her. *But don't we imagine ALL love objects?* reflected Gale.

Worse than this for Samantha, though, was that her father was having an affair with one of his students at the college. Gale shuddered in her chair thinking of how this was affecting Samantha. She had not gained back any of the weight she'd lost since coming back from Vermont, and these new developments were not helping.

Gale poured herself another cup of coffee and thought of Phoebe, who was afraid of gaining weight because she held in her mind now what seemed like a permanent image of a huge wedge of devil's food cake. Phoebe told the group she thought Daryl was getting engaged because there was something about her that was not good enough. The process of accompanying Phoebe through this, thought Gale, was going to be hard. Phoebe was dissecting herself like a lab specimen, like a pathologist doing an autopsy on herself. No body part, no aspect of herself escaped her merciless scrutiny. Was it her fingernails, her thighs, her eyelashes that were defective? Was it the plaid flannel pajama bottoms she wore that day to have coffee with Daryl? She thinks that maybe only thin girls can get away with that kind of outfit. Was she too serious? Was she too jokey? Should she have most of her breast tissue lopped off? Should cartilage be added to her chin?

It's exactly what I was like until I was in my thirties, thought Gale as she stood to stretch. *Just because Gerard and I have a good thing going now doesn't mean I still don't have self-doubt. I still eat to soothe myself. It made my mother happy to see me eating when I was unhappy, because she didn't WANT me to be unhappy, and I wasn't when I was eating. So SHE felt relief from my eating, too. As though cheese Danish could keep me safe,* thought Gale as she watered the geraniums on her windowsill.

* * *

The Fat Barbees, none of whom were fat, and all of whom were blonde and had met in rehab, sang the sixth track of their CD, *Duh You're Acting Blonde,* as Phoebe climbed onto her bed, preparing to write in her journal. Tom and Nicole leapt up onto the bed after her, pushing their small bodies against her, snuggling close. Phoebe had just read an article about the Fat Barbees in *The National Enquirer*. Lead singer, Rosetta Stone, was normal-sized, the height and weight of the average American woman, five foot four and 146 pounds. Compared to Barbie, and the gang at MTV, Rosetta looked fat, and she said she felt fat sometimes, but she told the interviewer that by using a mixture of self-help books, psychotherapy, yoga, meditation and a month in an addiction rehabilitation facility, she'd learned to say, "So what! I love lasagna. I'm singing anyway." Phoebe turned up the volume:

> *One two three four*
> *Check your brain at the door.*
> *Five six seven eight*
> *Time to learn to meditate.*
> *Scotch, bourbon, vodka, stout*
> *Alcohol is soooooooo out!*
> *Pot, cocaine, crack, smack*
> *Why be dull and out of whack!*
> *Lose the crack, lose the meth,*
> *Because you're boring me to death!*

Phoebe opened her journal and looked at the blank page as Rosetta sang:

Thinking only brings you grief,
Time for some mental relief,
Do some yoga, find your bliss
Om is where the heart is.
Go there go there be with pain—
Ticket to the freedom train!

Phoebe wrote:

I think Billy has a crush on me. I caught him looking at me with these googly eyes in group the other night. I think Scott has a crush on Sam, too. It's probably normal for that to happen in group. How could you NOT fall in love with someone you know so well who is so willing to be vulnerable and everything. But if that's true—then I should have a crush on Billy, and I don't.

UGH—why hasn't Daryl called me? I thought we were friends. I don't know whether to call him. I am getting into that game-playing frame of mind. I can't stop thinking about him. Why is this? I feel deranged!

DERANGED BY DARYL!!!

FRIENDS FEAR FOR PHOEBE'S SANITY!

Dr. Pauline Priestly smiled when she saw Hannah walking toward her. Hannah was headed for the seat in the classroom she liked best—the aisle seat on the right, six rows back, about a third of the way toward the back of the room.

"Good morning, Hannah," said the professor as Hannah walked past her on the way to her seat.

Hannah was surprised that her teacher had remembered her name after only three classes. There were over thirty students in the 7:30 A.M. class, which Hannah attended on Tuesday and Thursday mornings before spending the rest of the day at work at the Botticelli Bakery. Devie opened the bakery on those mornings, baked the breads and manned the counter ("womanned the counter" as Devie liked to say) until Hannah arrived there at ten.

The first time the class had met, Dr. Priestly had asked the students to write three pages about something they were either afraid or ashamed of. She said those were the only two themes worth writing about no matter what the subject matter of the class might be. This was a class in the English department called "The Literature of Death."

Hannah had written about her bulimia, something about which she had always been ashamed and fearful. But when she read what she'd written, it wasn't sounding right, or true. She thought that was probably because she had purged only once in the last four months. Sometimes, she forgot what her life had been like during her senior year of high school, when she'd purged daily.

She felt herself emerging out of a dark lonely tunnel into another life. She knew, but did not understand why, that her emergence from the darkness was somehow connected to her abstinence from purging. She did not know why this should be true. When she purged (she did not know if this was her imagination) she noticed that her ability to see would change, her whole world narrowing, as though she'd lost her capacity for peripheral vision.

She began to view her bingeing and purging from another point of view. It was as though food signified life, and if she ate she was alive, and if she was alive she was bad because she was alive while her mother was dead. So she'd have to throw up the food as an apology to her mother for her own aliveness. But during these past few months, she was surprised to notice that except for that one time the previous week, she no longer felt as though she would either choke or fly apart in all directions if she did not throw up what she had eaten.

This was what she'd come to after almost a year of group therapy, hundreds of e-mails and dozens of hours talking on the phone with Phoebe, Kaneesha, Samantha, Billy, Scott and Faye.

Hannah didn't throw away her first attempt to fulfill her assignment by writing about her bulimia, but she put it aside and wrote another. She called it, "She, Herself and I."

It began: "On November 6, I will be nineteen years old, and I have never had a boyfriend or a date. It isn't because I'm ugly, though I often feel I am. I'm average looking, tall, with good skin and eyes, and with above-average hair. Guys have asked me out, but I've always said no. It's not because I'm afraid of them. It's because I'm more interested in girls. I'm not interested in sex, though. So that confuses me even more, because if I'm a lesbian, shouldn't I be interested in sex at least? I feel as though I'm not even a normal lesbian.

"So it's being a lesbian that is shameful and scary. And I am an ABNORMAL lesbian. I don't know if that is better (at least I haven't done anything disgusting yet), or worse (I'm abnormal in all possible combinations). I'm afraid and ashamed of being so different."

The minute Dr. Priestly said "good morning" to her, Hannah assumed it was because the professor had singled her out because of her essay, and her lesbianism, and her weirdness in general and she regretted the whole thing—having registered for the class, having written the essay, having handed it in—and a feeling of despair engulfed her.

* * *

Scott thought of Samantha as he weighed himself for the first time in two months. Samantha used to weigh herself six times day. It was a chilly, late-September day and the white tile bathroom floor was cold beneath his bare feet, the weak light of early morning filtering in through filmy white curtains. The scale occupied a place beneath the counter in the center of which was the worn sink, its porcelain gray and pitted, faintly stained in places. He could feel his heart beating hard as he stepped onto the scale, its black plastic surface dull with wear. His feet, as he gazed down at them standing there, looked grotesque to him. Feet were, he admitted, funny-looking, but his own seemed ridiculous. He noted the configuration of his toes, the second toes longer than his big ones. He noted the blond hair just above his ankles. He was furry! The idea of his having smooth, hairless legs appeared suddenly attractive, startling him, causing him to close his eyes involuntarily. When he opened them again and looked down, his feet and the hair just above his ankles did not seem so terrible, though nothing about them had changed.

He looked at the numbers. He hadn't eaten breakfast yet, of course, and expected the scale to be kind. It was not. He was up three and a half pounds. He'd intensified his weight-lifting routine, but did not allow for the increase in muscle mass, which could have accounted for the extra pounds.

His shame about the weight gain added to his disgust that he cared so much about his weight, and thrust him into a deep gloom. He was like a girl, he thought, not a real man. He wanted to quit his weekend job at *www.university.com* where he helped customers, mostly senior citizens, learn how to use computers. He wanted to drop out of EMT school, out of life. None of his male friends could understand what he went through every day. Hannah and Samantha understood the hunger that threatened to consume him. They understood the overwhelming disgust—that sinking, queasy sensation in the center of himself that came when he felt the flesh at his midsection, soft and doughy and imaginary.

Twelve miles from where Scott stood looking down at the numbers on his scale, Gale reviewed her group notes. She held a white ceramic mug of green tea flavored with stevia extract, the noncaloric herbal sweetener she liked. Diplomas and certificates hung on the sage green wall behind the pine desk at which she sat, and beyond the desk were the armchairs arranged in a wide semicircle around the stone fireplace, chairs which that evening would be occupied by her Tuesday group. Scott, Faye and Billy had formed the core of the group after two other members had left it, one to go away to college and one because she wanted to try life without therapy for a while.

Phoebe McIntyre had been coming regularly for just over a year. She'd made great strides since Gale had met her. Aside from having lost over forty-five pounds, she had learned to speak up when her father, noted commercial photographer Michael McIntyre, made disparaging comments about her appearance.

Gale felt a surge of satisfaction when she thought about Phoebe. For one thing, she identified with Phoebe's plight, as she herself was recovering from compulsive eating. She liked Phoebe's sense of fun and admired her creativity in her struggle against compulsive eating. Gale's notes from the previous week recounted an incident in which Phoebe's mom had thrown a birthday party for herself, and there had been lots of leftover cake. Since neither of Phoebe's parents had a problem resisting cake, they felt comfortable keeping the cake in the freezer rather than giving a slice to each of the their guests to take home with them. One afternoon when Phoebe had come home from school, she felt the cake calling to her from the freezer. It was chocolate cake with a rich mocha buttercream icing and bittersweet chocolate mousse between the layers. Phoebe, in a valiant and, happily, successful attempt to avoid eating the frozen cake, sprayed deodorant on it before putting it into the garbage can. She knew herself, knew that she had taken cakes and cookies and all manner of delectables covered with coffee grounds out of the garbage can before. The deodorant story brought applause from the group, and even Phoebe's hard-to-please father, when he'd looked for the cake and was told what Phoebe had done with it, had commended her for her strong resolve and quick thinking.

Gale liked Samantha Rosen, too, though working with her was often frustrating. Each small step forward was achieved only after a long battle with Samantha's fears. When Samantha had first come, her boyfriend, Brian, had just broken up with her and she'd been self-mutilating, making small cuts on her arms, legs and shoulders, and starving herself. Her parents had separated after Sam had been in group for a couple of months and her new boyfriend, Len, had left for college in Rhode Island soon after that. Her daily regimen included fourteen lettuce leaves and an apple, though she complained bitterly about how fat she felt.

Gale repeated her anorexic theme song to Samantha: that a gain of one pound of body tissue could be achieved only if a person consumed 3,500 calories beyond what was required by one's basal metabolic rate (the number of calories required to run the body's involuntary activities—beating of the heart, blinking of the eyes and providing fuel for the manufacture of energy by the cells).

Anorexics found it difficult to grasp this principle. No matter how little they ate, it was always too much. For most anorexics, having bodily requirements of any kind—any need—was considered a sign of weakness. For the anorexic, the concept of the need for food being as non-negotiable as a car's need for gasoline was difficult to grasp. It was exasperating to Gale, and sad, and some part of her understood the fear that obstructed reason.

In group, Samantha had discovered that she could allow people to know her, let them come a bit closer than her comfort zone dictated. She hadn't cut herself since Len had left for college. But Gale feared that Sam might never break out of the prison of fear she had created within herself that kept her safe but prevented her from eating.

Faye Thomas, emphysemic and anorexic and more than twice Samantha's age, lived in fear of food, feelings and fat every day. She lived in fear of the unpredictable, of anything that might make her lose control of her feelings and compel her to eat. She breathed with difficulty and chain-smoked. And she was a nurse.

Hannah Bonanti had been doing extremely well, considering her challenges. Hannah had committed to removing purging as an option, while remaining accepting of herself should she binge or purge. Accordingly, she had noticed that her bingeing had scaled down, so that instead of eating eight doughnuts, she'd eat two. Her weight had not changed significantly, going up or down only two pounds or so, and she was beginning to trust that when purging is not an option, the size of the binge does diminish.

She had admitted to the group that she probably was a lesbian, that she hated the word "lesbian" and that even thinking about sex made her feel gross. She even hated those nature shows where animals mated right on TV. She supposed, she said, that she'd be one of those asexual gay people, like Andy Warhol.

Gale thought about Scott and was grateful that he and Hannah had been talking often outside of group, cheering each other on. Scott had been bulimic throughout high school while he'd been on the wrestling team, and he and Hannah were excellent sources of mutual support, especially since Scott's mother, too, had died within the past two years. His father had been drinking more heavily than usual since the death of Scott's mom, and Scott, knowing his dad thought nothing of driving while he was drunk, worried about him.

Billy Boeklin, thought Gale, was funny, compassionate and wise, a young man who had excelled at everything he'd chosen to do except lose weight. When Gale looked into his twenty-five-year-old brown eyes, she saw a much older person inside, someone who knew important things learned through pain. His father had abandoned the family of four children when Billy was seven, the oldest, and he had never seen his father again. Billy, who had been working for a builder since graduating from high school, knew how to frame a house and build a deck and repair a roof. Gale was impressed with this young man, who had cared to learn such vital, ancient skills.

He had been much too attached to his mother, so Gale was glad he had plans to move away. He wanted to go around the world, which he felt was practical, since people everywhere needed houses. Gale knew Billy could be happy no matter what he weighed. She hoped Billy could let himself know it.

Gale sipped the last of her tea, straightened the papers on her desk and placed the group note folder back into its locked drawer. She could hear footsteps on the stairs, and her first client of the morning coming into the waiting room.

❋　❋　❋

Phoebe felt Daryl's breath close to her face, his skin smelling like milk and honey. She breathed in and imagined that some of the air she was taking in had been inside him. His hand rested lightly on the back of her chair. The Brookdale University library was almost empty at six-thirty in the evening.

The art-history book, opened on the table before them, was huge. Daryl leaned toward Phoebe as she turned the pages. She stopped at a page that showed a painting by Vermeer of a woman beside a table with a pitcher on it.

Daryl leaned closer to the book to study the painting more carefully. Phoebe could smell the clean shampoo fragrance of his hair.

"Look," he said. "See how there's a single source of light?"

Phoebe felt as though Daryl were HER single source of light, and when he took himself away, it was hard, each time, for her to adjust to the darkness in his wake. He came home from college for weekends to be with his girlfriend, but today Gabby had been obliged to spend the afternoon at a family reunion, and Phoebe had enjoyed the luxury of an entire day with him.

"What time is it?" asked Phoebe. All she could think of was that Daryl had to meet Gabby at seven and that she would have to watch him go, the back of this head so beautiful with his long dark wavy hair curving above his broad shoulders, the slight bounce in his walk.

They had spent the day shopping. Daryl had helped Phoebe choose a dress for Bree Martin's wedding, which was going to take place in Las Vegas the following weekend. Bree was one of the models with whom Phoebe's father often worked. She was marrying her boyfriend of four years, who was an Elvis impersonator.

Daryl had been a perfect shopping companion. She found that she was not as self-conscious as she'd expected to be each time she'd come out of the dressing room to show him her selection, and was amazed that Daryl had been willing to walk all over the mall with her looking at dresses. In one store, whose window featured fluffy dresses the color of sherbet, Phoebe had tried on a pink pouffy strapless dress with a full skirt, imagining herself with a waistline in some sort of fairy princess fantasy, with Daryl, of course, as the prince. Only she'd felt more like the frog than like the princess in the dress. Daryl, seeing her in the pouffy pink dress, tactfully but firmly had said, "Uhhhhmmmmm-no."

"Why?" asked Phoebe, turning sideways to study herself in the dress.

"No," repeated Daryl. "Because pink is not you. THIS is you."

He presented her with a black and silver dress, a shimmering column of a dress, a shift, that made her look a foot taller than she did in the pink one. When she'd wriggled into it and stepped out of the dressing room, Daryl said, "That's it. That's you."

"Is it?" asked Phoebe skeptically.

"It is," said Daryl. "It's the you that you haven't met yet. It's the you I see."

Phoebe sat up straight in her hard library chair, turning toward Daryl. He was looking at his watch in response to her earlier question about the time.

"It's 6:40," he said, standing up. "I gotta go."

Boldly, Samantha rested her hand on Len's large square one. It was bold because Len was in one of his tense, silent moods. When he felt her hand touch his, Len sighed, as though he had been holding his breath until the moment she'd touched him. Samantha thought the sigh sounded pained, a sigh expressing anguish rather than the standard sigh of relief.

I'm sitting here thinking I'm reading his mind, thought Samantha. *At least I'm reading my OWN mind,* she noted.

Her moment of self-congratulation for observing the workings of her own mind—a skill Gale was encouraging the group members to practice—shifted instantly back to the assumption that Len's silence, his sigh, his refusal, so far, to turn toward her, to look at her, even after she'd touched him, meant that he was going to break up with her.

They were sitting in Len's car where, it seemed to Samantha, most of their important talks occurred. Except this was not a talk; it was a silence. Len wore a tan leather jacket, a white T-shirt and jeans. Samantha was in her black size-one jeans, her pink turtleneck, a black denim jacket and her black clogs.

The car windows were closed against the evening chill, and there was a full moon. Samantha felt like a moon revolving around Len. She felt stuck in an orbit in which she could neither get closer to him to gain comfort, or break away to find safety.

"Samantha," said Len.

There it was! He was using her full name. He never did that. No one who knew her well did that, ever. That's what Brian had done when he'd broken up with her.

"I have to tell you something," Len said, finally turning toward her.

Hannah finished reading the last paragraph on page eighty-three of *A Year to Live* and took a deep breath. She was sitting on her bed, propped up against two pillows. Her back ached. Reading the book reminded her of Dr. Priestly, who had given the book as a reading assignment, and when Hannah thought of her professor, she felt agitated. The professor KNEW. These were the words that would fly into Hannah's mind, unsettling her, when she thought of Dr. Priestly reading her paper about her lesbianism.

Dr. Pauline Priestly, forty-one years old, had a tall, sturdy body and long, straight black hair that she wore parted on the side, so that when she bent her head to read from a book in class, her hair formed a dark shining curtain around her face. She favored long black skirts, loosely fitting dark-colored sweaters, soft leather boots, and chunky silver and turquoise jewelry.

The agitation that accompanied the realization that Dr. Priestly knew her secret made her hungry. The hunger followed the agitation naturally, as though it made perfect sense that when a person was unsettled about something, food was the first thing that entered his or her mind. It was as natural to Hannah to eat when she was anxious as putting on a sweater when she was cold.

Hannah remembered the discussion in group one night having to do with adrenaline and food, how if someone was anxious, because anxiety was a form of stress, the person felt the need for extra fuel for fight or flight.

Dr. Priestly had asked the class for reactions to Stephen Levine's book about the virtues of living each day as though there was only a year left to live.

"I wish I was in MORE denial about death," Hannah had said in class, surprising herself with her honest sharing. "I think about death all the time—my mom's, my own, everyone's. It doesn't feel good, it feels weird."

"I don't think about death much," said Mark, a six-foot-four black man from Kenya. "At least not as something bad." He pronounced bad as "bod."

"When I think about death, it seems at a safe distance," said another student. "I'm still young."

"My philosophy professor told us that Socrates said we should practice dying every day, so that our lives would not be spoiled by the fear of death," said another student.

Hannah was starving. The tightness in her lower back worsened. She sat up straighter and rotated her shoulders in all directions, leaning forward, away from the scrunched-up pillows behind her. Her left shoulder ached. She thought she might be having a heart attack. The slender paperback book felt suddenly heavy in her lap. Squeezing and massaging her shoulder with her right hand, she wondered if she should eat something or go for a walk. She knew she ought to go for a walk, as she had eaten dinner at the diner on the way home from the bakery only an hour before.

She didn't want to walk. She wanted to eat. She wanted to eat a bag of popcorn, a cheese omelet with several buttered English muffins, and a pint of vanilla fudge ice cream with an entire can of mixed nuts and some hot fudge sauce on top of the whole thing.

I need to get out of here NOW, thought Hannah, as she slid off the bed. As she headed out the bedroom door, she stopped. At the end of the hallway outside her room were the stairs that led down to the little alcove outside the kitchen. She'd have to pass the kitchen on her way out the front door.

The sensation that she was not safe hit Hannah with unexpected force, exploding in her solar plexus as though she'd been struck there. Her heart pounding, she sat back down on her bed and reached for her phone. She'd call Kaneesha to ask her to come and get her, to usher her safely out of her own house.

Hannah felt humiliated that she had to go to such lengths to take care of herself. She had committed to Gale, to the group and to herself that she would go to whatever lengths necessary to stay safe. If Kaneesha wasn't able to come, she'd call Sam, and if Sam couldn't come, she'd call Phoebe or Scott or Billy or Faye. She would not abandon herself.

As Hannah dialed Kaneesha's number, she thought, "This experience gives the expression 'home alone' a whole new scary meaning."

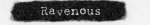

The beautiful woman sitting beside Phoebe on the plane was reading a book entitled *Anatomy of the Spirit*. Phoebe saw the title when the olive-skinned young woman with the long kinky dark hair placed the opened book face down on her seat before climbing over Phoebe, in an aisle seat, to get to the bathroom.

Phoebe, along with her father and his crew, were on a nonstop flight to Las Vegas, where her father was going to shoot a shampoo commercial in which the model, Bree Martin, was going to be part of a magic act. Before the shampooing, her hair was going to be a dull, drab brown. After the "magic" of the shampoo, the hair would be a sparkling chestnut with glints of auburn, extravagantly thick and silky. Phoebe could already imagine it swinging in slow motion across the TV screen.

Bree Martin had enough hair for three people's heads, Phoebe thought as she looked at an ad in *Vogue* in which Bree appeared. Her hair was naturally magnificent—heavy and glossy and perfect. The beauty of Bree's hair had nothing to do with shampoo. It had to do with genes. Raphael, the hairdresser, would have to make her hair look drab in the "before" shots with different kinds of glop so that it could be returned to its natural gloriousness for the "after" shots. Phoebe was missing her Friday classes, but wanted to be able to go to Bree's wedding.

The young woman who'd been reading *Anatomy of the Spirit* came back down the aisle toward row twenty-four. Phoebe noticed the graceful way she slid herself neatly between the stewardess and the seats as they passed each other in the aisle. The woman had a large mole near the outside of her left eyebrow, and greenish eyes, forming a startling contrast with her dark complexion. She wore jeans, silver Nike Airs and a green top that fit snugly around her shapely upper body. She was slender, and had a gamine-like quality that reminded Phoebe of Audrey Hepburn.

"Excuse me again," she said, and smiled as she climbed over Phoebe to get back to her seat.

"Interesting title," Phoebe remarked as her seatmate closed the book and placed it in her seat pocket as she sat down.

By the time the plane had touched down at McCarran Airport in Las Vegas, they had been talking for over three hours. Annemarie had learned about Phoebe's struggles with her weight, her father and her love for Daryl. Phoebe had learned dozens of things about Annemarie Santeneco, but the one thing Phoebe found most interesting about Annemarie, a graduate student in psychology at UCLA, was that she was writing a paper on how compulsive behavior— whether it was related to drinking, or shopping, or eating, or gambling—was connected to shame.

Annemarie sipped from a small bottle of spring water the stewardess had given her. Phoebe noticed the beauty of her hands, the long delicacy of the bones of her fingers, the length of Annemarie's neck as she leaned her head back to sip from the bottle. Phoebe wanted to know more about Annemarie, wanted to be wearing the soft, narrow well-worn jeans and the poison green sleeveless turtleneck in which Annemarie looked so relaxed and comfortable and slender and perfect. Phoebe wanted to be Annemarie.

"I'm coming to New York a few weeks from now," said Annemarie, as she took the book out of her seat pocket and slipped it into her carry-on bag. "I'd love to come see you and meet Daryl."

* * *

Len sat with his sketchpad opened on his lap while his Steely Dan CD played. His assignment had been to design a telephone. He'd not started on the phone design, though. He wanted to finish his drawing of Marika LaRue first.

Marika LaRue, he thought. *What a remarkable name. Could anybody really name an infant baby girl "Marika LaRue"?* He assumed this exotic person's parents had normal names—Jack and Shirley, for example. Jack LaRue. Shirley LaRue. These names had none of the sequined, feathered, neon glamour, though, of the name they'd bestowed upon their child.

Len had drawn Marika, whom he had never met, from memory, as accurately as he could. She had full lips and big square teeth, slightly too big, with an overbite. She had a big body and lots of dark hair that fell onto her shoulders in a chaos of waves that swung and bounced when she walked. Almost six feet and made taller by her inevitable platform sneakers, she glided down the halls of their school with confidence and flair, seeming to Len like the Queen of the World. Her laugh was big, too, and so were her earrings and the brightly colored shawls she wore casually wrapped around her shoulders. She had style, thought Len as he sketched in the line of her left hip in leggings.

In this sketch (he had already made two others) he would dress her in the shawl that made her look like a gypsy, cream-colored with huge red roses and a silky red fringe. Len drew her carefully, his soft Venus pencil caressing the textured surface of the paper, working slowly, savoring particularly the shadowy contours of her prominent collarbones.

I t's pretty good," said Michael McIntyre as the model's gleaming chestnut hair swung luxuriously across the monitor as the photo crew watched the results of the day's shooting. The hair looked heavy, and its glossiness suggested that it would feel cool and silky to the touch.

"But it's not perfect," he continued. He looked at his Rolex. "Let's do it again to make sure we got the dove in the background for long enough."

"Oh NO!" groaned the crew in unison. Then, resigned, they began to move lights around again, as the model and the magician, holding his dove, returned to their original places on the stage.

Phoebe watched as Bree took her place. She looked supremely confident and serene.

Later, as Phoebe drove with the crew to the wedding chapel for Bree's wedding, Phoebe thought, *I will never, ever feel so confident and serene.*

The wedding chapel was painted white and looked from the outside like a giant square piece of wedding cake, the building's pink trim looking like icing. Bree was dressed in a big, fluffy, white satin dress with a high, white lace collar and a hundred satin-covered buttons down the back. Phoebe had often imagined herself in such a dress, standing beside Daryl like the figures on top of wedding cakes. As she conjured this image now, she experienced a heavy, sinking feeling; she'd look huge in such a dress! Anyway, Daryl was engaged to Gabby. It was ridiculous for Phoebe to think about Daryl as a candidate for lifetime companion.

Phoebe's "little black dress," the one Daryl had selected for her, was not as little as she would have liked, though it was two sizes smaller than her last dresses had been. Bree's groom, Layne, was dressed like Elvis, in a white, bell-bottomed jumpsuit, complete with multicolored gems, gold studs, fringes and a wide belt with a gigantic round gold buckle. His sideburns reached to the tips of his earlobes, and his pompadour was pomaded to a stiff sheen. Phoebe could smell the coconutty fragrance of Layne's hair gel mixed with the scents of roses and freesia with which her father had filled the chapel in a tribute to the happy couple.

Her father was paying for everything. Phoebe admired her father's generosity. But she sometimes regarded this otherwise excellent trait with cynicism because she suspected it came from his need to be indispensable, noticeable, the center of attention. Phoebe shooed that thought away as the wedding march began and the dozen of them stood to honor the bride and groom. Phoebe looked at her father and felt a mixture of hate and admiration that confused her.

The couple wanted to have the reception at a buffet. So, after the ceremony the wedding party trooped through the buffet at The Bellagio Hotel, piling their large white dinner plates with slices of prime rib, king crab legs, succulent shrimp, wood-roasted baby quail stuffed with saffron rice, cured Virginia ham with pineapple slices, lime-marinated scallops, Peking duck, fried chicken, perfect tiny bite-sized pizzas, sushi, lamb shank, mushroom pie, Tandoori game hen, tender breast of turkey with gravy and cranberry relish, wedges of vegetable tart, pasta primavera, ravioli stuffed with lobster, Chilean sea bass, poached salmon, smoked salmon, oysters, seafood bisque, herring in cream sauce, sliced pieces of succulent fruit-marinated pork, roasted pheasant, veal chops, asparagus hollandaise, grilled Portobello mushrooms, truffle risotto and four kinds of mashed potatoes: sweet, spinach, beet and garlic. They had five desserts each.

Everyone but Phoebe, that is. Because her father watched her every move, her every bite, her every CHEW, Phoebe, in an effort to avoid the probability that her father would humiliate her in front of the entire group if she ate as luxuriantly as everyone else, chose several varieties of salad and some turkey breast with a tiny dollop of cranberry sauce.

Then she returned to her room, her head swimming in afterimages of little satin-covered buttons and flashing neon. She felt lonely and resentful, as though she'd been sent to bed without supper.

❈ ❈ ❈

When, after Hannah's fourth class, Dr. Priestly invited Hannah to the Morgan Library to see some of Freud's original manuscripts, Hannah was confused. As students rushed down the halls, she felt flustered and unable to answer as she stood beside the older woman just inside the door to the classroom. Hannah didn't know what the Morgan Library was, or where it was, or whether it was appropriate for her professor to be inviting her on a field trip. It wasn't as though the whole class was going.

"We can go on a Saturday," Dr. Priestly was saying. "Do you work on Saturdays?"

"Uh—yes, I do," replied Hannah nervously, looking at her watch to find somewhere to focus her eyes.

"Oh," said the professor. "Well, is there some other time that might be better for you? I teach only part-time, so I could be free when it's convenient for you."

Hannah wanted to ask, "Why are you asking me to go out with you? Will there be a quiz after the trip?" Instead, she said, "Where's the Morgan Library?"

"It's in Manhattan, on the East Side. We could have lunch afterwards."

"I guess that would be all right," said Hannah. She couldn't think of a reason to say no, though she felt frightened about having agreed to go.

"So what's a good day for you?" continued the professor.

"Wednesday is my day off," Hannah said.

"Good," said Pauline Priestly. "We'll go on Wednesday then."

Len held Samantha. Her soft blonde hair felt like silky feathers against his face and her small, lean body, so thin and insubstantial, made him hold her softly. He could feel her backbone, so exposed that it evoked in him a need to protect her, a need which only increased his confusion.

Why had this happened to him, to them both? Was he so disloyal, so insensitive? Sam had shown him nothing but devotion. She was physically frail, but in her heart was a fierce, unwavering determination to have a long-term loving relationship. She was in therapy; she was doing the best she could. Guilt filled him suddenly. It felt like a need to disappear, to distance himself from the conflicts that had triggered it.

"Sam," Len said, pulling himself away, releasing her from the circle of his arms. "It's getting late."

They were sitting in the dark in Len's car, at the edge of the Maple Ridge High School athletic field. Beyond the field was the gym, and beyond that, the school buildings and the bird sanctuary. Samantha remembered the bench where Brian had ended his relationship with her. The bench was right there, across this same field, and she recalled how she'd felt that day, after he'd said he couldn't be with her anymore.

Len hadn't told her he couldn't be with her. He'd said he still loved her, that the girl he was drawing was someone he'd never spoken to, never even met.

But if this girl meant so little to Len, why was Samantha hurt?

* * *

Samantha, Hannah and Scott sat sipping cinnamon-scented coffee concoctions at Java Station.

"How could he DO this to me!" wailed Samantha. "How am I going to get through this Marika LaRue thing? I don't know how I'm supposed to feel about it!"

"How DO you feel about it?" asked Scott, setting his white mug of coffee down on the round white Formica table next to his cell phone, his car keys and his ever-present roll of sugarless mints.

Samantha sat up straighter for a moment to ponder this. "I feel worthless!" she said. Then she slouched back down, burrowing her chin into the soft knitted collar of her gray turtleneck. She exhaled a long breath.

"I feel worthless! Not important enough to him. Not big enough to him. Not small enough to myself. Not pretty enough, or interesting enough, or sexy enough, or fun enough. I have a headache."

"You know how you said you get headaches when you don't eat," said Hannah gently, not wanting to sound scolding.

"You haven't eaten anything in two days," Scott reminded her.

"I know," said Samantha. "But I'm not ever hungry anymore."

"How could you not be hungry when you haven't eaten anything in two days and haven't eaten enough in two years?" asked Hannah. She wore a dark green sweatshirt that said "WE TELL YOUR FORTUNE AT THE BOTTICELLI BAKERY" printed across the front in an Oriental-looking typeface.

Samantha, who had been looking at her lap, raised her eyes and looked straight at Hannah.

"I feel like cutting myself," she said.

* * *

As the group (minus Phoebe who was still in Las Vegas) assembled around Gale's big stone fireplace, even before Billy and Faye were settled into their chairs, Samantha blurted, "I cut myself again. About an hour ago. I just had to get out of here," she explained, pointing to her head to punctuate the word "here."

The group remained silent, waiting to see if she would continue.

"I'm hopeless and stupid and disgusting, and I'm NEVER going to get it. NEVER! I don't even know why I come back here. What's the point? You're all probably bored with me by now anyway."

Billy said, "I'm not bored. I'm interested in you."

"I'm not bored," said Scott. "I care about you."

"I'm glad you're here," added Faye. She coughed for a long minute, then cleared her throat. It sounded painful. "I'M the boring one," she said when she could speak again.

Gale said, "You know Samantha, when your life feels like a root canal, as it must right now, why would you expect to go through it without novocaine?"

"I know! I know about the novocaine thing," said Samantha. She had heard this novocaine analogy from Gale before. "But DUH! Cutting myself? Why can't I find a DIFFERENT pain killer. One that doesn't HURT so much. One that isn't so—so—STUPID!"

"It really bothers me when you call yourself stupid," said Scott softly. "You're not stupid. You're just in pain, and you're doing the best you can."

Scott looked at Samantha with undisguised adoration. Since that night in group the year before when he had done a role-play with Samantha, in which he had played Len and Samantha had practiced telling him, as Len, that she cut herself, Scott had fallen in love with her.

"Well, I'm sorry if it bothers you!" said Samantha harshly. "I'm not a perfect person!"

Scott stayed quiet. He had never heard Samantha express anger. One part of him was glad she had, because he had come to understand that when she cut herself, she was expressing anger, among other things. Another part of him was horrified that the comradely feelings she seemed to have for him would be erased by this one remark.

"You ARE working on finding other ways to soothe yourself; you're working on that here," Gale reminded her. "And you HAVE improved. You've learned that it's okay to ask Len what he is feeling instead of making assumptions, thinking you can read his mind. You have such a much better relationship with your mom and sister now."

"Whatever I do, it will never be good enough. I know I'll never be able to eat enough. Enough is way too much!"

"For me," said Billy, "too much is not enough, Sam. I could learn something from you. When you say it's pointless to come back here to group, I feel really bad, as though you don't care about me, about all of us, as though you don't realize that you're a part of something that wouldn't be the same without you."

"I never realized how self-centered I was!" said Samantha sadly.

"How self-centered you ARE!" said Billy smiling at her.

They were quiet for a minute. Then Samantha said, "SO you're saying you'd miss me? The way we all miss Phoebe tonight?"

"I'd miss you a lot," said Hannah. "I'd miss how funny you are sometimes."

"Oh yeah!" Samantha said, smiling. "I'm a laugh riot!"

"I'm going to Manhattan with Dr. Priestly tomorrow," said Hannah. "How should I feel about THAT."

"How DO you feel about it?" asked Faye, in the midst of recovering from another fit of coughing.

"I don't know why I'm going," said Hannah. "I don't know why she asked me."

From Phoebe's journal:

PHOTO CREW STORMS LAS VEGAS
Hairdresser Wins $12,000 Playing Slots!

Raphael Fernandez, hairdresser extraordinaire, won thousands last night at a slot machine in the posh Bellagio Casino, while his coworkers from Manhattan cheered.

Sluts Strut and Strip on the Strip!

Topless dancers abound.

Hunk Daryl Morgenstern Sets Wedding Date!!!!!!!

Daryl Morgenstern told friends, who called Phoebe at her hotel, that he and Gabriella had set a wedding date.

Phoebe McIntyre Mourns— Pigs Out at Bellagio

Friends once again fear for fat Phoebe's sanity since she heard of the handsome hunk's plans.

"He could have told me himself!" she complained after an unnamed source broke the news.

Phoebe sneaked away to the magnificent buffet at the Bellagio Hotel and comforted herself with four kinds of mashed potatoes, Tandoori game hen, truffle risotto, poached salmon, fried chicken, and seven desserts, including chocolate mousse and crème caramel.

❋ ❋ ❋

Oh my God, she's a lesbian! Hannah thought when Dr. Priestly placed her hand on Hannah's left thigh as they drove through the tunnel into midtown Manhattan.

Many thoughts followed this realization: *There is something wrong with this woman. She's a lesbian! There is something wrong with lesbians. Sex is frightening no matter who is having it. And finally, there is something wrong with me.*

Hannah experienced these thoughts as Dr. Priestly's powder blue 1964 Chevy Impala convertible sped through the final mile of the Midtown Tunnel into the brightness of Wednesday afternoon.

Hannah did not remove the professor's hand, nor did she remark on its presence on her thigh as the car cruised up Third Avenue. She looked around at the people walking; she tried to imagine herself calling Dr. Priestly "Pauline," as Dr. Priestly had asked her to do. She noticed that Dr. Priestly—Pauline—had on dark red leather boots with her brown tweed slacks and brown turtleneck sweater.

She noticed the people on the street again. They were so different, she thought, from the people in her small town, so different from one another. Where Hannah lived, most of the women dressed similarly in expensive-looking clothes. Most of the people in her town had that well-groomed sheen of wealth, had all their teeth, no matter what their age. City people, she noticed, were all so different: different colors of skin, wearing turbans or saris or torn jeans or business suits, and not all of them had all their teeth and some of them didn't look clean.

Hannah was grateful for these distractions since Dr. Priestly still had her hand on her thigh as she steered the car into a parking lot on Lexington Avenue.

"You look nervous," she said to Hannah, turning toward her after she had put the Chevy into park and they waited for the parking attendant to move the white Jeep directly in front of them.

"M-Me?" Hannah stammered. "Oh—uh—well, yeah," she sighed. "I am."

She felt better once she'd spoken and said something true.

"This is your first time, isn't it?" asked Dr. Priestly. It wasn't really a question.

"Time?" repeated Hannah.

"With—another woman," said the professor. "Your first date."

"Yeah," admitted Hannah. "How did you know?"

"Because of your essay," Dr. Priestly replied.

"Is it all right that we're—um—together today?" asked Hannah nervously. "I mean because of school and everything?"

"No," said the teacher. "It isn't. I can't seem to get myself to resist falling in love, though. Life is short. It makes one appreciate things more, don't you think?"

She's IN LOVE with me? thought Hannah, completely horrified at first, then less so, then pleased. Hannah smiled inside. Life WAS short. That was how she always felt.

The Las Vegas Elvisarama Museum had just opened, and Bree's new husband, Layne, would be appearing there six days a week. Bree had confided her anxieties about the marriage during a break from shooting when Bree, Phoebe and Raphael had strolled through the Fashion Show Mall looking at sparkly sweatshirts and sequined T-shirts.

Bree had seen a documentary on The Learning Channel about Elvis impersonators in which Layne had appeared. A statistic was mentioned which concerned Bree. The statistic indicated that the number of Elvis impersonators was climbing so high, so fast, that if the number of new Elvis impersonators continued to increase at its current rate, by the year 2008, three out of every ten people on earth would be an Elvis impersonator. This, she felt, did not bode well for the sound financial future of a newly married couple intent on raising a family.

Raphael was a huge Elvis fan so they went to Elvisarama. Phoebe followed him into the museum, its cool, quiet interior a welcome contrast to the blindingly bright warm day outside where cars sped past on Industrial Road, the silhouettes of the huge luxury hotels rising up beyond it. Elvis sang the song, "I Want You, I Need You, I Love You."

Raphael had stopped at a glass display case full of Elvis's things and was reading something. When Phoebe caught up with him, she began to read the document over his shoulder. It was a handwritten letter from Elvis to his father. The last paragraph read:

"I want to thank you for giving me intangible gifts from your heart—understanding, tolerance and concern—gifts of your mind—purpose, ideas and projects—gifts of your words—encouragement, empathy and solace."

"This letter—it's amazing," said Raphael. "I didn't know Elvis was such a poet!"

"Respect is avid," the letter continued. "It wants to contain everything and to retain everything. For you my father, my friend, my confidant, I have an avid respect."

Phoebe did not try to suppress the tears that sprang into her throat and up into her eyes. Raphael turned to her just as she was wiping one away.

"Terrific, huh?" he said. "I did not know my own father," he told her in his heavily Spanish-accented English.

Again, Phoebe thought of her own father. She supposed she was lucky to have a father. But the father she had continually, often even without words, projected toward her the feeling that she was not okay just the way she was. She felt ungrateful and disloyal for not appreciating her father, the fact of his presence in her life. Still, Elvis had written such an eloquent letter to his father that it made Phoebe envious, filled her with longing, then confusion, and then shame. She told herself again how ungrateful she was.

Raphael looked at his watch, then at Phoebe. "We are late for the next shoot!" he shrieked in his usual overdramatic style. "Your father will take his revenge by hating all the hairs I do!"

*　*　*

Samantha, Lacey and Hannah sat at the edge of the pier beside an enormous white yacht called *Defense Rests*. The girls held their jackets closed and scrunched up their shoulders against a late afternoon chill. The late-September day had started out unseasonably warm and sunny, but had quickly turned gray when four o'clock came.

Hannah had on a denim jacket, the front of which was dusted with flour and powdered sugar where she had handled it in order to put it on. Her jeans were baggy and this pleased her. Even though she had not been purging, her weight had stayed pretty constant, since her binges had mysteriously reduced in size. No longer did she eat entire pints of frozen yogurt and whole boxes of cookies. Now, a binge consisted of half a pint of frozen yogurt. It was miraculous to her that she could stop eating the delicious dessert while there was still some left in the carton. Maybe all the breathing was having some effect on her, though she couldn't understand why, or how.

Gale said that staying present to one's body was a crucial tool for getting a grip on compulsive behaviors. Hannah could certainly see how breathing took her from her mind, where she imagined herself fat, her mother dead, her father remarried to the girlfriend and herself letting her father know that she was gay—to her body, where, when she was breathing, she actually felt safe, at least in that moment.

Lacey and Samantha both wore their old high-school cheerleading jackets, white satin with Maple Ridge Cheerleading in green on the back and each of their names embroidered on the front. Lacey had on a black cotton turtleneck and ankle-length black boots, and Samantha wore a white T-shirt, khakis and her favorite black clogs. The girls had been in the tea shop, but Lacey wanted to have a cigarette, which was why they had come outside and

were huddled together on the pier beside the big yacht.

"Do you think *Defense Rests* belongs to a lawyer?" asked Lacey idly as she exhaled smoke. She was never without her box of Merits and her hot pink Bic lighter. She pulled her jacket more tightly around herself, snuggling her neck into its satiny collar.

"Why did he DO this to me?" repeated Samantha for the third time, continuing the conversation they had begun in the tea shop.

The first time she'd recited her lament, Lacey had said, "He didn't do it TO YOU. He just DID it. He's drawing someone, not DATING someone."

Samantha had asked the question again as soon as Lacey had completed these remarks, exactly as though she had not heard Lacey at all, or as though Lacey had not spoken. Lacey was afraid it sounded as though she had been defending Len. But she hadn't meant it to sound that way. It just seemed to her that Len hadn't set out to hurt Samantha. He had just gone on living, and things had happened to him and one of the things was Marika LaRue.

Lacey sighed and carefully put out her cigarette. She stubbed it out on the piling, thoroughly, and then placed it into the pack of Merits for disposal later.

The next time Samantha said, "How could he do this to me?" Hannah had answered.

"It must feel awful to be you right now, Sam. I'm so impressed with you that you haven't cut yourself again over this."

Samantha said, "Cutting doesn't help. It helps nothing. It just makes me look like an idiot with a bunch of weird scars. Nothing helps. I'm a complete loser."

The three of them continued to sit in silence while Lacey lit another cigarette and Hannah picked at her cuticles, a new behavior for her since she had stopped purging. The fact that this was a form of "cutting" had not escaped her. She didn't know what to do with this information, though. However, noticing herself now made her realize how much her fingers hurt, throbbed where the skin had been ripped away leaving the pink exposed flesh swollen, irritated and vulnerable to the slightest friction.

"How could he do this to me?" wailed Samantha again.

I have so much shame," said Scott when the group had settled down for their Tuesday night session.

"How do you know that what you're experiencing is shame?" asked Billy. "I never know what I'm feeling, just THAT I am feeling."

"I read John Bradshaw," answered Scott, "and I identified."

"What does the shame feel like?" asked Gale. "What goes on in your body, in the center of you, that you are calling shame?"

Scott closed his eyes. He took a long, slow breath. "It feels—I feel—nauseous," he said. "Sick."

"That's how I used to feel when I needed to throw up!" said Hannah.

"Why don't you feel that way anymore?" Scott asked.

"I do, sometimes," Hannah replied, "but not as often. I'm starting to think I might be good at something, at baking, as though I AM something. I think I am finding out what self-esteem feels like. A little."

I wish I felt that way, thought Samantha, wondering what Len was doing right at that moment.

"I have disgusting self-esteem," said Faye. "No . . ." she coughed violently for a minute, ". . . that's not right. If I had disgusting self-esteem, that would mean I HAD self-esteem. I don't think I have ANY."

"Self-esteem is one of those things you don't want to leave home without," said Billy wryly.

"How do you GET self-esteem?" asked Scott.

"You have to find out about yourself," said Phoebe. "Know who you are, what you're good at, like Hannah said."

"But how do you DO that?" wondered Faye.

"Writing is good," offered Phoebe. "It helps me see myself. Mirrors lie. Sometimes when I'm writing in my journal or writing an article for the school paper, I get such a kick out of myself that I forget how fat I am. Until my father reminds me."

"I sometimes imagine that I'm merging into other people," admitted Faye. "I wonder if I even truly exist."

"There's only one thing special about me," Samantha announced. "It's that I can *not* eat."

"What does it feel like to be you when you're not eating, Sam?" Gale asked.

"I feel strong and proud. When I eat, even if I eat lettuce, I feel empty. It's weird because it's backwards. When I eat I feel emptier."

"What else?" prodded Gale.

Samantha looked up at the ceiling.

"Are you looking at the ceiling to find out how you feel? Are you looking outside yourself?"

"Where should I look?" asked Samantha.

"Inside," said Gale.

* * *

Doesn't this feel good?" asked Gabby.

"Yeah," said Daryl. He pressed himself closer to her. "Are your feet still cold?"

"No," she said.

They were in Gabby's big white bedroom, stretched out on her white divan. Both of them were naked, and Gabby rested her head in the curve of Daryl's neck.

"Then why don't you spend more time with me when you come home on weekends?" Gabby complained.

"I drive for hours and hours to be with you!" said Daryl defensively. "And then I drive hours and hours back to school! I can't study while I'm in the car. I have to study, Gab!"

"I know, but you spend time with Phoebe and your other friends."

"Oh—so now I can't have friends?"

He pulled away from her and reached for his T-shirt.

"I didn't say you couldn't have friends."

"Yes, you did. That's what you ARE saying," said Daryl as he stood and pulled on his jeans.

Gabby sat up. "I'm not! I'm just—I just want to see more of you," she said forlornly.

"Your mom's a judge, your dad's a doctor, and you're their precious princess, Gabby. You've always had things exactly the way you wanted."

"Is that a crime?" protested Gabby, pulling her white sweater over her head.

"I can't do this now. I gotta go," said Daryl. "I'll call you later."

* * *

Gale took a deep breath and walked into *Computers.com*, a small shop on Main Street in Maple Ridge. It had taken her a long time to gather enough courage to face learning something new, complicated and difficult. She was attached to her old Smith Corona electric portable type-writer, which Gerard thought was perfectly Jurassic. After seeing so many people's home offices with sleek laptops on their desks, the old machine looked big and clumsy even to her. She couldn't keep her Smith Corona on her lap on a plane, either!

The reason she had chosen this particular morning to appear at the computer store was that she had had an "a-ha" experience the previous evening. She'd been saying good-bye to a client, with whom she'd been exploring the impor-tance of taking risks. She smiled to herself when she thought of how she used the word "explore" when talking with a client. She knew, when she said to a client, "We need to explore your fears of intimacy as a possible explanation for why you cannot sustain a functional relationship," that

what she was actually saying was, "It IS your fear of intimacy that is the central core of all your misery."

Gale realized, at the end of the session, that SHE needed
to take a risk, that in order for her client to do something
new that scared him, SHE needed to do something new
that scared HER. She had to go that distance, to step
beyond her fear. Only then could she "create a space" for
her client to do the same.

She had to go there first. She needed to take the map, the
directions, and the flashlight and forge ahead to the
unknown. Only then could the client, too, go there. That
would be how she would create the space for him to do it.
Then, all she would have to do once she had stepped into
the dark, beyond her own fears, was to wait for him in the
clearing.

Sometimes, when she sat listening to a distressed client,
wondering what she could say to help, she forgot this step:
She had to go there herself first.

What did this mean? What would she have to do to help
Hannah and Samantha and Phoebe and all the members of
the Tuesday group, she wondered, as she looked around the
computer store in perplexity. She didn't yet know. She didn't
have to know right now, this minute. Right now, she had to
decide if she wanted a laptop or a big clunky piece of beige
plastic in her life.

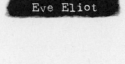

* * *

Daryl had fallen into the habit of calling Phoebe after his dates with Gabby. He would come home from college late on Friday night to be with Gabby, but would not stay at her house overnight on Saturday because he'd have to study, so he'd go back to the place he was staying to read organic chemistry.

"The trips home are becoming a hassle," Daryl said to Phoebe as he settled down on his friend's pull-out sofa with a glass of iced tea, the phone wedged between his head and shoulder. He was wearing blue plaid flannel pajama bottoms and a gray T-shirt that showed the bulge of his biceps and the power in his forearms. Once, when Phoebe had seen him holding a phone, she'd marveled at how small the receiver looked in his hand.

Daryl's buddies at school kidded him about how he drank nothing stronger than iced tea. But Daryl was serious about his studies and about being the best premed student he possibly could.

Phoebe had already had "the discussion" with Daryl about why he had not called her in Las Vegas himself to let her know he and Gabby had set a wedding date: June 17 of the following year. They now called this "the discussion" because Daryl HAD finally called her in Las Vegas and said, "We need to have 'the discussion' now. It's about the setting of the wedding date and the fact that you heard it first through someone other than me. It's just that I had not had a chance to call you yet, that's all Phoebe. Please don't be mad at me about that. One woman constantly mad at me is enough."

"Does Gabby know you're feeling that the weekend trips home are a hassle?" Phoebe asked, trying fiercely to keep the excitement out of her voice. She was so ashamed of herself for feeling happy when something seemed not to be going well with Daryl and Gabby.

"No," Daryl sighed, sipping his tea out of a tall glass with Ronald McDonald painted on it. "You know how she gets, how insecure she is about me. It's as though I can't do anything right, never do enough to prove to her that I love her. It's a major bummer."

"Does Gabby know how often we talk?" Phoebe asked.

"Oh yeah," said Daryl, putting the glass of tea on the end table and plumping up the pillows he could then lean back against. "I tell her stuff. Remember you told me about that talk show where the psychologist said it's important to share stuff? So I do that. But that's another example of where I can't do anything right, because she says she doesn't like that you and I have such a close thing going."

Daryl looked around at his friend's living room. The green plaid pull-out sofa had worn spots on the arms, and smelled strongly of nicotine and stale beer. Beer cans cluttered the end table so that there was barely space for the lamp and the phone.

"Gabby doesn't appreciate what an effort I make to be with her every weekend," he said. "I could be visiting my sisters in Pennsylvania. I could stay at school and study instead of driving all this way in both directions."

"Why doesn't Gabby drive up to school to see YOU?" asked Phoebe.

"You know what a princess she is. She doesn't want to drive all that way alone."

Phoebe thought she herself could take some lessons in how to be more of a princess. She could hear ice cubes tinkling in the glass as Daryl took a sip of iced tea. She knew that Gabriella was just trying to feel in control by expressing her fears about Daryl's other relationships. Gabby was only trying to feel safe. But in doing that, she was actually creating the very thing she was most afraid of—distance between herself and Daryl.

Phoebe suspected that if Daryl ever DID leave Gabby (which she doubted because Daryl was a stand-by-your-woman kind of guy) that Gabby would probably blame his leaving on her weight. And in blaming his leaving on her

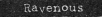

weight, she would be entirely missing the important lesson about how needing to be in control was really what caused the most pain. Gale had remarked one night in group that the risk of loss is embedded in every living moment. Phoebe reflected that to hold on too tightly in the controlling way Gabby was doing, was likely to create the very loss she was trying to prevent.

Phoebe couldn't help feeling glad that Gabby was acting so unwisely. She couldn't help being gratified that Gabby was not in therapy, otherwise her therapist would certainly be coaching her through all this.

"So, do you want to go to the movies with me next weekend? Gabby has to go to a family thing in Chicago on Saturday night, and I don't want to go with her. So she and I will just get to spend Sunday together. Of course she's mad at me for that, too."

"I'd love to go to the movies with you," said Phoebe, light-headed with joy at this prospect.

*　*　*

There was a small bakery for sale in Vermont, and Devie had always wanted to move to that leafy mountainous state. She felt confident that she could place Hannah in charge of the bakery in Long Island, hire an assistant for her, and then move to Vermont with her family to run the new one if it turned out to be any good. She was taking the trip to Montpelier to see it the following week and was going to invite Hannah to come along to help her decide what work might need to be done in the kitchen, offering to pay her regular per hour wages to accompany her. Devie's sister, also a baker, would do the essential baking while they were gone.

Devie came into the bakery's delivery entrance at the back, through the short, dark hall that led into the big, gleaming kitchen. Hannah kept the bakery spotless. This was especially important since the health inspector had visited them unexpectedly the previous week. The inspector had no complaints about the conditions in the bakery and had even commended Hannah on the excellence of her lemon poppy-seed cake. He'd also reminded Hannah that her name was palindromic and explained that a palindrome was a word or phrase that was spelled the same way forward or backward. He said he was aware of palindromes because his wife's name was Ava.

Hannah felt more confident about her work at the bakery after the health inspector's visit. He'd been so pleased with the condition of the bakery and so friendly toward her. Devie had expressed anxiety to Hannah in anticipation of the inspector's visit because the bakery had been cited for

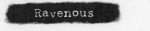

health-code violations a number of times when Devie's for-
mer assistant had not been as careful as Hannah.

When Devie came into the large, bright room, a machine
was mixing dough and the fragrance of baking bread filled
the air. Hannah was standing near the mixer beside one of
the long stainless steel counters.

Devie looked at Hannah with the admiration women
have for models and movie stars, believing Hannah possessed something she'd never had, something she never
would have, and this knowledge made her look at Hannah
with a fascination made bitter by envy.

She looked at Hannah's thick dark hair and her strong,
slender legs in the black leggings she wore beneath the long
white apron she baked in and tried to imagine how being
beautiful must feel. Hannah, Devie thought, was extremely
pretty, but not in the usual American way with small, sym-
metrical, Barbie doll features. Hannah was beautiful in a
more European way with her strong straight nose, dispro-
portionately large, upward-tilting eyes and glorious masses
of dark hair. Her blue eyes had flecks of gray in them, but
only sometimes.

Devie had often observed Hannah at work, focused on
weighing flour, or applying pink frosted roses to the edge of
a white birthday cake. Devie, now thirty-nine, had never
felt pretty, even at Hannah's age. It was hard for her to

imagine what beauty felt like. She imagined that pretty people spent hours looking in mirrors admiring themselves. She wished her own complexion was as smooth and as permanently tanned-looking as Hannah's and that she had Hannah's high, prominent cheekbones and square chin. Hannah was tall and had broad shoulders so that she looked elegant, even in a sweatshirt. Devie felt forever excluded from this form of feminine power. The best she could do to shine, she knew, was to succeed in her business.

Hannah looked up from the mixer and greeted Devie, having to speak louder than usual to be heard above the mixer's whir.

"Come into my office when you're done, okay?" said Devie, mouthing the words in an exaggerated way so that Hannah could lip-read them in case the noise was too great for her to be heard.

When Hannah had finished the next step in the baking of her cranberry walnut muffins, she went into the small office and sat opposite Devie, who was on the other side of the desk, deep in concentration, reviewing the day's receipts. A small line that Hannah recognized as anxiety had formed between Devie's dark eyebrows. Hannah studied Devie. Her round dark eyes, thin lips, and sallow face did not add up to beauty, but there was something about her, Hannah thought, that made her want to look at Devie for a long time.

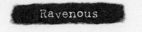

Devie finished her work on the computer, stood, closed the lid of her laptop and picked up her purse from the floor. Hannah stood, too. Devie looked at her watch and started to move toward the door.

"Was there something special you wanted to discuss with me?" Hannah asked, confused.

"Oh, yeah," said Devie. "Be sure you clean up really well tonight."

"But you know I always do that. The health inspector . . ."

"Yeah, well, he's quite the flirt," said Devie. "I don't trust him."

Hannah felt sudden fury. She thought, *There she goes again with remarks about keeping the bakery clean.*

"You think he didn't cite us because he has a crush on me?" said Hannah, barely able to suppress angry tears.

"Maybe," said Devie, "on you or on your lemon poppyseed cake."

Hannah was furious, then felt guilty for being so angry. After all, this WAS Devie's bakery, she HAD been cited before with the warning that if the violations were not corrected, her bakery would be closed down. This was Devie's chief source of livelihood since her husband had been so badly injured at his construction job that he was on disability.

Still, Hannah took so much pride in her work. She treated the bakery as though it was her own. Devie had even said as much to Hannah after Hannah had been working there for only a week.

"Okay," said Devie looking at her watch again. "I gotta go."

She took a step toward Hannah and, leaning forward, placed her cheek against Hannah's flour-smudged one, startling Hannah. Devie had never done this.

"Bye," said Devie. "The fortune cookies are selling well, though."

What did she mean by that? thought Hannah. *That the fortune cookies are selling well even though you yourself are a tremendous slob about how you keep the bakery?*

Devie moved toward the rear exit, walking past the stainless steel shelves, drums of flour and just-baked trays of corn, bran and blueberry muffins. Hannah watched Devie's short dark hair swing as she walked away, watched her use her shoulder to push open the heavy door of the bakery's back entrance. When the door closed behind her and Devie started her silver Mazda pickup truck, Hannah felt suddenly breathless, as though she'd been punched in the stomach. She looked longingly at the muffins.

How could Len DO this to me?" moaned Samantha in Tuesday night group. Her face seemed very pale above her purple turtleneck.

"So, do you want to pick someone to be Len and ask him?" asked Gale, predictably.

Samantha felt irritated at Gale. She was always asking someone to pick someone else to play someone else. Samantha was sick of group, of Gale's constant positive outlook, sick that Billy and Scott and Hannah and Phoebe all seemed to be getting better while she wasn't. Samantha could always depend on Faye, though. She was the same no matter what: emaciated, coughing and fearful.

"That would be too painful," said Samantha. "He might tell me. It might make me feel all fat and blobby inside."

Samantha blotted at her eyes with the shredded, balled-up tissue she'd been clutching.

"What do you feel inside you now?" asked Gale softly.

"Nothing," answered Samantha. "Pain."

"Is it nothing, or is it pain? Is feeling nothing painful?"

"I do feel SOMETHING," said Samantha, irritably. "I feel an ache."

"Where?" prodded Gale.

Samantha's right hand rose and rested over her heart.

"In my chest. I think."

"And what would the pain in your chest say if it could speak?"

There she goes again, thought Samantha. *Asking parts of our bodies to speak. UGH.*

Samantha sighed. "It would say—'I'm tough and strong and nothing can hurt me.'"

"So if you could take that ache that is tough and strong and unable to be hurt out of your chest and put it right next to you, there would be a space in your chest for something else to come in, right?"

"I guess so," said Samantha, annoyed by all this.

"So what else would come into your chest once you took away the ache and the toughness?"

This is SO annoying, thought Samantha, taking an involuntary breath. She looked up toward the ceiling, thinking about what else would come into her if there was no ache and no need to remain tough and strong and unable to be hurt.

"Look down instead of up, Sam," Gale said. "Look TOWARD your body instead of away from it. See what comes."

"Uhhhmmmm, let's see. If the hardness and toughness were taken away, what would come into my chest then?"

She looked up again, then remembered Gale there. Gale was SO annoying. Samantha looked down into her lap.

"I'm scared," she said. "Alone. A loser. Sad."

"And what else?" urged Gale.

"There's more?"

"Look and see," said Gale.

"I'm ugly. I feel ugly."

"What else?"

"Confused. Humiliated!"

"If you took away the ugliness and fear and sadness and confusion and humiliation and made a space in your chest for something else, what else comes?"

Samantha closed her eyes. A deep breath came. "I'm angry!"

The entire group cheered.

❋ ❋ ❋

From Phoebe's journal:

Big Night Has Arrived!
Phoebe FREAKS!!!!!!

Phoebe McIntyre, about to go out on the first actual date of her young life, is waiting for handsome hunk, Daryl Morgenstern, to arrive in his chariot to take her to their cinematic tryst. Dashing Daryl is engaged to the glamorous Gabriella Allibrandi, who is spending the evening in Chicago at a family affair, freeing Daryl to accompany the fat, frightened, about to become fabulous Phoebe to the movies.

* * *

Phoebe stood in the center of her bedroom. On the blue carpeted floor at her feet was every article of clothing she'd had since she was twelve. Some of the T-shirts were new, but most were vintage, picked up at a shop in Manhattan specializing in T-shirts featuring bands whose popularity had peaked when Phoebe was in diapers.

The BIG NIGHT had arrived. She and Daryl were going to the movies, and she needed to look amazing, so striking, so electrifying that when he saw her, he'd drop to his knees and propose right there in the foyer, in spite of the fact that Gabby was wearing a modest, tasteful diamond signifying their engagement.

She tried on a T-shirt she'd bought recently announcing the appearance of a band called Nefarious Potato, a band that had performed at a local club. The T-shirt was a vengeful shade of red, and when she put it on, it looked as though all the color had drained from her face. She tried on her trusty black Pink Floyd T-shirt, but Daryl had seen her in it a million times, and he'd never been so moved that he'd dropped to his knees and proposed. She wanted to look as though she had just thrown something on and looked effortlessly, unself-consciously fabulous in it. This was going to take a tremendous amount of effort, sort of like when the models would arrive at her dad's studio looking like skinny, faded, not exceptional young women and, after three hours of primping and fussing by hair and makeup people, lighting geniuses, wardrobe stylists and her perfectionist father, one photo of the hundred photos taken turned out wonderful.

She'd tried on half a dozen outfits and still had about ninety to go.

The phone rang, and Phoebe had to step over a pile of leggings and T-shirts to get to it, the clothes tangling around her ankles, the poodles weaving themselves into the knot.

"Phoebe, listen," said Daryl as soon as Phoebe had picked up. "Gabby didn't go to Chicago; she's here, and we're going to dinner and a movie. Do you want to join us? I told her I'd asked you to go to the movies with me, and I didn't want to disappoint you."

Phoebe's mind raced, and she was aware of her eyes going out of focus. Her heart felt like a tight fist, while the rest of her went limp.

"Phoeb—are you there?" Daryl asked when the silence lengthened.

"Yeah," she said. "I'm here."

And I'm going to be here forever because I'm NOT going to the movies with you and your fiancée because you feel sorry for me.

"I'm going to pass," she said. "Thanks for calling."

Phoebe, beyond tears, looked blankly out the window past the large lawn to the houses across the road, where warm lights of television sets emanated their golden glow in what she imagined were cozy living rooms. Images of cookies sprang into her mind.

She imagined eating them—giant chocolate-chip ones, big round oatmeal-raisin ones, and a box of ginger snaps, with several glasses of cold milk to numb her throat as the gobbled cookies went down.

She imagined how she'd feel afterwards. Gale had suggested she do that: to fast-forward an imaginary videotape to the end and see what would happen then. She did that; she saw how she felt afterward! It was not a pretty sight: There she was, full of self-recrimination, collapsed on her bed in a mess of clothes in which Tom and Nicole were also tangled, her stomach distended full of half-chewed ginger snaps, and aching, hating herself for having eaten the stupid cookies.

It was so boring! It was SUCH A BORING MOVIE! She had seen it too many times.

* * *

The first thing that came into Hannah's mind when she awoke in Vermont was, *Wow, I am lucky not to have died in my sleep.* Sleep was like death anyway, since you didn't know you were sleeping when you were sleeping any more than you knew you were dead when you were dead.

The second thing she thought was how lame it was that she, a young person, would have such morbid, deathy thoughts. It was her mother's premature death that caused these sorts of things to spring into her mind, of course. She had checked this out in group: None of the people in group had thoughts like this, at least not first thing after waking up, especially on a day with the sun pouring through lace curtains held back from the windows with bows.

Hannah glanced to her right across the few feet of space toward Devie's bed to see if she was awake. Devie's face was turned toward the window, so Hannah couldn't tell if her employer was still sleeping. They had arrived in Montpelier at 2:00 A.M. and gone to bed right away. Devie hadn't even undressed or brushed her teeth; she'd just fallen into bed in her tight black short-sleeved T-shirt and soft, worn jeans and fallen immediately to sleep.

Hannah looked at Devie's beautiful muscular arms, and a thrill raced through her, but she noted that she didn't want to do anything about it. She just wanted to have the feeling. It occurred to her that she had never known lust. Was THIS lust? She didn't think so, because she didn't want to DO anything, she just wanted to be in the experience. Was lust a testosterone-driven emotion? If women were supposed to have it too, was she abnormal about yet another human phenomenon?

She thought about having a naked sexual encounter with her boss, forcing herself to forget, for the moment, how Devie had hurt her feelings. She visualized the actions that would look sexual if someone were watching those motions in a movie. But that's all they were—motions. Hannah didn't feel the need to perform these actions. She just wanted her boss to love her. She wanted to be important to her. What did having an orgasm have to do with that? What was wrong with her? WAS there something wrong with her? Or was she just afraid of losing control? She didn't know.

What she did know, what she was learning in her therapy, was that there was one single thing that was more important to her than anything else, and it wasn't about having friends or being able to afford a car. It was about keeping herself safe. She did not feel safe with Devie now since Devie's remarks about keeping the bakery clean. Why had she come to Vermont with her? She never should have come. But she'd been afraid to refuse. She'd have had to lie about why she couldn't come. What would have been so horrible about lying? Her life was full of lies.

Her back ached, and her foot had fallen asleep so it was numb and tingly. She wiggled it, trying to bring feeling back into it. Her neck was stiff, and she wondered if she had multiple sclerosis. She sat up slowly, moving with great care, and rolled her head around; it felt so heavy, she wondered how she had been walking around holding it up all these years.

She looked around the room and noticed that it was afflicted with bows. The cords from the lighting fixtures mounted on the walls were wrapped in metallic gold ribbons that were tied into bows beneath each sconce. The chandelier in the center of the bedroom had a wide gold ribbon tied into a big bow around the chain connecting it to the ceiling. A basket full of potpourri on the table in the sitting room beyond the foot of Hannah's bed was wrapped in a burgundy velvet ribbon tied into a bow.

Devie said "Urrgh" and turned over to face Hannah, but her eyes remained closed. Her hair was tousled, and she looked like a teenager to Hannah rather than the thirty-nine-year-old mother she was.

Hannah crept slowly out of bed, taking care to fold the sheets and bedspread down carefully so the fabrics wouldn't rustle and wake Devie. She moved quietly to the bathroom, closed the door gently, and stood in front of the mirror. She took off her clothes in order to do what she had done every morning since she could remember: She looked at herself, taking stock.

Hannah had always hated her breasts. She'd constantly compared them with the breasts of other girls—in the locker room at school, in the shower at the gym, with pictures of women in magazines. In all cases, she felt she did not measure up. She hated their smallness but even more their shape—triangular and scrawny in her view—like the breasts of old tribal women on the Discovery Channel. She longed to have the sorts of breasts that looked swollen all the time, that pressed against sweaters and T-shirts and bras, breasts that formed cleavage, that looked perpetually engorged, threatening to break free.

You did not have to be a psychology professor to realize that breasts symbolized mothers, womanhood and nurturing. Hannah was able to admit that she often felt angry at her mother, but not that she hated her. But it was the size and shape of her breasts Hannah hated, not their meaning. Still, Hannah realized that a psychoanalyst would speculate that Hannah, in hating her breasts, really hated her mother—for leaving her, for being self-absorbed, for starving herself to death.

Hannah sighed and turned to look at herself from the side. Her butt was flat, too. So, there it was, clear as day: She did not have decent breasts, or a nice, round butt, or full lips, or any of the traits that made you a whole woman in America. Maybe in another country, Hannah thought, she could feel all right about herself.

She rummaged around in her handbag looking for the makeup case in which she'd packed her toothbrush. Crumbs of chocolate were bunched in the bottom of her makeup case, nestling into a crevice in the green satiny lining, and they were stuck beneath her fingernails when she withdrew her toothbrush from the bag. She hadn't bothered to brush her teeth when they'd arrived so late, and her teeth felt furry.

As she brushed her teeth, she wondered what Devie's plans for breakfast would be. Mealtimes were scary because she never knew if eating would lead to bingeing. She wondered when she would binge again. That was how she spoke to herself in her mind; she wondered "when" and not "if" she would binge. She knew herself well enough now to know not to say "never." Her resolve to stay sane about food was strong, but she still had no evidence that it was safe to trust herself.

There were still too many things she knew that she didn't want to know. When those things penetrated into her consciousness, she had to pretend she didn't know them. She had to lie to herself, and it felt terrible to do that, and that was when she needed so badly to binge. Hannah knew that it was only a matter of time before her father would remarry, and she didn't want to know this. She knew she was attracted to women, and this was something she definitely did not want to know.

She was in flight from her own truth. This was one of the things that compelled her to eat so wildly. She knew that, too. But she didn't want to know that she knew the reasons for her bingeing, because if she admitted to herself that she knew, she would have to look at what it was she was running away from. And in that knowing, it would have caught up with her.

* * *

Billy sat with his sister, Dee, the day after she'd turned eighteen, listening to her favorite band, The Fat Barbees. She'd spent her birthday at the club in Manhattan where the group had performed and gotten their CD *Wish She'd Never Given Birth*.

Dee was all in black, wearing a black dog collar a friend

had bought for her at Hot Topic. Her short spiky hair looked startlingly red against the whiteness of her skin. She was sprawled on the flower-patterned sofa with one of her short, thick legs folded beneath her and the other leg dangling over the edge. She and Billy were close, especially since he was able to understand how she felt about weighing more than "normal" teenagers. They enjoyed listening to music together, too, especially enjoying Rosetta Stone's strong voice singing that song, "Don't Like It in Here":

Don't like being in my body, hate being in my body, can't stand being in my body
Don't like it in here, don't like it in here.
What's the point of staying on Earth, if you just don't have self-worth?
Do not like being on this Earth, wish she'd never given birth!
Fat legs, hips, thighs, can't stand even having eyes
To look upon these ugly things
Wish to God I had some wings.
Don't like it in here, don't like it in here.

Part of the song sounded like rap music and part of it sounded like Latin dance music, and Dee thought she could hear what sounded like a ringing telephone in it somewhere.

Phoebe loved that song, too, Billy remembered. Phoebe was so beautiful to him. He wished she could see herself the way he saw her. An image of Phoebe's thick brown curls, rosy skin and curvy upper lip came to him, shocking him with a sudden longing.

*　*　*

Do you want to go to the movies?" asked Scott when Samantha picked up the phone, almost a week after she'd found her anger in group.

"Scott? Is this—Scott?"

"Who else?"

"I don't know. It's just—you've never called me before."

"I know, Sam. Gimme a break here, I'm REALLY nervous."

Samantha, in the midst of her gloom, laughed, surprising herself.

"The movies?" she said.

"Why do they call it 'movies' when it's only one movie?" said Scott. "So—do you want to go or not?"

"To a movie?"

"One movie. Yes. Sam—I'm in agony here."

"Okay," answered Samantha without enthusiasm.

"I'm not going to take you if you're not in the mood, because it doesn't sound like you're in the mood," said Scott.

"I am," Samantha said half-heartedly. "I'm in the mood."

"Is this how you sound when you're in the mood?" asked Scott.

"I guess so."

"I don't think you're in the mood," Scott said.

"I'm not," Samantha agreed, finally.

"Have it your way," said Scott. "See you in group. Bye."

Scott asked me out," said Samantha to a cloud of smoke behind which Lacey's narrow face with its pointy features was barely visible.

"That cute Scott?" asked Lacey, coughing, frantically waving away the smoke by batting her hand back and forth in front of her face. "The one in your group that drove us to that club—the whatchamacallit—The Bayou? The one with all the hot sauces on the tables and those drinks they serve in jars?"

"That Scott," said Samantha.

"He's so cute!" exclaimed Lacey. He's so—blond! That's great!"

"If it's so great, why don't YOU go out with him?"

"He didn't ask me," Lacey replied. "He hardly knows me."

"He hardly knows me, either," reflected Samantha.

"You're in GROUP together! Of COURSE he knows you!"

"Nobody knows me. Because I don't even know myself. When I even get CLOSE to knowing myself, I get scared. I'm so—so MEAN! I'm so mean in my head. If you heard the things I say in my head about myself and about other people, you wouldn't WANT to know me."

She paused. "You know who knows me? Len. Len knows me. I'm not gonna let THAT happen again."

* * *

Scott decided he would never go back to group again if he'd have to see Samantha there, and of course he'd HAVE to see Samantha if he went back to group. So he couldn't go back.

As he hoisted the free weights over his head, he felt some relief. The effort he had to expend each time he pressed the heavy, cold chunks of metal above his head made him exhale hard, and with each new breath in, and each hard breath out, his shame dissipated.

How could SHE, of all people, DO this to me? he thought.

She KNOWS how much shame I have, she hears about it once a week!

He kept hearing her words, "Not in the mood." Couldn't she have gone to the movie anyway—to save him from humiliation at least? How selfish was she? It was only a movie. A stupid movie! *Would it have KILLED her to sit there next to me? Today is Tuesday—group night. How can I go there?*

Another set of eight repetitions with heavier weights, and he'd decide.

Scott was not in the waiting room with the rest of the group when Gale opened the door to her office and asked Billy, Faye, Phoebe and Samantha to come in. Hannah was still in Vermont.

"Where's Scott?" asked Faye as she settled herself into the blue brocade armchair she always selected. "He's never missed a single group in three years, and he's never late."

"Well, he hasn't called," Gale replied. "Has anyone heard from him?"

A gentle knock was followed by Scott coming timidly into the room, his bearing so constricted that it seemed as though he wished to remain invisible.

"Sorry I'm late," he mumbled as he sat in the chair to Billy's left, opposite Samantha. He kept his eyes lowered, his voice soft, as though this would protect him from being a target someone could shoot at. He regretted having come. Then he was glad he had.

At least I feel safe with everyone else here, he thought.

"I'm sick of hating myself so much," announced Samantha. "I'm just sick of MYSELF. It's always me, me, me. I can't escape myself! I understand suicide now."

"Sam!" exclaimed Phoebe.

Scott knew exactly what Samantha was talking about.

"I know what you mean," Scott said, raising his eyes to look directly at Samantha.

"You DO?" said Samantha, looking at him for the first time that evening.

"You really hurt me, Samantha."

"I know. I know I did. I'm so wrapped up in myself. I don't know how to get out."

"What's keeping you there?" asked Phoebe.

"I think I'm afraid. I'm afraid to come out," admitted Samantha. "I was afraid to go to the movies with you," she said to Scott.

"But what could have happened to you? Couldn't you just have sat there next to me? I have feelings, too."

"I was afraid," said Samantha simply, as though repeating

herself explained something. "And sad. I'm—I'm . . ."

"Grieving," said Faye. "And not presentable."

Samantha nodded.

"You could have let yourself be comforted, then. Aren't I good for THAT at least? I mean, I know I'm a disgusting guy who cares too much about my muscles and my weight and stuff, but—"

"You're not disgusting. I'll go to the movies with you any time you want to," said Samantha.

"You're just saying that because you think I'm pathetic."

"No, I don't think that. We'll go to the movies."

"Don't do me any favors," said Scott angrily.

And he stood quickly and left.

* * *

It's not as if she even knows who I am!" insisted Len as he and Samantha sat beside each other in his car, illuminated by moonlight. "I'm not having a RELATIONSHIP with her! I'm just drawing her. And I'm NOT breaking up with you. Why do you keep SAYING that?"

"I don't care if she knows you or not!" said Samantha. She noticed how solid she sounded.

Len hunched up his shoulders and crossed his arms, turning slightly away.

"So you've been DRAWING her," she continued. "That's like—that's like LOOKING at her over and over again! That's like THINKING OF HER the WHOLE TIME you're drawing her. That's like LOVING HER! It's like you're making love to her with your charcoal and colored pencils!"

Suddenly, Samantha felt thin.

"I still love you, Sam," Len said meekly, uncrossing his arms and turning back toward her.

"I don't know if I care whether you do or not."

I broke up with Gabby," Daryl said as soon as Phoebe answered her cell phone.

She was at the mall shopping for a gift for Samantha's birthday. She'd just been coming out of Express and was heading across the corridor to Sephora when Daryl's news stopped her, causing the young mother right behind her to bump into the backs of Phoebe's sneakers with her stroller.

"What happened?" said Phoebe.

"I've had it with her control thing," said the handsomest, kindest, most sensitive young man in the state—maybe even the country, as far as Phoebe was concerned.

"She's used to getting everything she wants," he continued. "She acts like her royal highness in her house up there on the hill."

Phoebe thought again how SHE would like to get some lessons from Gabby about how to feel more deserving. She remembered well a long-ago conversation with Daryl about how nice Gabby was to herself, and how treating herself well was so attractive to him, how it made him respect himself more for having chosen her. He'd said how it made HIM want to treat her well, too, as though she was famous or powerful or something and treating her well was the right thing to do.

"She had me running around like a lackey," said Daryl.

"Uh huh," said Phoebe, basking in the news of Daryl's new freedom, instead of saying what she really felt, which was, "Yippee!"

* * *

It occurred to Hannah as she brushed her teeth on their second morning in Vermont that she was letting the water run while she did so, and that this was a waste of water. But she liked the sound of the flowing water; it seemed, every morning and every evening, to help her forget whatever was troubling her, as though life was momentarily taking a break as long as the water was running. Wasn't there some scientific stuff about negative ions and running water, too, something about how water in motion elevated people's moods, and this was why they liked being near the ocean?

Hannah turned off the water and heard Devie moving around outside the door, humming faintly to herself, some cheery melody Hannah didn't recognize. Hannah loved the fact that Devie was humming. She sounded happy. Hannah's mother was tense at all times of the day. Hannah had certainly never heard her mother hum or sing a single word of any song.

Sadness suddenly spread through her. She could feel it in the tightening of her throat, and when she thought of her mother's constant anxiety, it made Hannah angry at Devie for having something her mother never had. Now she felt as though Devie wasn't intelligent enough to worry about things. Wasn't she nervous about buying a new bakery in a community in which she had never lived? Why wasn't Devie more anxious?

They had spent the previous day looking around. Devie

said she didn't even want to bother looking at the bakery unless there was a possibility that she'd want to live in Montpelier. So they'd spent the day looking into shops and strolling the residential neighborhoods and browsing in the two small bookstores. Devie liked it there.

She'd made one comment to Hannah, though, about Hannah's height that made Hannah feel guilty about being tall. She'd simply said, as they both stood up from their seats at dinner the previous night, "You're so tall!" Hannah was at least seven inches taller than Devie. But the way Devie had delivered the observation sounded like there was something rude about being tall when the taller person found herself beside someone barely five feet two.

Later, Devie asked Hannah not to say anything during their meeting with Janelle, the owner of the bakery in which Devie was interested, especially warned Hannah against saying how nice everything in the kitchen was if it was indeed wonderful. Devie said remarks like that gave sellers the idea to raise the asking price.

Hannah had not intended to say anything to the owner of the bakery during their inspection of it. Devie, thought Hannah, was treating her like an eight-year-old who needed to be shushed.

"Are you ready to go downstairs for breakfast, Han?" asked Devie when Hannah emerged from the bathroom carrying her toothbrush. "They have this culinary school right here in the village, and the students bake breakfast stuff."

"So—pastry for breakfast?" Hannah asked. "We're having breakfast at a bakery?"

"Yep!" Devie replied, taking her overnight case off the floor by the door and heading for the bathroom. "We can spy on the competition."

"Uh—I'm not really that hungry this morning," said Hannah, who didn't want to eat cake for breakfast. Devie didn't know about Hannah's bulimia, not yet, and Hannah was not eager to present this information now.

"Well, can't you just have a cup of coffee or something?" asked Devie hesitating at the door to the bathroom and sounding disappointed.

Hannah didn't want to displease Devie. And she could understand that Devie wouldn't want to eat breakfast alone, so she said she'd join her. She wore her Keds so she wouldn't be adding any inches, since Hannah was self-conscious about her height with Devie now.

"You're not going to be tempted by a chocolate croissant or a lemon poppy-seed muffin?" asked Devie playfully.

"I don't like eating bakery stuff in the morning," Hannah said. The bulimic Hannah could think of nothing better. The recovering Hannah had to be careful.

"Okay then," said Devie. "I'll just have a quick shower, and then we'll go downstairs and brave the bows."

✳   ✳   ✳

With fierce concentration, holding onto the red marker so tightly that her knuckles were white, Phoebe drew the outline of a heart onto a piece of pink paper. Then she colored it in a childlike scribble. She wanted it to look like the fourth-grade art that parents displayed on their refrigerator doors.

When she was satisfied with the heart, she pierced it right in its center with a lightning bolt that she drew in black and yellow and purple. Underneath the heart struck by lightning, she used the same yellow and black markers to write: BE MINE—Phoebe. Then she scanned the drawing and e-mailed it to Daryl.

Annemarie had encouraged Phoebe to take this big risk, to announce her love for Daryl. There was, Annemarie said, no time like the present to be first in line now that he was a free man. After all, she'd said, Valentine's Day was less than four months away.

Annemarie put me up to this, thought Phoebe. I may need her to help get me through the disaster of what might happen next!

*　*　*

"Boy, there sure are a lot of lesbians here in Vermont," said Devie as she stuffed the receipt for their Ben and Jerry's peanut-butter-crunch ice cream cones into her dark red eelskin wallet. Hannah had only coffee for breakfast. Devie had encouraged her to help herself to bites of each of the breads, rolls and scones in the basket on their table, but Hannah had managed to resist, though it seemed to irritate Devie that another baker would not be curious about someone else's muffins.

They'd met with Janelle, the woman who was selling her bakery, and Devie had insisted they celebrate her decision to buy it by having real Vermont ice cream in Vermont. Hannah was annoyed that Devie was so insistent.

Hannah swallowed hard, the lump of ice cream feeling too cold as it went down, making her throat ache.

"Do you—mind them—the lesbians?" Hannah asked when they were outside the shop on Main Street.

"Oh no!" said Devie reassuringly. "My sister's a lesbian."

"But would you—hire a lesbian?" asked Hannah, licking melted ice cream from around the edge of the scoop where it met the cone. It tasted too sweet.

"Sure! Of course I would!"

"Well—what about in the front of the store, where they'd be with customers all day?"

"Of course they could wait on customers. You know, my sister told me that the American Indians recognize four genders: men, women, men that are like women, and women that are like men. Are you trying to tell me something?"

Hannah hadn't realized how quickly the ice cream had been melting. Her fingers were sticky and the cone was soggy where her fingers were wrapped around it. The morning air seemed unnaturally clear, more luminous than a cloudless morning ever had, the air more transparent, the colors of the signs and of people's clothing looking brighter, more saturated with purple and yellow and green and red.

"No," Hannah answered. She felt exhausted. Her whole life was a lie, and it was so tiring to keep it going. The only thing good and true about herself was her baking—her muffins, breads and pies.

"So—where should we have lunch?" Devie asked, taking Hannah's arm and walking them both toward the center of town.

All she ever does is eat! Hannah thought. *We had breakfast AND ice cream and now we're going to have lunch!* She was wondering if she should tell Devie she had a toothache, or a tummy ache, or something that would relieve her of the need to eat yet again. But then she realized it would make

Devie suspicious. Hannah had already thrown away her melting ice cream cone. Devie had a hamburger lunch that included hot apple pie with Vermont cheddar melting over its top crust. Hannah had only a bite of her own burger.

But by the time they'd arrived back in Long Island at midnight, Hannah was ready to eat everything in the refrigerator, the freezer and the cupboards. She had rehearsed the binge many times during the long drive from Montpelier to the ferry in Connecticut, and continued to plan as the ferry crossed Long Island Sound. She had visualized herself enjoying maple-walnut granola with cold milk and bananas, buttery grilled cheese sandwiches, a whole jar of macadamia nuts and some English muffins with raspberry jam.

But when she actually let herself into the dark house, she was so exhausted she had only a handful of macadamia nuts and a slice of Swiss cheese and went to bed.

I told Len how I felt," announced Samantha in the next meeting of the Tuesday group.

Scott sat beside Samantha; they had talked on the phone a few times. It had taken several conversations to soothe the hurt that had arisen between them. Once, Scott had hung

up in the middle of Samantha saying, "But what about ME?" after she had said how sick she was of being so self-centered. Then she'd called him back, laughing.

"What did you tell him?" asked Scott.

"That I didn't care if that girl knew who he was or not, that he knew who SHE was, that drawing her was like CARESSING her. He said he still loved me, but I said I didn't know if I cared. Then something amazing happened."

"He gave you a ring," suggested Faye after her coughing fit had subsided.

"No," said Samantha. "I felt thin!"

"Why?" asked Faye.

"Why did I feel thin? I'm not sure. It just felt really good to take a stand."

"You told the truth," said Scott.

"Telling the truth feels good. Of course, how would I know? Anyway, Sam, you ARE thin," said Hannah.

"And you know what else?" Samantha continued. "I didn't feel like cutting myself."

"YAY!" cheered the group.

"Actually, I felt like cutting HIM—I wouldn't, of course."

"It was appropriate to feel angry," said Gale.

Hannah, sitting beside Samantha, reached sideways for her hand and squeezed it.

"Actually, I feel like cutting him myself for hurting you so much," said Scott.

* * *

Why am I so depressed?" Scott asked Gale as they sat together in an individual session. "There isn't anything THAT horrible about my life that I should be this depressed! It's gotten to the point where I feel depressed that I'm so depressed!"

Scott had been seeing Gale in group for almost three years. He'd first come when, as the star of his high-school wrestling team, he'd confided to his coach that he was purging by vomiting in order to keep his weight down. But he had never seen Gale in an individual session before.

Gale remembered when she'd met with Scott for an initial interview three years earlier, before he'd come to his first group meeting. She's asked him if there were any other compulsive people in his family.

"You mean besides my alcoholic dad, my pill-popping mom, my pot-addicted brother, my obese grandmother, my OTHER obese grandmother, and my compulsively gambling grandfather?"

Now, Gale said, "Well, in your case I'd say there are probably at least two things operating. There's a good chance that you have a genetic tendency toward having imbalanced amounts of neurotransmitters. Look at how many irresistibly strong cravings members of your family have. The other thing going on is that there are unresolved childhood wounds."

"I can see that," said Scott. "I feel irritable a lot of the time, too, even when there isn't any present reason for it. So, you're also saying that I may not have enough soothing chemicals circulating around in my brain to calm me down and stuff?"

"Exactly," said Gale.

"So, I'm gonna be another Prozac statistic?"

"You have a few options there: You could take pharmaceutical drugs—a psychiatrist would have to help you decide about that. Or you could try herbs. Or you could try amino acids—a nutritionist could help you with that. You could learn to meditate, which also changes your brain chemistry. You're already exercising, so that's good. The other option is crucial: You and I could work on helping you grieve your losses. Unresolved grief can make people very cranky!"

"What if nothing works?" asked Scott anxiously.

"You're afraid that none of these things will work."

"Yes," said Scott.

"When you get some help looking at stuff that you've been keeping out of your awareness, it really can lighten you up. We can do that together. Everyone knows things they'd rather not know."

"So what would be MY stuff that I don't want to know?"

"Only you know!" Gale said, and they both laughed.

Oh, get over yourself, girlfriend!" said Kaneesha as she, Hannah and Samantha sat in Kaneesha's father's black Sebring convertible in Orient, Long Island, waiting for the ferry to Connecticut. The girls were going to visit Kaneesha's sister, Tanya, who was working as a nanny for a large family there.

Hannah had been talking, again, about how ashamed and weird she felt about her deepening realization that she was attracted to women at the same time as she was repelled by the idea of sex.

"There's a huge galaxy out there!" Kaneesha continued. "You're a small girl compared to that. Smaller than a grain of sand. It doesn't matter if you want to have sex or not. NOBODY CARES."

"So you're getting sick of me then," observed Hannah, dejectedly.

"Not sick! Just want to give you some perspective! Who CARES if you're a lesbian. So is Lily Tomlin! So is Melissa Etheridge, and so are a lot of other people we never even heard of!" Kaneesha said, turning the key in the ignition in readiness for driving onto the huge car ferry to New London, Connecticut.

"But I'm a WEIRD lesbian," insisted Hannah. "I am a lesbian who doesn't ever want to have SEX with anyone." Hannah did not mention that Pauline—Dr. Priestly— would probably be putting pressure on her soon. This gave Hannah great anxiety. They had had several dinners and lunches and trips to Manhattan already. Wouldn't the day come soon when Pauline would expect the relationship to evolve the way other people's did?

Samantha was looking out the window, surveying the long line of cars waiting to drive onto the ferry. She had heard Hannah's laments enough times in group and was not going to expend any more energy trying to talk Hannah off her ledge of despair. Of course, Hannah was just as tired of hearing Samantha saying, "How could he do this to me?" So Samantha supposed she and Hannah were even. Kaneesha, though, was just warming up.

Kaneesha was wearing red, her favorite color, in which she looked, Samantha thought, fabulous—like a firecracker, with her now shorter hair all braided and sticking out at stiff angles from her head, like the Statue of Liberty's crown.

"So what if you don't want to have sex with anyone!" said Kaneesha.

"You don't think it's weird?" asked Hannah.

"DAMN RIGHT IT'S WEIRD!" agreed Kaneesha. "YOU'RE ONE WEIRD GIRL!"

Hannah, curiously, Samantha noted, seemed relieved that Kaneesha had reached this conclusion, as though Hannah had won the argument. People, she observed, were eager to be agreed with, even if the outcome of the dispute had them winding up weird.

* * *

There's a voice in my head," said Hannah, "that keeps saying, over and over and over, 'You're not good enough!'"

Hannah, Phoebe and Samantha were hanging out at Phoebe's house. Michael and Molly McIntyre were celebrating their twenty-fifth wedding anniversary in Scotland, where Molly had never been, and Phoebe had invited her friends to spend the rainy evening at her house. She'd lit scented candles and made a fire in the big stone fireplace. Having friends around her reminded her of campfires and roasted marshmallows and ghost stories. What Hannah was talking about sounded like a sort of ghost story, because it was about voices she was hearing in her head.

"Whose voice do you think it is?" Phoebe asked.

"It's my mom's voice for sure," said Hannah without hesitation. "That was the way she talked to me when she wasn't being loving. She was horrible then, would say the most awful things to me about myself. It was like she had two different parts, and you never knew which one was going to be there."

"I'll bet that was your mom talking to herself out loud about herself," Phoebe said. "I'll bet SHE didn't feel good enough. I think that about my father sometimes when I'm in my right mind, that he just criticizes me and is so perfectionistic and everything because HE doesn't feel good enough about himself."

"When you say that, I know it's supposed to make me feel better, but it just makes me feel worse."

"It makes you feel guilty or something, doesn't it," said Samantha. It was not spoken as a question but as something she already understood.

"It makes me feel guilty that I was so angry at her," said Hannah. "I feel as though my anger killed her."

"Sometimes, I get scared that my anger toward my dad will just make him keel over and die," Phoebe said.

"Then I get mad at her even MORE because she MADE me be so angry at her," continued Hannah.

"And then you want to binge," said Phoebe.

"And then I want to binge to bury my anger, yeah. I want to bury MYSELF in the food because I feel so bad about myself."

The fire was going out so Phoebe got up to put another log on. Samantha rearranged her legs beneath her on the soft, dark green leather sofa.

"And then I want to purge because I can't stand feeling so DEAD from having buried myself in food," Hannah added. "I want to bring myself back to life."

Hannah waited, looking inside herself. She was looking at the afterimage of her words. They had burned a mark inside her mind, like when she'd looked at the sun too long and she could still see it shining after she'd closed her eyes and turned away.

From: *Annemarie@ultrasw.com*
Date: Mon 16 Oct 2000 11:31:43 PT
Subj: Makeup and men
To: *PhoebeM@optonline.net*

I'm so mad at Dominick. He teaches at an art school so he thinks he knows everything about appearance and design and clothes and stuff, but you know what? He tells me not to wear foundation or lipstick or mascara because he says women who wear makeup look like female impersonators, so we go to dinner and I DON'T wear makeup and he spends most of the evening looking at the hostess at the restaurant who IS wearing an INCH of makeup and BIG FALSE EYELASHES. He practically sprained his neck twisting around to glimpse her every time she walked people to their tables.

I just came back from the mall where I bought EVERYTHING at Sephora. They had a special offer where they give you free stuff. I am sending you everything they gave me.

How's school? Oh who cares about school. How's Daryl?

A. XOXOXOXOXOXOXOXOX

From: *PhoebeM@optonline.net*
Date: Tues 17 Oct 2000 10:42:47 EST
Subj: Elvis, Daryl and Dad
To: *Annemarie@ultrasw.com*

A: Phooey on Dominick for not giving you his undivided attention. You deserve that whether you're made
up or not. I still can't stop thinking about Las Vegas. It
was like a big Styrofoam breast. Everything was fake but
irresistible at the same time. Raphael and I went to the
Elvis Museum and there were postcards in the gift shop
with recipes from Elvis's kitchen, like one for peanut-
butter-and-banana sandwiches. I am sending you one
(the postcard, not the sandwich).

Daryl has not acknowledged that he got an e-love letter from me. It's bizarre that he hasn't because we've
talked on the phone a million times since I sent it. I am
half-hoping he never GOT it. I don't know what to do
next about that. I'm scared to do ANYTHING.

Put on your crisis-intervention hat and await further
news.

With love everlasting—P.

P.S. My dad is impossible. He follows the models around
criticizing everything about everyone. At least I know it's
not just me he picks on! That was QUITE a revelation.
He insulted Bettina's manicure yesterday. She had a mil-
limeter of cuticle showing, and somehow it got into the
picture, and he went ballistic, and she wound up crying.
I'm totally scared of him more than ever now. Raphael is
keeping me from killing him and myself. Only kidding.

✳ ✳ ✳

Phoebe sat looking at her computer screen, slouching, a
glum expression on her face, her hands resting limply
in her lap. She willed something to appear there, a response
from Daryl. She had pressed SEND almost a week ago, the
SEND that had flung her e-love letter toward him through
cyberspace. Now there was no turning back. But he had not
acknowledged receiving it.

Her BE MINE message might have reached Daryl, and he
might have chosen not to answer her until he could think of
a tactful way to reply. Or, it might not have reached him for
one of those computer reasons. It might still be out there in

the mysterious ethers of the cyberworld, stored as an electronic speck in a huge computer somewhere in California, waiting to be catapulted across space onto Daryl's screen.

The phone ringing jarred Phoebe from her anxious reverie. Obsessing, she reflected as she picked up her phone, was exhausting.

"Hey, Phoebe, it's Billy," said a familiar voice. "What's shakin'?"

"I am," said Phoebe, listlessly.

"Why is that, young princess?" replied Billy with his customary playfulness. He had begun to call Phoebe "princess" ever since Phoebe had shown up in group one evening wearing a little rhinestone crown she had borrowed from a photo shoot. Annemarie had suggested that Phoebe take firmer charge of her life, that she imagine herself as Queen of the World, of her world, and Phoebe had indeed felt stronger in herself when she began to think of herself as the chief executive officer of her own life.

"I sent Daryl an e-mail over a week ago, asking him to be mine. I drew a lightning bolt through a red heart. He hasn't acknowledged getting it, even though we've talked dozens of times on the phone since then. I'm scared."

Billy's sadness threatened to reveal itself in his voice. He hesitated before replying. Finally he said, "It's good to take risks. You've been crazy about him for a long time."

For almost as long as I've loved you, he thought.

"But he is only just out of his relationship. I don't want to create a rebound thing. I'm really scared. Why couldn't I have waited!"

"Because you were afraid if you waited, someone ELSE might have grabbed him!"

Phoebe sighed. She'd wanted Daryl to grab HER! "Exactly! Besides, I don't have much time left before I am going to turn nineteen, and I HAVE to get kissed before that!"

"Is the kiss more important than the kisser?" asked Billy. *If just anyone would do. I could have kissed you a long time ago,* he thought.

"NO! But you know what I mean!" said Phoebe impatiently. "Anyway, enough about me. How are YOU doing? What's up with you?"

"Same old, same old. Trying to avoid the cookies. Trying to stop postponing doing my Spanish homework. You know me, doing everything at the last minute. But I have to know Spanish if I'm going to go around the world." Billy was taking Spanish at the community college.

"Do you want me to come over and keep you company?" Phoebe suggested. "That helps sometimes."

"Would you?" said Billy, with amazement and delight.

"Yeah, I would, if I could figure out a way to keep my eye on my e-mails at the same time. Any ideas?"

"Yeah, sure. You could use my sister's computer. She's at a sleepover."

* * *

Samantha sat glumly in her room, staring at her collection of zebras, torturing herself with thoughts of Len.

Sure, she'd told him how she felt, but telling him didn't make the hurt go away. She felt fat again.

Len wouldn't tell her anything about the girl he was drawing over and over again. He reiterated that she was not his "new girlfriend," as Samantha had insisted. But Samantha wanted to know who this girl was, what it was about her that was so compelling that Len, who had seemed so devoted, could be so intrigued.

Because Len wouldn't tell Samantha anything about her (he said he didn't KNOW anything), Samantha had to make her up.

She's taller than me, thought Samantha, *but the same weight. So she's MUCH thinner. She has thicker, blonder hair than I do, and nicer eyebrows, and prettier hands, and better breasts, fuller ones, even though she's skinny. Her knees aren't as knobby as mine and her eyes are Elizabeth Taylor violet. She does a thousand crunches a day and kick boxes, so she has*

a better middle than I do and a prettier belly button. She has whiter teeth than I do, and she laughs more.

Samantha had eaten twelve leaves of iceberg lettuce that day. It was ten-thirty at night, and she was waiting for Scott to pick her up. She was sorry she'd said she'd go out with him; her heart, so full of the confusion that Len had started, was not in it.

And she was starving. Her hunger had shifted from a vague, expanding, hollow ache to a definite sharp pain. She had gotten used to the lightheadedness. She liked it.

* * *

El Sueno was rocking that night. As they cut across the crowded club, Scott kept his hand on Samantha's elbow, steering her through the maze of dancers moving in time with the Latin rhythm of the music. The club was a current favorite among the twenty-somethings in their own and nearby towns. A track from *The Buena Vista Social Club* CD was playing, and Scott had to speak loudly to the bartender to be heard above the music.

Scott ordered cranberry juice for himself and a club soda for her. Scott drank beer when he was with his friends.

Sometimes he drank too much beer. But he didn't want to be driving Samantha around with any alcohol in him.

Samantha looked at the people on the dance floor and noted that the women were what she considered "chunky" but realized they were probably average, maybe they wore size twelves or fourteens. Samantha was a size one, and though it was hard for her to find clothes that fit unless she shopped in the kid's department, she considered a size one too big and was heading for a zero. That was how her life felt, too—as though she was headed for a big zero.

"Do you think these women are fat?" she asked Scott when he'd turned away from the bartender to face her.

Scott considered the dancers closest to them, two women in short, tight dresses—one a blue and yellow floral print with a ruffled hem, the other red. Both had ample breasts and hips and solid-looking legs, and they moved skillfully to the Latin beat. Their breasts bobbed with each vertical movement.

"Yeah, I think I do," Scott said, adding an "I'm sorry" because he knew Samantha so well, knew she did not need her distorted perception of her own and other people's bodies validated. He wanted to tell the truth though. And the truth was that he, too, considered any body with flesh rippling even the slightest bit to be fat, as Samantha did.

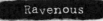

He was suddenly ashamed of himself and regretted having told her what he thought.

"I know," said Samantha. "The thing is, their bodies are probably normal. So, I think I'M not normal to feel the way I do."

"You're NOT normal," said Scott, playfully pulling the end of her hair. "You're not a 'normie.' Neither am I, I guess."

"How can we live in the world this way?" asked Samantha sadly. "It's not as though I think I'll ever change. I know I won't. Anyway, I don't even WANT to."

"Me, neither," Scott admitted. "I mean, I'd LIKE to change, be different about how I feel about my body and stuff. But I can't imagine that ever happening. Why would it?"

"I know," agreed Samantha.

It was so easy to be with Scott. She could be exactly who she already was and didn't feel she had to hide or lie or pretend.

* * *

From Phoebe's journal:

Despairing Damsel Despondent

Why hasn't Daryl responded to my e-love letter yet?!?!?! I sent it last Wednesday. I spoke to him on the phone last Thursday and Friday. We talked about Gabby and his guilt because she was SO devastated. Why is he surprised that she is devastated? DUH. She's been sending him books and CDs every day, and long, loving letters, he said, full of apology and pleas for mercy, full of reminders of the big white wedding they were planning, full of memories.

If he got my little red heart pierced by lightning, maybe he's just too preoccupied, too stricken to respond? I don't think so. I'd like to think so.

I'd RATHER think so than that he got it and is too horrified to tell me, "No, I will not be yours. I CANNOT be yours for the following reasons:

- I am still crushed over no longer being HERS. I still love her.
- I am feeling like I have been a very bad cowboy, deserting this woman.
- I do love you, Phoeb, but do not want to touch your face, or stroke your body, or entangle my limbs with yours.

* * *

Hannah and Pauline routinely met for coffees or lunches or dinners, and they spent hours talking. Hannah was relieved that Pauline had not only not pressured her into exploring sex but didn't even bring up the topic in their conversations, which centered around their histories.

Hannah spoke of her mother's illnesses—the cancer, and the anorexia that had killed her. Pauline spoke of her brief marriage to her high-school boyfriend, and the abortion she still suffered over. Hannah explained that her father had recently met, and quickly thereafter fallen in love with, a woman he was planning to marry whom Hannah had still not met.

Hannah was surprised that this growing friendship had not made her anxious enough to purge. She'd binged often in the past months, but had not purged except for once. Somehow the importance of the size and shape of her body had receded a bit into the background—not entirely, but enough to leave a spacious foreground to contain this growing friendship. This, thought Hannah, must have been what Gale meant when she suggested to Hannah that one day she would understand that appearance was not the most important thing, that relationships were.

On a rainy Wednesday, Hannah and Pauline went to

Pauline's house on the other side of town from where the university was, about forty miles from where Hannah lived. Pauline's house was not at all what Hannah had expected. Based on how Pauline dressed, Hannah expected something stylish, perhaps southwestern in flavor.

"So what do you think?" asked Pauline when she let them into the brown, cedar-shingled ranch house through the door that connected the garage to the kitchen.

All the furniture in Pauline's house was brown: the sofa was brown brocade with matching armchairs, and the carpet, which did not look entirely clean, was brown. The afghan that was draped over the back of one of the armchairs was brown, beige, orange and white, and Hannah just hated everything. It was the house Pauline had grown up in and contained all the furniture and knickknacks belonging to her parents, including a collection of ceramic frogs. Hannah hated the frogs; she couldn't understand why anyone would collect ceramic representations of what she felt was an exceedingly ugly animal.

"Who collects frogs?" chirped Hannah cheerfully, making a valiant effort at tactfulness.

"My mom collected them," said Pauline, dropping her keys onto a small hall table before turning to Hannah and taking her into her arms.

She held Hannah for a long time, rocking her back and forth.

* * *

Phoebe fidgeted with her watch strap, buckling and unbuckling the red leather band over and over. She hated expectant waiting of all kinds. Today she was waiting for her parents, who were coming to meet her at Gale's for a session. Her father would come straight from his studio in Manhattan, and her mother would come from the assisted-living community where she'd recently bought her parents an apartment.

Molly McIntyre was very sad about the steady progression of her parents' aging. Phoebe sometimes walked into the kitchen to find her mother staring out the window at nothing. One day she told Phoebe that she had been thinking about when Phoebe would be coming to visit HER in an assisted-living community.

Molly came into Gale's waiting room flustered, her lime green silk scarf wound stylishly around her neck and her long, graying dark hair gathered into a gray velvet scrunchy. Phoebe's mother had been a model; her figure was still slender, and she looked wonderful in clothes, which often made Phoebe feel even more like a lumpy potato than usual.

I take after my father's side of the family, reflected Phoebe, as she watched her mother remove her short, flared black wool coat to reveal gray tweed slacks and a gray cashmere sweater. Her mother was forty-four, and she did yoga and worked out in their fully equipped home gym almost every day. Molly had even starting going to tai chi classes. She'd asked Phoebe to join her, but Phoebe had declined. She couldn't imagine herself performing the smooth, flowing movements without looking and feeling ridiculous.

Her mother placed her coat on one of the pegs on the wall beside where Phoebe was sitting, and leaned down to kiss her daughter's forehead.

"You have such beautiful skin," said her mother. "So clear and rosy."

Phoebe actually hated her skin because it was so rosy. And anyway, her mother tended to compliment her only on features not associated with weight. Her mother, in the last several months, had told her she had beautiful hair, hands, eyes, lips, teeth and feet. Phoebe was too tense, at the moment, to take in her mother's most recent compliment. Her father was late.

She and her mother had been talking for a few minutes about how Phoebe's grandparents had been adjusting to their new life when Michael McIntyre arrived, full of himself as usual, Phoebe observed, blabbing a mile a minute about cabs and traffic and last-minute phone calls. This recitation was delivered after he had completed his cell phone call, which he'd been in the middle of when he'd walked in. He was always, Phoebe reflected, attached to one of three appliances: a camera, a phone or a TV remote-control device.

As he was removing his tan suede jacket, Gale came out to collect them, and they moved slowly—mournfully, Phoebe thought—into Gale's office.

"Phoebe is still at least forty pounds overweight," said her father, even before he'd sat down. "Maybe fifty pounds."

"Overweight compared to what?" asked Gale as she settled herself in an armchair beside him.

"Uh—you know, height and weight tables. How she looks. Not normal. I'm afraid she'll be unhappy."

Gale said, "Mr. McIntyre. How do you feel about doing something a little different than what you might have expected?"

"All right, I guess," said Phoebe's father, settling himself, finally, into his chair.

"I want you to switch chairs with Phoebe. Switch roles with her. Phoebe—how do you feel about being your dad?"

"Uh—okay, I guess," said Phoebe, but truly hating the idea. She didn't like saying no to Gale, though.

"Be him," Gale continued. "Say what he just said to you. And you, Mr. McIntyre, you be Phoebe, and listen to what her father has just said to her. See how, as Phoebe, it makes you feel. Okay?"

Phoebe, playing her dad, said, "Look at her. She's still forty pounds overweight. Not normal. Fifty pounds overweight, maybe."

"How did that make you feel?" Gale asked him.

"Stricken," said Michael McIntyre, blinking. He paused, reorganizing himself. "Struck."

"Okay, now switch back. Phoebe—do you have anything to say to your dad?"

Phoebe and her father changed chairs again.

Phoebe turned her chair to face her father and sat up straighter.

"Dad, your creation of me—your design of me, your styling of me—was finished the moment you impregnated my mother. I'm not going to continue to be molded by you and criticized by you and disapproved of by you."

Phoebe sounded triumphant, towering, jubilant—even to herself. But inside, she felt panic.

Phoebe wrote:

Friends Horrified!

Phoebe McIntyre's Eating Nightmare!

A day of missed classes has Phoebe's friends worried that the editor of the school paper and the best student on campus may jeopardize her academic future AND her weight-loss goals!

Insiders say Phoebe spent the day at The Mink Tulip, the campus eatery, chomping on doughnuts and washing them down with vanilla milkshakes.

Pals say part of the problem is McIntyre's turbulent home life, which features her famous pop, who clicks pix of slick chicks, and his constant remarks about her weight.

"Criticism from her father is devastating to her," said a pal. "She's in therapy, though. I hope that will be enough to get her through this."

---

* * *

"Why did you really ask Dad to leave?" asked Samantha. "Is it true that he is dating a student of his?"

She sat with her mother in their kitchen, on a bright autumn day with the sun pouring through the window above the sink, illuminating the pots of ivy and geraniums that lined the high sill. It was not easy for Samantha to ask these questions; part of her didn't want to know the answers.

Marge Rosen put down her coffee mug and sighed. "It's true." She hesitated; she touched the handle of the shiny dark blue ceramic mug but didn't pick it up, holding onto it as she continued, as though for support.

"But the trouble began way before. He was always flirting with the baby-sitters. Maybe it wouldn't have been so bad if he had flirted with ME once in a while, too," she said.

The group members and Gale herself had encouraged Samantha to have this discussion with her mother. Marge's therapist, a colleague of Gale's, had urged Marge to be honest with Samantha if the subject should ever arise. Marge held onto the handle of the mug.

"It's going to be hard for me to visit Dad now," reflected Samantha. She was surprised at the neutrality in her tone when she heard herself voice this observation. She was surprised at the neutrality of her emotions, too. It was as though the small measure of compassion she had cultivated toward herself and her own self-destructive behaviors had grown to include her father and his behavior.

"You'll do the best you can," observed Marge. "He can't help who he is."

But who IS he? thought Samantha. *He is not the Dad I thought I had all these years.* An image of her cuticle scissors formed in her mind with a speed that startled her.

Sharp objects are not going to save you, she said to herself. *Putting more scars on your body is not going to keep you safe. It is just a temporary high from the soothing chemicals that come after. Cutting is not going to save you!*

It felt enormously calming, she realized, to be sitting with her mother, talking with her! Maybe talking would save her.

❖ ❖ ❖

On a bleak, blustery, overcast afternoon, Pauline led Hannah down the dim hall of her brown house, turning on lights, until they arrived in the back bedroom, also carpeted in brown, where Pauline pulled the drapes over the windows, enclosing the two of them in darkness. She lit a candle on the night table, and Hannah was aware of the faint aroma of vanilla. She liked that: It helped dispel the gloom of the uninterrupted brown and the anxiety that came when she realized she felt obliged to allow Pauline to be close to her physically.

There was an unpleasant smell about the house that the vanilla candle made less sharp, a swirl of smells she could not identify, a mixture of aspirin and woolen blankets and heated dust and orange juice. Perhaps Pauline's father had died in this house.

Pauline said, "So—are you ready?"

"No," said Hannah. "But I don't think I'll ever be ready. And I want to be normal really badly."

"What does 'normal' mean to you?" asked Pauline as she stepped out of her black skirt, sat down on the bed, and pulled off her soft black leather boots.

"It means getting naked with another person occasionally," said Hannah

"So," asked Pauline. She was in a black bra and pantyhose now, with black panties underneath. "Are you ready?"

Hannah noticed the length of Pauline's strong legs, her long neck, the slightly softening flesh around the elastic waistband of her pantyhose. *She has such beautiful skin,* thought Hannah, *so smooth and the same color all over.* Though Pauline's thighs were substantial, they were not plump. Instead, they had a pleasing muscular solidity that made it hard for Hannah not to want to stare at them.

"No," said Hannah, disappointed, sitting down hard on the bed. "The only thing I feel like doing is moping. I just want to be here with you."

Actually, I just want to be here looking at you, Hannah thought.

She looked at Pauline apologetically. "At least I don't want to leave."

"Why don't we just be here together then?" suggested Pauline.

"It's okay?"

"It's fine," said Pauline. She slid back on the bed to recline against the pillows and motioned for Hannah to join her.

"Can I keep my clothes on?" asked Hannah nervously.

My father wants to know why you aren't telling me to eat less and exercise more," said Phoebe. She and Gale sat in their armchairs in front of Gale's fireplace.

"If I tell you to do something different than you're already doing—to change in any way—then I'll be doing the same thing your father, and the magazines, and the makeup ads are telling you to do: 'Change! Be taller! Be thinner! Have longer eyelashes! Smell like a cookie! Smell like flowers! Be perfect. Be MORE perfect! Do crunches. And floss!' I'm not going to do that."

"My parents think I need guidance."

"All growing organisms need guidance. Here is yours: Be yourself," said Gale.

A car alarm went off somewhere down the street. Phoebe felt unsettled in the presence of the sound, which was designed to evoke anxiety. But she felt good that Gale wasn't asking her to be different than she was at that moment.

"But who IS myself? I don't think I know yet. How do I find out who I am?"

"Are you breathing?" asked Gale.

"I don't think I was when you asked," Phoebe reflected. She breathed. "I am now."

"Breathe," said Gale, "and notice what comes, what images, words, sensations."

"If I breathe, then I can find out who I am?"

"It's one way. Another way is to ask yourself if you feel opened or closed. Get to know yourself."

Phoebe took two long, slow deep breaths. She felt self-conscious, breathing with someone watching her.

"I feel self-conscious," said Phoebe.

"You won't when you're alone," Gale reassured her.

"I never just sit and breathe," observed Phoebe.

"Few people do. We're all in constant motion. If we're not moving, we're collapsed on the couch watching TV."

Phoebe yawned.

"How is this conversation making you feel?" asked Gale.

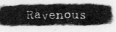

"Bored. I don't mean to hurt your feelings."

"You wanted to turn off my voice?" Gale asked.

"Yes, I think so," Phoebe confessed.

"Who else's voice do you need to turn off?"

"All of a sudden when you said the thing about collapsing on the couch watching TV, I thought of my father. I want to turn off HIS voice. It's always in my head. It's like that car alarm!"

"If you could talk back to that voice of his right now, what would you say?"

"SHUT UP!!!!!!!!" cried Phoebe.

The car alarm continued to sound. Phoebe breathed. The car alarm had been going for too long; breathing felt good.

* * *

Samantha stared at the formula for calculating her basal metabolic rate that Gale had given her. She knew she needed to eat more calories, and she was terrified. She tried to take her mind off her simultaneous need for and fear of change.

She vacuumed the already spotless carpet in her room. She rearranged all her zebras. She put her trophies for track in the closet—she didn't want to look at them; they were from another lifetime, "B.A."—before anorexia. She went through all her T-shirts, refolded them, and put them back on the shelves in her closet according to color. Len had not called or e-mailed or written to her that day—yet. She hated that.

She turned to the back of the magazine on her bed and read her horoscope.

"Pisces: Today your focus is on a romantic object who is far away. Do not get lost. Give thought to your goals. Do whatever you can now to define your goals for the future and begin to move toward them. Your life is in your hands."

Samantha was despondent; she'd forgotten how to have goals. For so long, her only goal besides being thinner had been to have Len adore her exclusively, and now she had forgotten what the point of that was. She guessed the point of having Len adore her was to finally feel good about herself. But why was she waiting for HIM to feel good about herself? What a loser she was being!

She picked up the phone.

"Han? It's Sam. Do you have a minute?"

"Sure. What's up?" said Hannah, who was in the kitchen, looking into the refrigerator. *Thank goodness,* she thought, *Sam had called her. Saved by the bell.*

"I'm having a breakthrough," announced Samantha.

"Is it one of those good breakthroughs, or one of those horrible, disgusting breakthroughs?" Hannah asked, closing

the refrigerator door and walking into the study, sitting at her father's desk. Samantha was having a breakthrough, and she had saved Hannah from a breakdown by calling her.

"I think it's one of the horrible, disgusting ones."

"Well, WHAT IS IT?" said Hannah. "The suspense is getting to me."

"Well, it's long story, but I was reading this magazine about dieting, and then I was thinking of Gale's formula, and then I was waiting for Len to call, and then I was vacuuming my room, and then I read my horoscope, and I realized that I am waiting for Len to give me a reason to feel good about myself and that I don't NEED his permission or his love to feel good about myself!"

"DUH," said Hannah. "I feel the same way about Pauline and Devie and everyone," admitted Hannah. "Doesn't everyone?"

"Probably," said Samantha, "but it's such a bummer. Anyway, I just finally DID Gale's formula, and I discovered how little I've been eating! I must be nuts."

"You got that right," agreed Hannah, good-naturedly. "I'm right there in the nut jar with you."

"I know I have to eat more now. I KNOW it. I don't know if I'll be able to DO it, but at least I actually KNOW it now. In other words, I BELIEVE it now."

"What's the formula that gave you this revelation?" Hannah wanted to know.

"I figured out that I could eat more than lettuce and STILL stay skinny. The formula is pretty interesting. It took me a while to figure it out. This is what you do: First, you change your weight in pounds to your weight in kilograms by dividing your weight by 2.2. Then you convert your height in inches to your height in centimeters by dividing it by .39. Then you multiply your weight in kilograms by 9.6 and multiply your height in centimeters by 1.85 and add them together."

"You're kidding," said Hannah. "You actually DID this formula?"

"Yep," said Samantha with pride. "It gives you the number of calories you need."

"Then you multiply your age by 4.68 and subtract it from the number you just got. Then you multiply THAT number by 1.5 if you are a little bit active, or by 1.7 if you are way active, or by 1.3 if you are a couch potato. Is this too complicated?"

"WAY TOO COMPLICATED!" said Hannah. "UGH!"

"If your mind is bent by the formula, you just go online and there's a Web site that will do the math for you. It's *www9.uchc.edu/departments/facdev/nutrition/cal.htm.*"

"Even the WEB SITE is impossible. But I'm trusting that you had a breakthrough, Sam," said Hannah, doodling on a pad on her father's desk.

"So I realized that the number of calories I need just to beat my heart and blink my eyes is higher than what I've been taking in! MUCH higher! I may be starving myself to DEATH!"

"DUH!!!!!!!!" said Hannah.

"So, after doing the math, I realized I can eat something with protein along with the lettuce and STILL be skinny. I'd BETTER eat. Just a little more. Very little. I think I can do it. I can't do it alone, though. I'm so scared, Han. I'm not going to do it by myself. I just know I'm not."

* * *

Ouch!" said Samantha. "My hip—move your arm!"

"Sam—my leg! Let me just . . . there!" Len said.

They were wrapped around one another horizontally in the back seat of Len's car.

"Wait! My neck!" said Samantha.

"Sorry," said Len.

"You're poking me with your elbow. My rib!"

Len moved.

"Wait—stop! Your knee!"

"Is this better?" said Len, once again rearranging his long arms and legs.

"I guess so." Samantha sighed. "Condom?"

"I forgot," admitted Len. "Do you have one?"

"No," said Samantha. "Why don't you just take me back home?"

"I wish I had a condom," Len said. "I wish we had somewhere to go."

"That's not what I'm annoyed about," said Samantha.

But she didn't say why she felt so annoyed. She wanted Len to read her mind because she didn't want to read it herself. She wanted him to understand that his obsession with the girl he was drawing had made her feel unsafe with him, and she was furious at him for making her want to distance herself from him. And she was angry with him for needing him. She hated needing.

Hannah looked out her bedroom window at the brown, shriveled leaves at the back of the house. Her mother had died in the fall, and now the gloomy look of the opaque sky, and the fallen, dried leaves, reminded her there was nowhere to go but toward death.

She stepped into her jeans and pulled them up over her narrow hips. The fact that they were still easy to zip surprised her. She had not purged for weeks, but she had binged.

Making herself throw up was something she'd experienced for so long that to not have it in her life, every day, made her feel as though she did not know herself. The familiar panic unsettled her.

What if she binged again today and didn't throw up? What if the calories finally stuck, blanketing her hips and stomach and thighs, even her neck and face, with soft, flabby flesh? Imagining her lean form being obscured in this way made her feel she was being buried alive, and she took an involuntary breath. Again and again, when she watched her own thoughts, no matter where the thoughts started, ultimately they took her to her mother, in her polished mahogany box, in the ground a few miles away.

What if this was the last time she was going to zip up her jeans? What if she went to work for the last time in her life and spent a half-hour of her morning sipping the strong coffee she loved, sweet, with lots of cream, after selecting the fortunes that she would put into her meringues that day?

Today, self-love can change your world.

You deserve happiness. Let yourself have it.

And what if, after selecting the fortunes, she died? What if this was the last day of her life? What if she knew this was going to be the last day of her life, and she lived it as though it was? How would she live it differently? She lived now as if she had all the time in the world, an eternity to worry and plan and postpone.

But what if she lived differently? How would this day be different?

When Devie came into the bakery, she'd say to her, "I don't want to be afraid of you. I can make bread rise. I can bake over 250 muffins a week and tens of dozens of cookies. I can frost a cake that winds up in people's wedding albums that they keep for the rest of their lives. I can binge without purging (most of the time). I'm not going to drag myself through the whole role-play thing in group where I have to pick someone to be you. I already have the real you here. I'm going to tell you how what you said to me made me feel. You hurt me when you told me you wanted me to keep the bakery clean. I already keep the bakery spotless. I don't want to feel guilty for being tall or bulimic or gay, and I hated it when you 'shushed' me even before I said anything to Janelle in Vermont. Furthermore, I'm longing for you to hold me. I'm going to die today. Would you hold me all day, until I'm dead?"

Phoebe was in her room listening to The Fat Barbees while the wind blew and the rain pelted against her windows so hard she had to turn up the volume. The fourth track on their CD was called "A Mother's Place."

You're not my mother, I don't know you
You're not my mother, you don't know me.
You're never home, always at work
When you're not there I go berserk!
BERSERK! BANANAS! One sandwich short of a picnic!
Some feminist she made a speech and you, Mom, got co-opted.
I really think I would have been much better off adopted.
My mother would know me, three sugars, one cream,
My mother would know me, you don't know me!
A mother's place ain't in the mall,
NO! You don't know me, not at all!
A mother's place is in the heart, YOU DON'T KNOW ME!

Phoebe thought about the song. She liked the Latin-sounding percussion that accompanied the line, "BERSERK! BANANAS! One sandwich short of a picnic!" as though the music had suddenly gone crazy, too. She liked the way the song sounded angry and gentle at the same time somehow. She identified tremendously with the lyrics. Even though her mother hadn't worked after she'd had her, Phoebe didn't feel her mother knew her, or wanted to know her, not really. She had never once defended Phoebe against her father's harsh judgments.

In her mind, Phoebe saw cookies: a box of shortbread and a cellophane-wrapped package of Oreos, the same cookies that her mother had placed in the very back of the pantry when she'd come home from the market earlier. From hundreds of feet away from where she sat in her bedroom, the cookies exerted their magnetic force, and the force felt to Phoebe like gravity.

Phoebe thought about the Oreos; she liked them best without the sugary paste sandwiched in the middle. She would scrape the cream off and eat only the chocolate wafers, their bitter, crumbly dryness pulling moisture from her tongue and filling the back of her throat with dark chocolaty satisfaction.

Then she remembered what Gale and Billy had been talking about once—that postponing the first bite would help. Remembering brought a spontaneous deep inhaling. She noticed that when she breathed in, she would breathe into her chest only, not wanting to allow her abdomen to round out when she breathed.

Gale said not to hold the stomach in when you were breathing. Phoebe breathed and let her abdomen expand; it

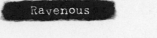

was not a good feeling. She felt enormous and balloony. Her belly button felt as though it was going to touch the wall opposite her before it exploded and flew off.

She persevered. Still sitting on her bed, she closed her eyes. She breathed deeply, letting the muscles of her abdomen push out.

It was as though she had been living outside her body, hovering somewhere nearby. Now she had definitely come INTO her body. She didn't like it in there! It was too big a body. She wanted to take it off, or forget it fast. She felt ashamed of how big she had let her body become. It was the wrong size for her, and she couldn't return it! But she COULD exchange it.

There was no way she was going to put cookies into this already-too-big body. She would e-mail Annemarie and hope the magnetic force of the cookies, still pulling at her so hard, would fade.

From: *PhoebeM@optonline.net*
Date: Mon 23 Oct 2000 9:41:42 EST
Subj: I'm breathing!
To: *Annemarie@ultrasw.com*

A: I am SO PROUD to tell you that I breathed just now instead of eating cookies. This is pretty amazing because my father was HORRIBLE to me in the therapy session that he came to with my mom. My mom didn't defend me! She never does. I talked back to him and everything, but after I did that I felt really guilty and scared and alone and I wanted to take it all back and just stay quiet and let him go on, just so that I could be near him.

P. XOXOXOXOXOXOXOX

P.S. Daryl! No news! Oy vey!

I can't let Pauline touch me without clothes on," said Hannah. "I just can't get myself in the MOOD or something. WHAT'S WRONG WITH ME?"

"I don't always feel in the mood," said Samantha. "I almost NEVER feel in the mood, in fact. I just need the love and reassurance, so I go along."

"Really?" said Hannah with relief, riveted by Samantha's news.

The two girls were waiting for Phoebe and Scott at the diner in Maple Ridge, the town most central to where each of them lived. The restaurant was nearly empty, and the

girls sat at the far end of the room, in a booth in the corner, away from the six other customers.

"So what do you DO when you're not in the mood then?" asked Hannah, eager for a solution.

"I don't do anything," said Samantha, sipping a diet soda through a straw. "I just—I don't know—breeeeeeeeeathe."

Both girls giggled. When Gale said the word "breathe" she elongated it like that, so the word itself would sound more like a breath. Laughing relaxed Hannah.

"You don't HAVE to be in the mood," Samantha continued. "Only one person has to be in the mood. That person can start. You just have to be willing to go along. It works for me."

"Am I taking this whole sex thing too seriously?" Hannah asked.

"I think you are," said Samantha. "What's so terrible about hugging and holding?"

"I don't know," said Hannah. "It's just that you see all these articles listed on the covers of magazines about how to be MORE sexy and have MORE sex, and I want to have LESS. I don't want to have ANY. What's WRONG with me?"

"You're asking the wrong person!" said Samantha. "You know what Gale says about me—that I'm interested in MY body more than anybody else's."

"It's not that I'm not interested in her body," reflected Hannah, "or that I'm more interested in mine so much, either. I just don't want anybody inside mine, or too close."

"Look—here's the gang," said Samantha, as Scott sat down beside her and Phoebe slid into the red leather seat in the booth beside Hannah.

"Wait—let me guess," said Scott. "Hannah is wondering what's wrong with her."

"Stop it!" said Hannah, her feelings hurt. "You're cruel! I have a defect, and you're making fun of me!"

"You don't have a defect. You just aren't interested in sex. It's no big deal," said Scott.

"Ya think?" said Hannah hopefully.

❋ ❋ ❋

Samantha, in baggy jeans, an oversized orange sweater and her black clogs, slid into the driver's seat of her silver Mazda and thought of her father. Tonight's drive over to see him would be torture, she realized, as she shifted the car into reverse and slowly backed out of the driveway.

She drove through the Maple Ridge business district, past the Roses Are Red florist shop, Blue Heron Real Estate, and The Moonlight Cab Company, and she thought about the rumor she'd heard about her dad dating one of his students at the college. Her mom had validated the news and did not seem shocked about it. So Samantha surmised that this must not have been the first time her dad had done something like this. Samantha shuddered, a feeling of disgust thick and aching in her throat.

Images of her father with a girl of twenty developed in Samantha's mind. Clearly, Samantha's was not the only young body that interested him. She had become used to her father monitoring the changes in her body as she moved from childhood through adolescence, making remarks.

"You're looking good," Nat Rosen would remark approvingly when Samantha walked through the house on the way out the door to catch the school bus. Or he'd say, "Boy, you're filling out nicely!" Samantha felt no particular way about the words her father said, but there'd be that tone in his voice of—of what?

Now, Samantha heard his words in her mind and the tone in them sounded flirtatious, as though her father were imagining HIMSELF enjoying her body, as though he WAS enjoying her body.

It had been at the age of fourteen that she'd begun to restrict her food, taught herself to take tiny bites and chew every bite thirty times, to return her body to its small, child-like boyishness.

As she drove out of the commercial district, past the store called Good Night, Irene, which sold sleepwear, and past the newspaper stand and the car wash, Samantha realized that as her weight decreased, her father still made remarks about her body.

"You look fantastic in that tank top," he'd said admiringly when she dressed for a July picnic with the family in a green top that matched her eyes.

But wasn't a father supposed to tell his little girl how adorable she was? As Samantha drove onto the entrance ramp of the Long Island Expressway, she felt a familiar confusion, recognized from a long time ago. Part of her loved how interested her father was in her. But another part of her felt invaded by the way he looked at her. There was a difference between his words and the tone of them. What father could fail to notice that his daughter was developing breasts? But it was the tone of his voice that had disturbed her.

Samantha realized that she couldn't feel okay visiting her dad without saying something to him about her discomfort about all that. She understood what that expression "an elephant in the living room" really meant, what it felt like.

There's a place inside me that wants to eat a roomful of bread and doughnuts and lemon poppy-seed cakes, and another place inside me that doesn't want to do that AT ALL," reflected Hannah during an individual session with Gale. It was windy and cold outside, and the windows rattled, and this gave the sanctuary of Gale's office an even cozier feeling than usual.

"Do you want to do some work on that?" asked Gale.

"What kind of work?" replied Hannah, apprehensively. Hannah felt unsettled imagining herself doing role-playing. The sort of "performance" she felt she was expected to deliver made her feel self-conscious, especially in an individual session with only Gale as her audience and only an empty chair playing another role in her drama.

"Why don't you pretend this chair is your 'hungry place'—the part of you that wants a roomful of bread," suggested Gale.

"With butter," Hannah added.

"With butter," echoed Gale.

Hannah tilted her head and listened to an inner voice. After less than a minute, it seemed she had heard enough. She nodded her head, and addressed the chair.

"What do you want? To make me a huge blob? What are you trying to do to me?"

"Switch chairs now Hannah. Be the hungry place," Gale suggested.

Hannah moved to the empty chair.

"I am helping you get through the minute! I am your best friend, and your most loyal companion. I am your best all-purpose medicine, too! I am your most comfortable easy chair when you are exhausted after a day at the bakery— I . . . I have to switch chairs again," said Hannah. "I have to talk back!"

"Go for it!" said Gale.

"Enough!" said Hannah, in the other chair. "You're lying! You are NOT my friend! First you want me to eat, and then you want me to THROW UP! You're DISGUSTING! You're DISGUSTING to me, and you're NOT my friend!"

Hannah's face was red, and she was full of emotion. "I need to switch chairs again."

"Do that!" said Gale. "Take charge."

"I am NOT disgusting," said Hannah as the part that made her need to eat a roomful of bread. "You know how good you feel after you throw up. You know how fuzzy and relaxed you feel, as though warm oatmeal is flowing through every vein after you throw up! I am your tranquil-izer and your sedative and your anti-anxiety pill! I'm like a soothing mother!"

Hannah was surprised when she heard herself say that. She remained silent. She could not argue with the truth of these observations.

Hannah took a deep breath. She closed her eyes. She looked inside herself for some clue as to how to disentangle herself from the confusion. The answer was there.

"I am SO hungry for my mother I could eat the world," she said. She opened her eyes. Tears came out of them.

"I'm eating for the part of me that needs my mother." said Hannah. "I knew that, but I didn't want to know it. But it's so OBVIOUS!"

"I know," said Gale softly.

"Phoebe once told me that she eats for the part of her that wants her father to accept her, to fill the empty space where his seal of approval would be."

"And Samantha once told us that she doesn't eat for that part of herself that wants to feel superhuman," Gale reminded her.

"It sounds as though each person has conflicting parts in them that need to have therapy," said Hannah. She sniffed away her tears and laughed with relief. She felt supported and accepted, and not so confused.

"I'm not as crazy as I thought," she said.

"Either that, or you are as crazy as you thought, and so is everybody else," said Gale reassuringly. "Everyone has parts that are in conflict with other parts."

* * *

Phoebe spent a sad, hopeful evening checking her e-mails, but no cheery words from Daryl in many different colors appeared on her monitor. Sam had sent her a funny forward about different kinds of Barbie dolls (a Barbie with unwanted hair on her upper lip, a soccer mom Barbie in a station wagon, a menopausal, wrinkly-faced Barbie complete with hot flashes), which Phoebe might have thought funny at some other time.

Her sadness about Daryl's lack of response to her e-love letter expanded to include her sadness about the sudden death of his mother the year before, about her feelings of hopelessness of ever being closer to him, about her father's treatment of her and her mother's lack of protectiveness. This larger sadness called out to all the other sadnesses inside her, and she thought of Jessica.

Jessica, Phoebe's best friend throughout high school, had died of self-starvation just before they were to graduate. She thought for a while about Jessica. She thought about Adrian, Jessica's mother, who was a television actress, about Jess's six-year-old brother, Matthew, and about how they'd moved away only a few weeks after Jessica had died. Phoebe wondered about how Matthew was doing. He and Jessica had adored each other.

Phoebe fed her frog, whose name was "Frog, Formerly Known as Prince." She tweezed five hairs from between her eyebrows. She watched a neighbor through the windows of his garage as he installed speakers into his white Acura. She was not in the mood to start her paper about Buddhism for her comparative religion class. She took a lavender-scented bubble bath. While she was in the bathtub she read an article in *O* magazine about speaking up, taking risks.

She got out of the bathtub and dried herself off, being careful to avoid glimpsing herself in the mirrors on the bathroom's opposite wall. Catching a glimpse of herself naked was so painful of late that it sometimes took her days to recover from constantly replaying images of her fatness in her mind.

She thought about the *O* article encouraging readers to dare to be bold. It was true, she thought. She'd felt worlds better when she'd spoken up to her father about the way he criticized her body.

She remembered the time last year when he'd humiliated her at the studio. Just as she'd been about to place a fork full of seafood salad dripping with olive oil into her mouth, her father had said, "WHAT ARE YOU DOING!" so loudly that everyone in the huge space had turned to stare at her. The entire crew, all the models, EVERYONE had turned to look. She'd run out of the studio. Then there'd been the family session with Gale where he'd been so mean again.

Later, with the confidence she'd gained from the group's support, she'd been able to tell her father how she'd felt and he'd treated her with more respect for a while. But only for a while; then he'd reverted to his old patterns. Gale said that was to be expected—people did tend to change back, and you had to remind them again and again until they got it— but it was painful.

Boldness. The article in *O* said to speak up. She HAD e-mailed Daryl the red heart pierced by a lightning bolt. But he'd never acknowledged receiving it, and she had decided it had gotten lost in cyberspace.

Phoebe had popped her Fat Barbees CD into the player when the phone rang.

"McIntyre—is that you?" Daryl said. He sounded tense to Phoebe, not like his usual mellow self.

"Yes, Morgenstern, it is definitely me," she replied.

"What's up?" he asked, without enthusiasm.

Phoebe should have waited a few beats, she knew. He did not sound at all like himself. Why had she chosen this particular moment, during this particular call, to be bold?

"You know I'm completely in love with you, right?" she blurted.

Daryl's silence hurt. A second, maybe two seconds,

just long enough, aching seconds passed to tell Phoebe everything.

"I got your lightning-bolted heart," Daryl admitted. "I didn't know what to do."

The silence stiffened Phoebe's neck and made her hands ice cold.

"I know you have feelings for me," said Daryl.

Of COURSE I have feelings for you! Phoebe thought. *Any woman who is not blind would have feelings for you!*

"I have feelings for you, too. But I'm afraid of ruining our friendship," he said sounding serious, and reluctant, and tense—like a banker refusing to give someone a loan.

OH NO, thought Phoebe. *What do I do now?*

She breathed. Daryl stayed quiet. She could hear him breathing. Did she hear it—or did she imagine him heaving a sigh of relief? She breathed, too.

"I understand, Morgenstern. I love our friendship. I don't want to ruin it, either. I just needed to let you know how I felt about you."

Still, he didn't speak. Phoebe's discomfort was tremendous. She could not allow the silence to continue, to just be there between them, around them, holding them softly, binding them closely together in a difficult moment.

"It feels better having let you know," she said.

It feels TERRIBLE having let you know, she thought.

D ad!" called Samantha, after she had let herself into the house her father had been renting ever since he and her mother had separated less than six months before. She said the word "Dad" crisply, with no hint of eager anticipation of his appearance.

The last time she'd visited, she'd fully intended to tell him her feelings about the rumor that he was dating one of his students, but she'd hesitated then because she didn't know if who he dated was any of her business. She'd talked it over with Gale, and Gale said that Samantha was entitled to have feelings about things and that it was perfectly appropriate for her to let her father know what those feelings were, especially if withholding this information from him would get in the way of her being with him. Gale said it was important to use "I" statements, to talk about her own feelings rather than about how disgusting she thought he was.

"I'm back here!" answered Nat Rosen.

She walked down the hall into the living room, where he was reading the paper. Samantha could smell meat cooking on the barbecue. Her father used the outdoor grill even in cold weather. It was the only way he knew how to cook meat. He lowered the paper and smiled when he saw Samantha.

"Dad," she said, "we have to talk."

"Sure, honey," he said, picking up a glass of red wine from the small table beside him. Samantha didn't remember whether her father always drank wine in the early evenings. She didn't remember if he liked detective novels or books about war, or if he wore shorts in the summer, or if he liked ketchup on his French fries. He'd become a stranger to her in such a short time. The only thing she could remember right now was how she'd felt when her mother told her he was dating one of his students.

"What is it?" said her father. "You look upset."

"I AM upset," Samantha said. She had rehearsed this talk in her mind, and she had rehearsed in group.

"I heard you were—" Here was where the rehearsals had gotten tricky. She didn't know whether to say "affair" or "dating."

"I heard you were dating one of your students, who is not much older than me, and I feel skeezy about it."

"Skeezy?" her father repeated.

"Weird! I feel weird about it. And I feel weird about how interested you have always been about how I look, about whether I've gained or lost weight, about what I'm wearing, about how I LOOK in what I'm wearing."

"I'm your dad! You're my little girl!"

"I'm NOT your 'little girl'—I'm your eighteen-year-old—almost nineteen-year-old—daughter, and it's not the words you've said to me about my body, it's HOW you've said the words."

"How have I said them?" said Nat Rosen, hurt in his voice.

Samantha was prepared for his defensiveness. The rehearsal in group had worked well.

"Look—Dad—if you don't know what I'm talking about, I'm not going to stand here arguing with you. I'm telling you I feel uncomfortable with you right now. Maybe I'll feel different down the road. I hope so. Right now, I can't visit you for a while."

❋ ❋ ❋

I feel guilty taking up so much of the group's time," said Hannah after she'd spent a few minutes talking about how ashamed she felt. "Nobody else here is a lesbian, so how could anyone be interested in this?"

"Here we go," observed Gale. "You're feeling guilty for breathing other people's air again."

"I DO feel guilty!" insisted Hannah. "And I SHOULD feel guilty!"

"This is guilt about your mother, too, I think," Gale said. She waited a beat so that Hannah could take that in. "And being a lesbian is only one way of being different. But I'll bet everyone in the group feels different in some way and can identify with your shame."

"Who?" challenged Hannah.

"I feel weird about feeling so fat when I know I'm so thin," offered Faye, coughing. "Not to mention my constant (cough) hacking, which I know would (cough) go away (cough) if I could just stop smoking. People move away from me (cough) on the subway, like I'm (cough) contaminated or something (cough)."

"I feel stupid about my bulimia," said Scott. "I mean, it IS getting better, but still."

"You mean YOU'RE getting better, not IT'S getting better," suggested Gale.

"Yeah," said Scott. "I'M getting better. But I still purge sometimes. Much less, though."

"I feel like such a loser," offered Billy. "I'm fat, and I don't like sports and I like to draw."

Hannah smiled at him. She could feel the tightness in her jaw and the back of her neck ease.

"I feel ashamed that I'm so self-centered," confessed Samantha. "Plus all you guys are getting better, and I'm still eating lettuce for meals. And I'm ashamed of my dad. I don't even want to see him anymore."

"Are you seeing him?" asked Faye.

"I told him I have to take a break from visiting for a while," said Samantha sadly.

Gale was impressed that Samantha had made this observation about her self-centeredness. She WAS extremely preoccupied with each detail of her physicality to the exclusion of an awareness of her place in the bigger world.

"So what do you think?" Gale asked Hannah. "Do you still feel so terminally different?"

"I guess not," Hannah conceded. "I guess everyone DOES have stuff they feel ashamed about." She sat up straighter. "But now I need to make an amazing announcement. It makes me feel REALLY weird to say this, but you know what?"

"What?" said Scott and Phoebe and Gale, simultaneously.

"I'm afraid to say it because if I say it, it might go away."

"WHAT IS IT?" said Faye and Billy.

"I feel beautiful. Sometimes," said Hannah.

"WOW!" exclaimed Phoebe. "What brought this on?"

"It's the way Pauline touches me," Hannah said. "She touches me like I'm the most precious, exquisite person. It makes me feel so valuable, worthy of attention. Beautiful. As though I even deserve that. Maybe."

The group was silent, taking in this unlikely recitation. Gale took a breath, as though readying herself to say something, but hesitated.

Then Gale said softly, "You know, your mom was so involved with herself for so long, I'll bet you didn't have the opportunity to feel you were the important center of things. Children need that."

"I think I'm getting that now," said Hannah, "that sense that I'm very important to someone. It feels REALLY good. Pauline doesn't even care if I don't take off my clothes. Maybe someday I'll be able to, but right now, it doesn't seem to matter to her."

Hannah hesitated, pensive. "I think I could take my clothes off if I could get drunk first or something. But drinking makes me want to throw up."

Scott looked at her quizzically. "And you feel HOW about throwing up?"

Hannah smiled, seeing the irony. "I don't like to feel nauseated, though. And I need to be in control."

"A-ha, the 'C' word," said Gale.

"Yeah," said Hannah.

"It's good that Pauline accepts you in the place you're at," said Phoebe. "That's what I wish I could have with my dad."

"I need that from MYSELF," said Billy. "I just can't accept how big my belly feels, how disgusting I am to myself. I see how abusive it is after hearing about how Phoebe's dad talks to her."

"Billy," said Gale turning toward him sitting beside her. "What do you believe the big belly says about you as a person?"

"Well—it says I'm sloppy and that I don't care about myself. It tells everyone who's looking what I do when I'm alone."

"And if your big belly were a separate person, what would it say about how it felt?" asked Gale.

Billy deliberated. "Let's see. My big belly would say that I'm not good enough. I don't measure up to other guys. I'm unmanly. I can't control myself. I'm defective. No one will ever love me or want to have a baby with me, and I'm going to be lonely for the rest of my life. And it's unmanly to even care about this belly stuff. Why would a real man be so concerned about the size of a belly?"

"What else?" Gale prodded.

"Well—my father left. That probably had something to do with me not being good enough. That's probably what my big belly feels."

"Probably," Gale agreed. "So when you're worried about the size of your belly, that's not what it's really about. It's really about all the feelings, the emotional pain that the big belly makes you realize you're in that bothers you."

"Yeah," said Billy.

"So, is it unmanly to be in emotional pain?"

"I think it's unmanly to TALK about being in emotional pain."

"What about John Bradshaw? Do you respect him?"

"He's awesome," Billy said, without hesitating.

"Good thing for John Bradshaw then, huh!" said Gale. "Because he says to talk."

Dear Journal, wrote Phoebe:

College Freshwoman Considers Entering Convent!!!!!!!!!

Honor student Phoebe McIntyre told sources close to her that she was considering entering the Our Lady of Lourdes Convent after the chubby coed watched a television program about Mother Teresa.

The troubled academic told friends of her humiliation since the dashing Daryl Morgenstern, recently split from the glamorous Gabriella Allibrandi, told her he would prefer to keep their relationship one of friendship rather than romance.

Phoebe, who has never missed a therapy appointment, completely forgot to show up for her last session, said unnamed sources.

"She spends all her time with her poodles," said a friend. "She hasn't even gone to yoga or to work at her father's studio."

*　*　*

Hannah was ready; and Pauline was ready for Hannah to be ready. Over the past weeks, they had spent countless afternoons lying in Pauline's bed for hours, holding one another. Hannah had buried her face in Pauline's silky hair that smelled of her rosemary shampoo.

Hannah had chosen a number of inspiring fortunes to place in her cookies that week.

Practice feeling as though you have already hit the home run.

She was ready. She could not remain an asexual being for the rest of her life, she had decided. She announced this to Pauline as they drove from the bakery, where Pauline had picked her up, to Pauline's house.

They came into the brown house through the garage. Pauline dropped her keys onto the little hall table, on top of an L.L. Bean Catalog and some unopened mail. Hannah noticed that it was hard for her to look at Pauline. As they walked down the hall to the back bedroom, Hannah felt as though she was walking the last few steps to the gas chamber, breathing her last breaths.

If you don't like this dream, dream something else.

Hannah was ready to begin her new dream.

But now she was too afraid. "Do I have to take my clothes off?" Hannah asked timidly. She sounded to herself like a four-year-old asking if she could have a candy bar.

"Of course not," said Pauline, pulling off her boots.

Hannah was so grateful for Pauline's patience; she felt a thickening in her throat and tears formed at the edges of her eyes.

Pauline had bought a new comforter from a catalog and Hannah was relieved that it was not any shade of brown, but a trellis pattern in green and white. They sunk into the center of the bed, the fluffy down comforter puffing up around them.

"I'm drowning in goose feathers!" laughed Pauline, flattening the puffy comforter around her with her arms. Hannah lay still, looking at the white ceiling, a heaviness in her chest.

"I'm not ready," whispered Hannah.

Pauline turned her body to face Hannah, her head in her hand, her arm propped up at the elbow.

"What's going on?" she asked Hannah.

"I don't know—it feels as though you're my MOTHER or something. I can't have sex with my MOTHER."

"How can I help you?" asked Pauline.

"You can't!" said Hannah sadly. "I don't think there's any way you can."

"I'm NOT your mother," said Pauline, unnecessarily.

"I could be ready if you were a stranger. But now—I just know you too well. It would be—embarrassing."

"I can't be a stranger to you. It's too late," said Pauline.

So what do I do about Daryl?" said Phoebe as she settled into her chair for her individual therapy session with Gale. "How am I supposed to feel when he tells me that dating me would ruin our friendship?"

"This tells you he values the friendship a lot," Gale observed.

"This tells me he is not hot for me," said Phoebe dejectedly.

"Not necessarily," Gale said.

"Necessarily," insisted Phoebe. She sighed.

"What do you know about the demise of his relationship with Gabby?" asked Gale.

"I think it ended because she pressured him to do stuff he wasn't ready to do. He's a college kid! He's not ready to

think of himself as a family man. Probably that need to think of himself as a cowboy thing was operating there, too." She thought for a minute. "And nothing he could do was right, was enough for her."

"So what does that tell you about being his friend?"

"I need to let him be wherever he is. I AM letting him do that. I have no CHOICE but to do that. I would never tell Sam to be closer to her father, or to eat more or anything like that. She isn't ready. It would be a—what did you call that—a 'boundary violation'—like you were saying last week."

"Bingo," said Gale.

"I need to be with him where he is, even though I might not like it," Phoebe said.

"You are becoming a good therapist," observed Gale.

"But I'm NOT his therapist!" wailed Phoebe. "I'm his FRIEND! And I want to be his lover."

"I think we need to explore that remark," said Gale. "I'm not sure you think you're ready for lover status. With any-one. What do you think?"

Phoebe pondered. She sighed. "You're right. I'd be terri-fied to have to be with Daryl in a sexual way. What do I know about that? Nothing."

"So, why not be grateful for where the relationship is right now?" suggested Gale.

Phoebe nodded her head thoughtfully.

"So then I need to agree with him very emphatically about remaining friends, about what a good idea it is to take it no further?" asked Phoebe.

"If you think he isn't ready to commit to Gabby, then how come it would be okay for him to commit to you?"

"I don't want any other girl to start something with him! Then he will stay with her until he IS ready, and I'll have missed out!"

"How much control do you have over what he chooses to do and over what he is ready to do?" Gale asked.

"Hmmmm," said Phoebe.

Later, Phoebe sat at her computer writing to Daryl.

"You're absolutely right about the friendship thing," wrote Phoebe, tapping out the letters quickly on her keyboard. "I value our friendship too much to jeopardize it by changing anything. Thanks for telling me how you felt."

Having reached this conclusion, however unwillingly, and having sent her conclusion to Daryl, made her feel calmer.

Only minutes later, Phoebe was surprised to find Daryl's immediate reply:

"Hey, McIntyre: Maybe we need to rethink this whole thing."

* * *

It occurred to Hannah, browsing in the bookstore, that every magazine she was looking at had articles about the size of the body and the condition of its various parts:

Beat Fat Forever—Lose 25 Pounds of Fat by Next Month

Sexy Breasts

Love Your Legs

Is Stress Making You Fat?

Make Over Your Entire Body

Love Your Belly Bulge

Easy Sexy Hair

Love Your Butt

Love Your Thighs

The cover of *People* magazine boasted that it contained photos of the Fifty Most Beautiful People in the World. Who decided, wondered Hannah, that these were THE most beautiful people in the world? Who made these determinations? Sometimes the faces in this "most beautiful people in the world" issue were not as pretty as people who never appeared in the magazine, or any magazine.

What about kindheartedness? Generosity? Why wasn't there a magazine naming the fifty most charitable, compassionate, funniest people in the world? She looked at her watch. She didn't want to be late meeting her dad; he was going to be introducing her to The Girlfriend for the first time.

Hannah had resisted the muffins—her own freshly baked ones—at the bakery. She had never binged on her own baked items since she'd started working there, and it seemed to her that as each muffin-free day she spent at the bakery followed the next, she felt a cumulative strengthening of her resolve to stay binge-free there.

Now her eyes slid to the right, where the pastry case in the bookstore's café displaying large, luscious-looking muffins, glazed doughnuts and small iced cakes seemed to pull her closer. She spent hours and hours, day after day, with cakes. She didn't feel so attracted by the cakes she made herself.

In this pastry case, the food seemed far more fascinating. Each piece sat atop a paper doily of lace, or on a pedestal, triumphantly proclaiming its own presence, its undeniable power. These cakes (for what was a muffin if not a small, unfrosted cake?) had the appeal of a woman who has spent an hour making herself up, fussing and fluffing and applying gloss. The same woman might seem plain first thing in the morning, and she might not even look all that different after primping. But the woman would FEEL different after

lavishing attention on herself, and that pampered feeling would exert an allure, just as the pastry presented so preciously now did, one luscious piece at a time seducing Hannah with its charms.

Hannah baked muffins every day. She knew what they were. And whatever they were, there was no magic in them.

Here, at the bookstore café, the chocolate-chip muffins were surrounded by a specific glow, like saints in Italian pre-Renaissance paintings. The lighting on the muffins seemed richer, not at all like the harsh fluorescence that fell on the thousands of books and dozens of people in the rest of the bookstore. The corn muffins had emanations of some sort, and the moistness of their golden tops glistened. Energy was flowing out of the muffins directly toward Hannah. It was as though they'd singled her out, shining just for her, speaking to her of comfort, of sweet oblivion, of close-eyed bliss, of nurturing, of home, and of a mother she could be close with, take into herself. The muffins spoke to Hannah, and Hannah believed them.

Two girls waited in line in front of Hannah. One of the girls coughed suddenly. It was not a smoker's cough, like Faye's. Hannah flinched. She visualized dangerous microorganisms spewing into the air around her, fanning out into a wide circle, settling on her lips, floating up into her nasal passages, spreading onto the surface of her eyes, invading her throat the next time she swallowed. She swallowed. She wiped her lips with the meaty part of her hand at the base of her thumb, imagining she could taste the bacteria, which, invisible to the eye, had been coughed into the surrounding air by the girl.

She had become used to Faye's coughing. The group was used to the way Hannah breathed through the fabric of her sleeve when Faye had a coughing spell. This didn't seem to bother Faye. But there was no food involved in group.

The girl's cough was nasty; and she did not look clean. Her long teased hair looked sticky. The cough was dry and hollow sounding, repeated at what seemed to Hannah to be predictable intervals. She hated people coughing anywhere near food. She believed people who coughed should not place themselves near food until the cough went away. Good thing the bakery items were in a case, she observed.

Anxiously, Hannah checked her watch. Her father had given her a cell phone as a graduation gift, and now she took it out of her silvery gray book bag and speed-dialed Samantha's number. Just as she was about to hang up, unwilling to talk to voice mail, Sam picked up.

"Hey, Han," said Sam.

Hannah walked away from the coughing girl in the line at the pastry counter to the far end of the store to get some privacy.

"Help!" she said. "The muffins are speaking to me!"

"You're at the bookstore across from the mall, right?" asked Samantha.

"How could you possibly know that?" countered Hannah, mystified.

"The muffins talk to me there all the time. Also, I remembered you told us in group that you were meeting your dad and The Girlfriend at the mall tonight. That's enough to make the muffins SING to you. In harmony."

"I'm so glad you were there, Sam."

"Meeting The Girlfriend has to be excruciating, right?" said Samantha.

Samantha, after a year of therapy, had learned well. She was getting less self-centered, and she'd learned to connect dots between what people were feeling and what they were doing. This skill, however, had had no effect whatsoever on Samantha's anorexia, since no matter what Samantha was feeling she always did the same thing. She didn't eat if she was anxious, and she didn't eat if she was sad, and she never ate when she was happy, and she didn't eat if she was mad.

"Do you want me to come over there?" Samantha asked.

"Would you?"

When Daryl came to pick up Phoebe to go to lunch on Saturday afternoon, he was wearing a black turtleneck sweater, jeans and his favorite brown tweed jacket (a thrift shop purchase) with a dried rosebud in his lapel. Phoebe found this floral touch incredibly romantic, and said, "Wow! I'm getting the rosebud treatment!"

"Yeah," said Daryl. "You are."

He looked into her eyes for just a second, then commented that she, too, had dressed carefully for the occasion. Phoebe was wearing her navy blue chiffon skirt with the little pink flowers all over it, a navy blue turtleneck sweater and lace-up black boots. Daryl liked that Phoebe dressed in a way that was both practical and feminine, without all the self-conscious, fashion-victim accessories that some girls favored.

Phoebe turned away to pick up her shoulder bag. They were standing in the entry hall in Phoebe's house. Her parents were out at an antique show. When she turned to face Daryl again, he said, "Phoeb, I think I need to be with you."

"I AM with you," said Phoebe. "We're going to lunch."

"I mean BE with you—as a couple," said Daryl.

Phoebe stood with her hand on the strap of her shoulder bag, holding her breath, holding her heart, her body very still. Her arms were tingling. She blinked a couple of times to reassure herself of Daryl's presence beside her.

He moved slowly toward Phoebe, so slowly that Phoebe at first thought she was imagining his approach. He placed his right hand lightly against Phoebe's left cheek. His hand felt cool, and she flinched very slightly with surprise, though his hand had landed there with extreme gentleness. He let his hand stay there and looked at her, and these images came to Phoebe, each scene fully formed in a milli-second, to be replaced by the next:

The wedding (they have eloped to avoid the danger of being photographed and therefore criticized by Phoebe's father), in which she is suddenly Audrey Hepburn—a lithe, long-waisted bride in a frothy white gown—with Daryl, inexplicably, in a naval officer's dress blues.

She and Daryl (she, lithe and ballerina-like, in a red one-piece bathing suit cut high on the thigh, he in surfer shorts printed with monkeys and palm trees) holding hands on the beach in Bermuda on their honeymoon.

Cooking pancakes for Daryl in their log cabin in New Hampshire.

The two of them, cheering madly for the Yankees.

The two of them taking a breather during a hike in the Grand Canyon.

Applauding as Daryl's twin sisters receive their high-school diplomas.

Immediately, she came back to herself, and she started analyzing everything. *Is he REALLY interested in me, or is he just being kind because he doesn't want to hurt me? How could he be seriously interested in ME? Why doesn't he pick one of those Barbie people? He could have any girl in the world, any WOMAN in the world. I think I'm having a heart attack— my whole chest is going to BURST.*

Daryl leaned further toward Phoebe and tilted his head slightly as he came closer.

Oh my God, thought Phoebe, *he's so close I can see each individual eyelash!*

She felt sick with panic.

"I think I may throw up," she said, and Daryl laughed.

The minute she pressed the END button on her cell phone after calling Samantha, Hannah regretted having called. She was being irresistibly drawn toward the mystical talking muffins, and she wanted to listen to more of what they had to say. There they were, pulling at her. Her throat longed for a big swallow of a buttery, sweetened corn muffin. Her mind hungered for the relief of finally having ended its conflict—to eat or not to eat.

Hannah looked at her watch. She had another twenty-five minutes before she'd have to walk across the road to the mall to meet her dad and Abbey—The Girlfriend—Abigail Jewett. Tony Bonanti's first foray into dating since Hannah's mother's death three years before had resulted in his being smitten with a school librarian from the next town. Hannah had seen a picture of Abbey—a redhead with freckles, a good-natured smile and slightly too-big teeth—who was only fourteen years older than Hannah, and whom Tony had met in his dentist's waiting room.

"My tooth fairy," was what her dad was calling Abbey. Hannah felt nauseated just thinking of Abbey and her dad together in the sun on his sailboat, or sitting in front of a cozy fire while her mother was in the cold ground.

Hannah sat on the closed lid of the toilet seat in the bathroom in the bookstore and ate two corn muffins and an entire lemon poppy-seed loaf. It was, after all, a small loaf, but Hannah was still eating the entire cake. She was in there because was she too ashamed to be eating cake when Samantha arrived. She wolfed down the cake, fiercely biting off large pieces of it and chewing hastily before swallowing.

✳ ✳ ✳

Do you have any condoms?" whispered Daryl as he held Phoebe in her bedroom in the dark. Strong white moonlight glowed at the edges of the window shades.

"Why are you whispering?" whispered Phoebe. "There's nobody home but us."

"I don't know," said Daryl, still whispering. And then he added, "Because it's so . . . quiet outside."

"I have condoms," said Phoebe sleepily.

Daryl waited, expecting Phoebe to get up to get them or to tell him where they were. He thought of the paper that Phoebe had written and e-mailed to him, in which she'd reflected about how easy it was to prevent unmarried teenage motherhood, how easy it was to prevent getting AIDS or other disease that was sexually transmitted. She'd even written an article about this in her "No Brainer" column for her school paper. All it took, she'd said, to prevent these dreadful things was a condom. Daryl remembered her adding, "But it's impossible to prevent becoming heartsick. There are no condoms for the heart."

Phoebe, nestled close beside him, made a garbled sound, something like "Hmphgh." She shifted toward him. They were spooning, and when she moved, her long heavy curls tumbled against his shoulder.

She's fallen asleep, Daryl realized, nuzzling closer to her as he received this revelation.

"Daryl and I—we're—together," said Phoebe to her parents at dinner the evening after her momentous lunch date with Daryl. He was back at his friend's apartment now, studying for a physics exam.

Michael McIntyre, absorbed in the careful carving of the roast beef, didn't respond at first when Phoebe made her timid announcement. She expected that her remark would elicit some reaction from her father that would evoke embarrassment, fury, frustration in her, or all three.

He put down the knife, tiny bits of bloody meat clinging to its serrated edge. The large carving fork still stuck straight up, pointing toward the antique brass light fixture that hung above the pine table that could comfortably seat fourteen.

"You and Daryl—you're sleeping together? Is that what you said?" asked her father, pushing his glasses back onto the bridge of his nose.

"NO!" gasped Phoebe. "I said 'we're together'—just that we're dating now that's he's broken up with Gabriella."

"We could see THAT coming," remarked Molly McIntyre, spearing an artichoke heart on the edge of her salad plate and popping it into her pink-lipsticked mouth. "I'm not surprised that he and Gabriella have broken up," she added, putting down her fork while she chewed, then blotting her lips with a white paper napkin. "Long-distance relationships are too hard."

While Phoebe admired people who actually put their forks down while they chewed, and then swallowed before picking up the fork again, she had never been able to master this seemingly simple skill.

"Gabriella is a beautiful name," reflected Phoebe's father, stabbing at a piece of roast beef with his fork.

"If you think Gabriella is such a beautiful name, why didn't you give it to me?" said Phoebe, annoyed to have to be hearing that name again.

"We named you Phoebe after your great-grandmother, Penelope," he said.

"Why didn't you name me Penelope, then?" asked Phoebe, becoming increasingly irritable with the direction of the discussion. She had meant only to announce this new development in her alliance with Daryl. She thought it would bring some congratulatory sounds from her parents. After all, she had never even had one date before, and now she was dating the cutest, most desirable guy in the Northeast.

Phoebe's father said, "Because Penelope is too old-fashioned a name. Anyway, why'd they break up? Was it her weight?"

"No," said Phoebe impatiently. "Because she was too bossy and possessive."

"Oh, you mean she was like your mother," joked Phoebe's father.

"Ha, ha," said Molly.

"So Daryl picked you, huh?" said Michael McIntyre.

"Yes!" Phoebe said. Her heartbeat accelerated. She knew her father was going somewhere with this, and it would be a bumpy ride. She could be bruised. She had been before. Why had she even bothered to mention it at all?

Her father sliced a piece of rare beef from the slab on his white dinner plate. It was so rare that blood oozed out of the meat when he pressed his knife and fork into it. He placed the morsel into his mouth. He put down his fork while he chewed thoroughly.

Phoebe waited anxiously, aware of her belly pushing painfully against the tightly fitting waistband of her jeans, which she was finally, but barely, able to fit into again. She became aware, too, of the fleshy heaviness beneath her chin, the solidity of her thighs spreading out onto the seat of her chair. She suddenly thought that in the event of an emergency, she could not use her seat cushion as a flotation device. An oxygen mask would not fall out of the ceiling above her head.

"He doesn't mind your weight?" her father said finally.

Phoebe had heard this sort of remark from her father before. His words, because she had endured so many similar ones before, brought her a sense of relief. At least he had not come up with a new way to hurt her. But she was still hurt by his words.

"NO!" she said. "He doesn't mind my weight!"

Then she helped herself to the largest, fattiest slab of beef on the platter and quickly cut off a larger than bite-sized piece, stuffing it into her mouth in the most bestial way she could devise. She chewed loudly, ferociously, looking straight at her father.

But he was looking down at his plate, scooping peas onto his fork.

* * *

When Samantha arrived at the bookstore fifteen minutes later, Hannah was nowhere to be found. She was not in self-help, or psychology, or in the diet section, or browsing the magazines near the front of the huge store where Samantha had expected to find her. Samantha knew exactly where she was.

Samantha recognized Hannah's red platform high-top sneakers when she looked for feet beneath the bottom edges of the doors to each stall. Hannah was the only one in the ladies' room. Her feet were pointing toward the back of the stall, so it was clear what she had been doing. Her feet turned to face forward, and the door to the stall opened.

"Sam," said Hannah, her voice flat, defeated. "I purged."

"Obviously," Samantha said, holding out her arms to Hannah, who moved into the embrace of the smaller girl and bent her head to place it on Samantha's shoulder. Samantha held Hannah, neither of them speaking. Hannah felt miserable and agitated.

"I need to get myself together," said Hannah, snapping into action. "I don't want to be late to meet The Girlfriend, and I need toothpaste or mints or something."

"I don't have any mints," said Samantha. "I never carry any kind of food with me."

"Mints are not food," observed Hannah.

The girls walked out of the bookstore to a nearby convenience store across the road from the mall where Hannah was to meet her father and The Girlfriend at a steak house.

"I hadn't purged in so long!" wailed Hannah.

"Don't worry about it," said Samantha. "It's normal to backslide. Of course, what would I know about it. I never have the opportunity to backslide because I never frontslide in the first place," she observed wryly.

"Don't you ever get tired of trashing yourself?" said Hannah, pulling open the door of the brightly lit convenience store, where she was faced with nine different brands of cheese puffs the color of life jackets. Hannah often felt as though cheese puffs WERE life jackets.

"Oddly, no," Samantha replied. "I never do get tired of that."

"Will you come with me to meet The Girlfriend?" pleaded Hannah.

Samantha considered. "I guess I could. Do you think your father or The Girlfriend would mind? I have nothing else to do tonight, except pray that Len calls and declares his love. If you think it would help you, I could come with you."

"Would you, Sam? That would be GREAT!"

Hannah found some sugar-free mints and popped three into her mouth.

"My mouth tastes so gross," she said. "Do I smell?"

She exhaled in the direction of Samantha, who sniffed, and then wrinkled her nose in response.

"I think you're okay. Don't breathe in The Girlfriend's direction though."

The girls headed across the highway toward the huge

indoor mall. It was tricky getting across the highway. Hannah followed behind Samantha, noticing her walk. Samantha had the kind of walk Hannah associated with robots, she realized. Her limbs seemed glued to her body so that they didn't swing naturally, rearranging themselves in relation to one another with each step. This is the walk of an extremely rigid person, she thought.

They were less than five minutes late for Hannah's eight o'clock date with her dad when they arrived at Peter Jane's, the steak house her father was fond of. Tony Bonanti and The Girlfriend had not yet arrived, so Hannah and Samantha sat at the bar where Hannah ordered a Virgin Mary with lots of Tabasco, and Samantha sipped a club soda.

"I spoiled my abstinence!" said Hannah despairingly.

"No you didn't," said Samantha. "Remember how Gale is always talking about how it's a natural part of the process to have a slip? She calls it 'looping.' Remember she was talking to Phoebe about that after Phoebe ate the leftover half of her cousin's birthday cake? Gale said that it's part of the recovery process to go forward for a while, and then to loop backwards. Then you come around and go forward again."

"Well, it FEELS awful! I hate looping! I just HATE IT!"

"Well," said Samantha, the ice in her glass tinkling as she sipped her soda through a red-and-white-striped plastic straw. "Get used to it."

"You know lots of psychology stuff," said Hannah. "It's a shame you can't use it on yourself."

"Isn't it though," observed Samantha. "Hey—isn't that your dad? And HER?"

Tony Bonanti walked toward them, holding Abbey Jewett's arm. Abbey was taller than Hannah expected, taller even than she was herself, even taller than her father—maybe five-foot-eleven. Her hair looked like it was naturally red, as she had the complexion to match it, fair and freckled, with those bald-looking eyelids because the eyelashes are so pale, and practically no discernible eyebrows. She was wearing a navy blue skirt and matching tailored jacket with a white shirt underneath it, and conservative gold button earrings. Her hair was pulled back and gathered at the nape of her neck. Hannah couldn't see what was holding it, but she couldn't miss how it fanned out frizzily in all directions in wild curls. She looked young. Hannah knew she was only thirty-two, but Hannah thought she looked even younger.

While Hannah looked at Abbey, Samantha was looking at Hannah's father. He looked so happy and alive, thought Samantha, compared to how her own father was looking lately. Her father seemed to have aged ten years in only six months.

"Hi, girls!" said Tony when he and Abbey reached the bar. "How're you doing, Sam?"

"Okay," Samantha replied. "I ran into Hannah in the

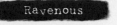

bookstore, and she invited me to join you. I hope you don't mind."

What have I gotten myself into, thought Samantha. *I have to sit through DINNER!*

"Not at all," said Tony. "Hannah, Sam—I want you to meet Abigail Jewett. Abbey."

"Hello," said Hannah, extending her hand. "Hi," said Samantha, while Hannah and Abbey shook each other's hands shyly.

"Well, should we get a table?" suggested Hannah's father.

Hannah was reminded of the many times she and her father would come to Peter Jane's for dinner before going to the hospital to see her mom during evening visiting hours. She was briefly horrified to realize that her father could have chosen another restaurant for tonight's meeting, one that had no associations to her mother, to those sad times.

But she quickly forgot her concerns when she noticed the tightness of Samantha's mouth, the tension in her whole face as she was handed the enormous menu. The specialty at Peter Jane's was the sixteen-ounce Porterhouse steak. What would Samantha order? Hannah fretted about her friend. Her father and Abbey, lost behind their menus, seemed very connected. They'd moved their chairs a bit closer together and their elbows were touching as they perused the huge, leather-bound menus.

Anger rose up in Hannah: How could her father have forgotten her mother so quickly! She couldn't sit there for the length of time it would take to order and eat an entire dinner. She wanted to leave, right now. But she couldn't leave Samantha sitting there.

While a white-shirted waiter was taking Abbey's order (Chilean sea bass with pureed sweet potatoes, caramelized onions, rice and a colorful vegetable medley was how the menu described the entrée Abbey had selected), Hannah regarded her future stepmother with the terror, hatred and disgust usually reserved for serial killers and swimsuit shopping.

When it was time for Hannah to order, she said, "I'm just going to have an appetizer as a main course. I'm not very hungry—I'll just have a shrimp cocktail."

Hannah didn't enjoy eating with other people. She savored eating only if she could eat large amounts, and only if she could then throw up the food. During the months she'd not been purging, eating had been a tense experience. She could not trust herself to eat appropriate amounts, since she'd never known how to do that. So she'd been eating only once a day, usually in the late afternoon. She'd choose plain foods, like tuna salad or scrambled eggs, and eat them in public. She would avoid bread, or anything sweet, because she found it so hard to not want to eat a whole roomful of those things. And she'd eat in public, usually at the diner. She'd spend the early evening with friends so she wouldn't be at home unless her dad was there, too. It was tricky on a daily basis to keep herself sane about eating, but she finally realized that this practice was helping her approach some semblance of normality where food was concerned.

Hannah prayed that neither Abbey nor her dad would say anything about how little she'd ordered. If either of them said anything to her, she could not even imagine what one of them might say to Sam when she ordered. What WOULD Sam order? Hannah turned her attention to Samantha, who was hidden behind the gigantic menu.

"Have you decided?" the waiter asked, his pencil poised over his pad.

Samantha put down her menu and said, "I'll have a glass of water and a side salad."

Then she turned to Abbey and Hannah's dad and explained, "I already had dinner. Hannah invited me at the last minute. I just ordered the salad to keep you guys company. I love salad anyway."

What a pro, thought Hannah.

Because she had never seen her eat anything, Hannah wanted to watch Samantha eat, but she didn't want to be noticed watching her, so she glanced toward Samantha's plate, and then looked quickly away. Samantha had asked the waiter to bring the dressing separate from the salad, and Hannah noticed that Samantha ate none of it with her soft Bibb lettuce. Hannah noticed Abbey sneaking furtive glances at Samantha, too.

Of more interest to Hannah was Abbey: her clothes, her makeup, her manicure—a dark red polish on her short nails, a color that reminded Hannah of the red of autumn leaves. Hannah watched her dad watching Abbey. Every few seconds, after he'd taken a mouthful of steak, he would look at her, his expression full of pride and satisfaction, something Hannah did not remember in him when he'd looked at Hannah's mom, whom he'd always regarded with tension and concern.

A sensation of tightness gathered swiftly in Hannah's chest when she thought of her mother as she watched her father watching Abbey. Samantha caught the strained look on Hannah's face.

She said, "Excuse me," and stood, intending to go to the ladies' room and hoping Hannah would come along. Hannah picked up on her cue and stood, too, and both girls walked past the bar to where the restrooms were, at the end of a long corridor hung with botanical prints of flowers. Once inside, Hannah sighed.

"How're you doing?" asked Samantha, unnecessarily. It was clear that Hannah was struggling.

"You know," Samantha said as she examined her complexion in the mirror. "When I heard my dad was seeing that girl in his class, I thought I would cut myself. Then I realized what I really wanted to do was cut HIM, and the need to cut myself sort of evaporated."

"And then what happened?" asked Hannah.

"I'm just saying that it's normal for you to be furious about this, about your dad wanting to marry someone, about her being so young and all, and your mother having died only three years ago."

"But what do I DO about the anger, though?" said Hannah, who had been looking at Samantha in the mirror over the pink marble counter, where thick, pink paper fingertip towels were folded in neat rectangles and arranged in a fan pattern, ready for use.

"What do I DO about the anger?" repeated Hannah plaintively, a vertical line forming between her thick, dark, pleasingly shaped eyebrows.

She sat down on one of the upholstered stools in front of the counter, as though the very question had suddenly exhausted her.

"Beeeeeeee with the anger," said Samantha, imitating the tone of Gale's voice. "Feeeeeeeel your anger, and remember to breeeeeeeeathe."

Both girls laughed. Hannah hadn't realized how tense she

was until the moment she wasn't, hadn't realized that her face had been all scrunched up, its features migrating toward each other, toward the center, her shoulders pulling in toward her neck, as though anxiety had made her smaller.

"But HOW? HOW do I feeeeeeel the anger when I'm not going to be allowed to DO anything about it?"

"When I get so angry that I want to cut myself now, I go to the beach and scream," said Samantha. "Gale told me to try that. It works sort of. I feel better after."

"Could I come along and scream with you?"

"Sure," said Samantha.

"I wish we could scream RIGHT NOW!" said Hannah, her throat tight.

Samantha imagined them in a scene from a movie: She and Hannah and all the other members of the group at the beach in the moonlight, screaming. They'd probably be arrested.

"But we're giving ourselves therapy, officer! We're doing anger-discharge work!"

Officer A: "Yeah, yeah, tell it to the judge."

Officer B, shaking his head: "Kids today!"

"I really can't STAND the idea of my father getting married again. It's hard ENOUGH that my mom died," said Hannah with a tone of resignation.

"I know," said Samantha. "It must be so hard."

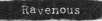

Hannah stood and put her arms around Samantha's narrow shoulders. Her body felt like all bones, and when the two girls hugged, Hannah could feel Samantha's rib cage. She felt she was holding a trembling baby bird.

"You're strong, Han. You'll get over this, too," said Samantha when they had moved apart.

"She's already dead," continued Hannah. "Now I feel as though she's dying all over again, as though he's killing her."

❋ ❋ ❋

Phoebe's poodle, Tom, jumped up onto Phoebe's bed and licked her face, her eyelids, her ears, her mouth. His little feet got tangled in Phoebe's long, thick, curly brown hair. Phoebe stirred. Nicole, Phoebe's other poodle, was curled up on top of Phoebe's feet watching Tom with interest. This routine was repeated every morning in Phoebe's large, second-floor bedroom.

The November sun had only just begun to brighten the sky. Phoebe groaned and turned over to go back to sleep. Nicole walked on her soft poodle feet to the pillow where Phoebe's head rested on a pattern of blue hydrangeas. She looked at Phoebe, willed her to open her eyes, to play with her. Phoebe suddenly opened her eyes wide, as though she could hear Nicole's thoughts. Tom jumped onto Phoebe's chest and crouched there in an attitude of waiting, like a runner at the starting line, ready to spring.

Phoebe's copies of *The National Enquirer* and *The Star* lay on the floor at the foot of her bed, their headlines proclaiming:

Liz Endures Another Surgery!

Liza Seeks Addiction Treatment!

Lose 30 Pounds in 30 Days with Celebrity Chicken-and-Cherry Diet!

Phoebe's reading glasses were on the floor near her journal. One of her black leather boots peeked out from beneath the bed's lacy dust ruffle.

Phoebe gathered her poodles close to her and heaved a deep sigh.

UGH! she said to herself. Even in her roomiest flannel pajama bottoms with their forgiving elastic waistband, she

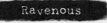

could feel the legacy of the previous night, the souvenir of her despair. She could not believe she'd eaten four pieces of the chocolate cake that Samantha's sister, Patti, had been given to celebrate her fourteenth birthday.

UGH!!!!!! Phoebe said to herself again. *How can I continue to do this? And WHY—WHY do I keep doing it? I have the cutest, sweetest boyfriend IN THE WORLD now! There is no excuse of lonely hopelessness anymore!*

Phoebe was keeping a secret from herself: She was terrified of this new relationship with Daryl. Where would it take them? What would happen when he got close enough to really see her? The food kept the answers to these unasked questions safely hidden.

She could hear her father walking down the hall, down the stairs, into the kitchen to begin his daily morning espresso ritual. She felt a wave of disgust flow through her belly, disgust with herself. Her father was right to have humiliated her all the time.

UGH! UGH! UGH! She flung the blue comforter aside. Tom and Nicole sprang off her from opposite sides of the bed and waited for her on the blue carpet, expecting fun. Phoebe sat dejected on the edge of her bed, listless, her shoulders slumped, her hair in disarray.

HOW COULD I HAVE EATEN SO MUCH CAKE? IT WASN'T EVEN MY CAKE!

She suddenly thought of Jessica. She always used to call Jessica at times like this.

❋ ❋ ❋

How can I be GAINING weight?" cried Phoebe, when her friends had arrived.

Billy and Scott had come in first, followed by Samantha and Hannah. Phoebe's new friend from school, Pearly Bodagian, who had a black eye from sparring in her Kung Fu class, was joining them, too, and they sat on big pillows around the fireplace. Phoebe was burning incense, and its exotic jasmine fragrance wafted around them. Phoebe's parents had gone to Mexico, and Phoebe was grateful for the privacy their absence afforded her.

"You don't look like you've gained weight," said Billy, who adored Phoebe no matter what size she thought she was.

"I have! I have!" she cried. "HOW could I be gaining weight when I'm with the guy of my dreams, of EVERY-BODY'S dreams! Am I scared of being close to someone because of what my dad is like? Or am I testing Daryl to see if he'll stay in spite of my blubber? Or am I just sabotaging myself because I am a loser?"

"You're with the guy of your dreams," said Pearly, her head

propped on a pillow. "It's scary. A 'too good to be true' scenario, so good you're afraid it's going to evaporate. You can't stand the suspense, so you're probably trying to MAKE it evaporate. Then you won't have to worry about it anymore."

Pearly had the shortest hair anyone had ever seen. She was warmhearted and easy to be with, the kind of person who, even after having met her only once, people felt they'd known for a long time. The group members liked her immediately.

"You're afraid to be close to him because of what your dad is like," said Scott.

"You're testing him," agreed Billy.

"But what if he FAILS THE TEST!" wailed Phoebe.

"Daryl won't fail," said Samantha. "Daryl is a great guy, and he's known you a long time."

"You're such good friends," added Hannah. "And that Gabby was such a control freak."

Like my dad is, thought Phoebe. *No wonder Daryl hated being with Gabby toward the end there. Sam and Hannah are right; Daryl IS the cowboy in the white hat. He's so great, so mentally healthy.*

Phoebe wrote:

Hot Gossip!!!!

Phoebe Coos As Lovebirds Lunch!!!!!!!!!!!!!

Dashing Daryl M. and fat Phoebe McIntyre spent the weekend in a love nest. Phoebe's folks, Michael (noted fashion photog) and Molly (his gorgeous ex-model wife) were in Mexico while the amorous Phoebe and enraptured Daryl played house at the McIntyre's Long Island mansion.

Daryl's mother died last year, and clever Phoebe's been whipping up his favorite dishes, such as meat loaf with egg noodles, and steak and mashed potatoes, to make him feel at home.

The lovebirds spend every spare minute together, and sources close to the couple say a delighted Daryl will soon be showing his appreciation with a ring.

Ringy, ding, ding.

"I'll believe it when I see it!" said Phoebe, according to a friend. "And when I see it, I'll faint."

* * *

Phoebe sat with her new friend, Pearly, at the tea shop in Port Franklin, and listened as Pearly described her latest decision-making problem. When Phoebe was reading her psychology textbook that morning, she could have sworn the chapter on the obsessive personality type had been written about Pearly.

The hallmark of the obsessive personality, the book said, was doubt. And Pearly was full of doubt. Should she study now—or later? Did she select the best shade of nail polish? Should she go out with Hector or did he smoke too much marijuana? Should she major in business, or social work? What should she wear to her sister's wedding?

As tiring as her friend's obsessing could be, Phoebe couldn't help loving the intelligence, humor and warmth that were the real Pearly inside the shell of worry and doubt.

Pearly's black eye reminded Phoebe of Jessica, and how she'd died of starvation at the age of sixteen last spring, less than a year ago. Jessica had suffered black eyes from falling and hitting her head on things. Phoebe wondered again what had become of Jessica's little brother, Matthew. The family had moved away just weeks after Jessica died.

Phoebe felt a surge of anxiety when she thought about Matthew. She should have found out where they were moving to, should have kept in touch with him.

The scones on the table in the tea shop looked good to her just then. She commanded herself to wait. She knew why they looked so good suddenly, even though it had not entered her mind to eat one before. Her anxiety about Matthew and sadness about Jessica made her perceive the raisins in the scones as succulently, plumply, irresistibly sweet all of a sudden.

She took two deep breaths and refocused on what Pearly was saying.

*　*　*

I feel horrible about myself! I ATE THE WHOLE SLEEVE OF OREOS! UGHHH!" wailed Phoebe, sitting with Gale in her afternoon session. Light streamed through the curtains, making lacy patterns on the table and floor.

"When you speak like that about yourself, it's very traumatic for you," observed Gale.

"Yeah, tell me about it!"

"I AM going to tell you about it. I HAVE to tell you about it. This is what you have to go on a diet from—this harsh, judgmental self-talk in which you tell yourself how horrible you are. You are NOT horrible."

"BUT I AM!" insisted Phoebe.

"Where does it get you to tell yourself you're so horrible?" asked Gale.

"I can't tell myself I'm WONDERFUL when I eat so many cookies!" insisted Phoebe. "If I don't tell myself I'm terrible, I'll eat MORE cookies."

"You are absolutely wrong," said Gale. "Telling yourself you're horrible will make you eat more cookies."

"How could I be wrong? I HAVE to punish myself when I eat too much. Otherwise, I'll just get worse!"

"No," Gale persisted. "Being mean to yourself is what will make you hungrier."

"HOW?" asked Phoebe suspiciously.

"When you're mean to yourself, it's traumatizing."

"Yeah? And?" said Phoebe.

"And when you are traumatized, it's very stressful."

"Duh!" said Phoebe, folding her arms across her chest.

"And stress produces a 'fight or flight' response," continued Gale. "And a 'fight or flight' response means the body has to mobilize for action."

"Action?" repeated Phoebe.

"ACTION," Gale emphasized. "And when the body mobilizes for action, one of the things it does is make sure it has enough energy to either fight or run away. It knows it will need extra energy for running away or fighting."

"Yeah," said Phoebe. "And?"

"So, when the body is in a state of stress, and it mobilizes to either fight or run away, it gets HUNGRIER because it needs EXTRA FOOD for the fighting or the running away!"

"So, you're saying that when I talk meanly about myself to myself, it stresses me and I need more fuel because of the stressing?"

"Exactly," said Gale.

Phoebe blinked twice. She uncrossed her arms. She said, "Hmmmmmph. I see what you mean." She thought for a minute. She said, "But how do I get out of the habit of telling myself how bad and wrong and hopeless I am when I eat so many cookies?"

"Practice," said Gale.

"So, does that mean I should eat more cookies just to have a chance to practice not telling myself I'm bad?" asked Phoebe coyly.

"Absolutely, if you find yourself eating cookies, do not tell yourself you're bad!" said Gale.

❋ ❋ ❋

Matthew Blaine, six and a half years old, missed his sister, Jessica, who'd been Phoebe's best friend. Jessica had died because of a heart arrhythmia caused by undereating, and Matthew remembered that Jessica was always trying to help Phoebe because Phoebe ate too many cookies. He wished he were taller—and older—because then he could leave his mother and her boyfriend and go back to Long Island and visit Phoebe.

"Matthew!" called his mother, Adrian. "Come to dinner!"

Matthew didn't want dinner. Jessica wouldn't have wanted dinner. She always had an excuse about why she wouldn't eat. She'd have a headache, or a stomachache or a toothache or an earache or she ate at school or at Phoebe's.

He wished Phoebe would write him a letter, but she didn't know his address. He knew hers, though, because he had Jessica's address book.

*   *   *

The snapshot showed Phoebe and Jessica on the patio at Jessica's house. In the picture, Matthew, in red shorts and a blue and white stripped T-shirt, was sitting on the lawn at the edge of the flagstone, his legs splayed, with a colorful pile of Legos and a half-finished Lego parking garage before him.

Matthew held the photo and dialed Phoebe's number. He hoped she still lived in the same place. Thinking about

Phoebe made him feel better, connected him with Jessica, who he missed painfully, missed every day. He hoped Phoebe remembered him.

He was alone in the big house to which he and his mother had moved only three weeks after Jessica's funeral. It was his mom's boyfriend's house, and Matthew didn't like it.

The phone rang four times, but Phoebe didn't answer. Her answering machine said, "This is Phoebe. If it's Daryl and it's Friday, I'll meet you at the bookstore café at the usual time. If it's anyone else, you know what to do."

Matthew was comforted by just the sound of Phoebe's familiar voice. Phoebe was always so nice to him when she'd come by so that Jessica could give her diet tips, explaining ways Phoebe could lose weight.

Matthew liked Phoebe just the way she was. It felt so good to have her hug him; her body felt soft and comfortable and pillowy, whereas when Jessica held him, the ends of her pointy bones felt sharp and poked him. Her back bones stuck out.

And Phoebe was alive. He hoped she remembered him, because he was going to be visiting her town, since his grandmother still lived there. He wanted to see Phoebe and let her hug him. He hoped she still wanted to.

He left a message: "This is Matthew Blaine. Do you remember me? If you do, please call me back. Call me back even if you don't remember me. I'll remind you about

Jessica and our dog Aladdin that you used to bring bones to. My mom isn't happy here. I'm not either."

He left his number and waited.

* * *

Matthew Blaine looked like a miniature adult thought Phoebe, as she watched him climb out of Adrian's black Subaru. Though he was wearing jeans and sneakers and a white New York Yankees T-shirt under his unzipped jacket, he had the bearing of a man in a suit and tie. And just before he'd flung himself into her arms and she saw his eyes, she realized that "the change" had taken place—that shift from feeling secure, to knowing there is no guarantee, ever, that makes safety from crushing disappointment and devastating loss a reasonable expectation.

Tom and Nicole, unused to having such a small visitor, jumped straight up and down like pogo sticks at Matthew's feet. Matthew's eyes, when he let Tom and Nicole lick his face, flashed with childlike wonder, but then, in an instant, his eyes returned to their dullness as though he'd gone away into a remote place inside himself again.

"I miss everything," said Matt later, sitting on a stool at the counter in Phoebe's kitchen, eating a peanut butter-and-jelly sandwich. Phoebe had been careful to spread the peanut butter, and then the jelly, all the way to the very edges of the bread, remembering that Jessica did that for him.

"I remember you like your sandwich with the jelly spread all the way to the edges," said Phoebe.

"I don't care about the jelly now," Matthew replied.

Tom and Nicole followed Matthew all afternoon, flopping at his feet the minute he sat down, then quickly scrambling back up to follow him when he moved around Phoebe's house, looking at everything.

"I was never in your house," he said. "It's a good house. I'm not happy in my new house."

"Why?" asked Phoebe.

"Because my mom doesn't pay attention to me the way Jess used to," he said, hugging both poodles, who sat in his small lap. "Why did Jess stop eating? Didn't she want to live?"

"I know she wanted to live," said Phoebe. "She made that amazing tie-dyed prom dress, remember? I KNOW she wanted to wear it. And she loved you, Matt. She wanted to live."

"So why'd she stop eating then?" he repeated.

"Because she didn't think stopping eating was connected to dying. To her, stopping eating felt like living, and EAT-ING felt like dying."

"I'm sad," he said. "I don't want to go home. Can I stay here with you?"

Phoebe wanted to say, "Of course, you can!!"

Instead, she said, "Your mom wouldn't let you."

"But she doesn't pay attention to me anyway!" said Matthew.

"Attention is the most important thing, isn't it," said Phoebe, more to herself than to Matthew. But then she thought of the kind of attention her father gave her and felt confused for a minute.

❋ ❋ ❋

Phoebe said, "Brrrrr," as she, Pearly, Samantha and Lacey walked into the huge discount warehouse store that seemed colder than the gusty autumn day. They'd decided to do some early Christmas shopping and Pearly, bored by the mall because she worked there on weekends, had suggested they use her membership card to buy things at a discount at the Thriftysave. Lacey wanted to get a watch for her boyfriend, and Pearly told her there were good buys on jewelry there.

"It's cold in here!" complained Samantha, pulling her old cheerleading jacket more tightly around herself.

Sam was always cold, thought Phoebe, even on warm days, because of her undereating.

As the girls walked down the long aisles of the high-ceilinged store the size of an airplane hangar past boxes of laundry detergent as big as refrigerators, Lacey suddenly stopped short, wide-eyed, in front of a giant economy-sized box of multicolored condoms.

"We have to have these!" she declared, pointing at the box.

"We?" said Samantha.

"Yeah!" Lacey replied. "We can split it among the four of us. We're all having sex, aren't we?"

"I am," said Phoebe, a dreamy vagueness in her eyes and voice."

"I am," said Samantha. "Every weekend. With Len. In his car."

"In his CAR?" said Pearly.

"We have nowhere else to go!" said Samantha defensively.

"Good thing you're so small," said Pearly, who was tall and big-boned. "I'm having sex with two different guys."

"At the SAME TIME?" asked Phoebe.

"NO!" said Pearly.

"Oh you're such a slut!" said Phoebe, teasing her.

"I'm not," said Pearly. "I just can never make up my mind which so I have to have both. I'm the same way with shoes and earrings."

"Oh—so men are a form of accessory to you?" said Lacey, smiling.

I've lost three pounds, finally," said Phoebe to Daryl, as she stepped off the scale and headed back to her bedroom from the adjoining gray, white and silver bathroom. Phoebe's dad had designed the room, as he had every other room in the house. Phoebe would have preferred wallpaper with big pink roses all over it, but Michael McIntyre said it would be fabulous to have a bathroom that looked like an enormous bathroom scale or the inside of a space capsule. Phoebe imagined what the cover of *The National Enquirer* would say about this bathroom:

> **Teenager Abducted in Bathroom That Is Actually Alien Space Vehicle!!!!**

"Three whole pounds," said Daryl, sitting on Phoebe's bed. He was bare-chested and the smooth, well-developed muscles of his arms, shoulders and hairless chest made him look more like a movie star than a college student.

"You have taken away three pounds of yourself."

"What do you mean?" said Phoebe. "Isn't it cool that I lost three pounds? Now I have only—oh—about fifty more to go."

"Yeah, it's great that you lost the weight," said Daryl, "'cause I know you wanted to. But now there's less of you! It's so mysterious when someone loses weight. Some of that weight is YOU!"

Daryl actually said wonderful things like this often.

Phoebe felt that glow of warmth spreading through her slowly, until it finally reached her hands and the tips of her fingers. It started in the center of her body and radiated outward, and it came when she felt most connected to Daryl, when she felt known and valued.

She marveled at how unlikely it was that a person as physically gorgeous and as intelligent and responsible as Daryl could also be so kind, sensitive and loving. The people in her Tuesday group often said Daryl sounded "too good to be true" and Phoebe would insist he WAS true, that he DID have these qualities. He DID say sweet things like this.

She scooted closer to him on the bed, pressing her body against his so that he could put his arms around her.

* * *

Samantha is always saying how she's not getting any better, or making any progress," said Hannah when the group had settled in front of the fire. "But you know what she did? She rescued me from a completely hideous evening."

"It was still hideous for you! I couldn't change that!" Samantha reminded her.

"But it was only moderately hideous," said Hannah.

"But that's what friends are for," insisted Samantha, minimizing, as usual, anything about herself that might be viewed as positive.

"Yeah," agreed Hannah. "But your rescue involved coming with me to a RESTAURANT, do you realize that?"

Samantha deliberated. "But I didn't even finish the salad," she argued, intent on proving how unrecovered she had remained in spite of all the therapy, and the role-plays and the self-help books that she had reluctantly read.

"And Sam and I are going to scream together," announced Hannah triumphantly. She turned to Gale. "Sam did the funniest imitation of you when I asked her how to deal with my anger about my dad getting remarried."

Gale shifted in her chair and crossed her legs. "Oh

yeah?" she said, making herself sound like a gangster.

"Yeah," said Hannah, racing ahead. "And I'm going to an Al-Anon meeting. Sam said her mom has been much less cranky and controlling since she's been going to those meetings. I need to be less cranky and controlling, too. My dad has his own life. I can't change what he feels or what he's doing. I wish I could, though," she concluded sadly.

The group listened attentively. This was one of the things Hannah found so helpful about group, that everyone listened, seemed so interested.

"That's one of the things I don't understand," Samantha said. "My mom has been so much better lately. She's easier to live with, and we talk now, and she isn't on my case all the time about eating, so why am I still starving? I'm not getting better fast enough. Or at all."

"You ARE getting better," Phoebe insisted. "You never used to return phone calls. You were the person in group who seemed to care the least about the rest of us. And we cared about you more than you cared about yourself."

"I didn't want you to care," reflected Samantha. She looked into the middle distance, as though she was watching something, watching herself in the past.

"I was afraid of being cared for." She hesitated again. "I was afraid if I let someone in, that would make me have less

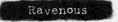

control, as though it would make me fat if I had another person's caring inside me somehow."

"But you finally let us in," said Scott.

"You were generous to help Hannah," observed Faye, coughing and turning toward Samantha. "You did something that would have freaked you out a year ago (cough). You went to a RESTAURANT." Faye used the word "restaurant" with awe, as though Samantha had placed her head into the jaws of a shark for her friend.

"I guess so," reflected Samantha, still not ready to admit that she had indeed made progress, even though her relationship with food had not changed much.

"The food is the last thing to shift," Gale reminded the group. "It's the tip of the big iceberg."

"What shifts things faster?" asked Billy.

"I read this great quote," said Gale. "It said, 'The difference between the ordinary and the miraculous is your undivided attention.'"

"Wow," said Hannah. "I'm going to use that in one of my fortune cookies."

❊ ❊ ❊

Phoebe sat down with the box of crunchy granola to watch TV. She liked to rummage around in the box to find the chunks of sweet granola that had stuck together, forming pieces the size of grapes.

She had decided to take a vacation from "being good." Gale had explained that every now and then you HAD to have a break, because you would naturally want one anyway (because of the "looping" phenomenon), and it was better to choose the binge than to feel deprived, because the deprivation would inevitably be followed by feeling you were possessed by some evil force that would compel you to stand in front of the opened refrigerator eating cold food out of plastic containers and not understand how you had gotten there.

So Phoebe had "chosen" the granola, and settled in for her deliberate binge. As she munched, she could feel that sense of vagueness build. That was what would happen when she ate sugar—or large amounts of starchy food like granola, cereal, pasta or bread all at one time—she would feel as though her eyes were going out of focus, and it reminded her of the expression she'd see in people's faces when they ate ice cream, a look of bliss, like infants looking up into the eyes of their mothers.

She thought about the vanished three pounds. She realized that in some part of herself, she missed them. They were a part of her that was gone now. It was as though she had agreed to have three pounds of herself amputated.

She mourned the loss of these several pounds of herself and of all the pounds that had gone before. She felt more exposed without her fleshy shield, and, even though the charts published by insurance companies said she should weigh fifty pounds less, Phoebe didn't agree that doing so would feel comfortable. Even now, she felt light, and the lightness felt like anxiety, a jittery feeling in her arms and shoulders.

"I don't know if I want to lose any more weight," Phoebe said to Gale during their next session.

"Good call with Thanksgiving coming," observed Gale.

"I feel too light already," Phoebe declared. "Like I'm going to leave the ground, like a kite without a string or something."

"So, you need a string," said Gale. "What about your dad? Is he a kind of 'string' for you?" asked Gale. "Maybe that's what serves you about his criticisms."

"Could be," said Phoebe, considering this, looking at her lap in black velvet wide-legged pants. Then she remembered what she wanted to tell Gale about.

"I had this great idea about that today," said Phoebe with enthusiasm. "I thought I'd move out of my house!"

"Good idea," Gale said.

"I could afford it if I worked after school, in addition to the weekends," said Phoebe. "I just need a room somewhere, not a whole apartment."

"Would you still work at the studio with your dad?" Gale asked.

"Oh no!" said Phoebe. "That would be a tremendous problem. If I don't continue to lose weight, my father is going to make my life hell. I'll have to work somewhere else. And I'm not sure I want to lose more weight. I'm not ready."

"Do you think there's anything you can do to help your dad understand you better?"

"No," said Phoebe. "There is absolutely nothing I can do about that," she said sadly.

Hannah had brought some fortune cookies from the bakery to Phoebe's house where the McIntyres were having a pre-Thanksgiving gathering. While Molly and Michael and Phoebe walked back and forth from the kitchen carrying platters that had held turkey and ham, and covered casserole dishes that had held sweet-potato pie, stuffing and creamed onions, the members of the Tuesday

group and Kaneesha dug into the huge bowl of fortune cookies, which Hannah had baked in autumn colors: rust, dark red, deep orange and golden yellow.

Phoebe broke open the first cookie:

Identity is your worst addiction.
Do something different today.

"I'm SO depressed," said Hannah, feeling that this fortune had been directed at her. She missed Pauline, but she had to say good-bye. She felt stuck in her life in some way she didn't understand.

Scott felt stuck the same way. He was on day eight of his abstinence from purging. Billy was trying low-carbohydrate eating and was in withdrawal from sugar and pasta. Samantha was having no success at all adding calories to her dinners of iceberg lettuce and an apple.

Change was the hardest, thought Hannah, when you were at the edge of some big possibility and one step forward felt as though you were going to be stepping off a cliff.

"I know what you're going through," said Faye to Hannah. "My husband—you know, the one who died? (cough)—he became so much like a parent to me that (cough, cough) I couldn't let him touch me after a while. My therapist in California said that was called 'Oedipal contamination' or some big fancy psychology term (cough).

So, I felt at least a LITTLE better because there was a name for what I had."

"But is there a CURE for it?" asked Hannah with a tone of bottomless desperation. "Is there a TREATMENT for it?"

"I never got around to that part," said Faye, "because Jack died."

"I think you have to PRETEND that you don't know the person," offered Kaneesha, who was now an honorary member of the Tuesday team.

"Pretend?" repeated Hannah. "That's kind of weird."

"You never pretend anything?" said Scott. "We spend our lives pretending! Don't you pretend you're not a lesbian and not bulimic when you're with your dad and Abbey? And don't we spend our entire lives pretending we're never going to die?"

"Yeah," said Hannah, "I pretend with them. But I don't have to have sex with either of them."

"What's so horrible about having sex?" said Michael McIntyre, coming into the big dining room with a tray of cups and saucers, followed by Molly carrying pitchers of milk and cream.

"DA-AD!" said Phoebe, making the word into two syllables. "We're not discussing this with YOU."

"I feed you delicious food all day, and you don't want to include me in your talking?"

"There are some things you just can't discuss with parents."

"Why?"

"Because—they're—PARENTS!" said Phoebe, exasperated when she realized that she couldn't explain something she nonetheless understood with great certainty.

"Because it feels like a boundary violation," said Kaneesha, who had been attending Al-Anon meetings to deal with her feelings about her mother having run off with her father's brother, then marrying him. Neither her mother nor her uncle drank, but it was something she had no control over, and Samantha's mother had told her Al-Anon was helpful for stuff you couldn't control. Sometimes Kaneesha wished her mother HAD a drinking problem; at least then there would be an explanation for what seemed to Kaneesha to be her mother's reckless behavior.

"A boundary violation?" said Michael McIntyre. "What's that? Is it like going through a stop sign?"

"Yes!" Phoebe said. "It's what YOU do when you are too interested in what I'm eating or in my weight or the shape of my chin and you SAY SOMETHING ABOUT IT TO ME! THAT'S a boundary violation. It's like you're crossing a line you have no business crossing. It's like you have NO RESPECT for me."

There. She'd said it. Perfectly. She felt excellent. She did not want any more fortune cookies. She didn't want any brownies. She didn't want any cinnamon pear cake.

"Anyone want some cinnamon pear cake, or brownies?" asked her father, seemingly unaffected by Phoebe's recitation.

"I'll have some of both," said Hannah, and the members of the group all turned to look at her, but no one said a word.

Hannah ate two brownies and a slice of pear cake in full view of everyone.

"So now what?" asked Scott, when she had finished. What Scott meant, of course, was: Was she about to go into the bathroom to purge? It was an odd thing for Hannah to have her friends know her so well, to have them so close. It felt strange, but it felt good. She was no longer so ashamed of her bulimia, so it was a silly charade to pretend it was a secret. Her lesbianism had replaced the bulimia in her "Hall of Shame" anyway.

"I'm going to read a fortune," said Hannah, feeling bloated, her stomach distended and pushing uncomfortably against the elastic waistband of her long, narrow black-wool skirt. She had started dressing like Pauline, though she wasn't consciously doing so. She selected a dark red cookie and crushed it. She removed the little tab of paper onto which she had printed the "fortune" and read what was written on it.

**The standard of success is not beauty,
fame or fortune. It's the happiness you feel.**

"I think it IS the beauty, fame and fortune," said Michael McIntyre.

"I feel like purging, but I'm not going to," said Hannah to Scott, after Phoebe's dad had left the room.

"Why not?" asked Scott, with interest.

"Because you guys are here. Besides, just because I feel like a disgusting pig, doesn't mean I have to do something even MORE disgusting."

"WOW," said Samantha.

Billy reached for a fortune cookie and crushed it. It was orange and broke into three pieces, and there was a strip of pink paper inside.

Find an excuse to feel good right now.

"That's a good one," said Phoebe. "I spend a lot of time longing."

"I'm longing to put my fingers down my throat right now," admitted Hannah, her voice shaky.

Annemarie—this is Daryl," said Phoebe proudly.

Daryl and Annemarie simultaneously extended their hands. Annemarie held Daryl's eyes with her own and said, "Hey, Daryl! I've heard so much about you, I feel I almost know you."

"Same here," Daryl said warmly.

The threesome seated themselves at the small, round, marble-topped table upon which the waitress had placed three small oblong menus with green plastic covers. Annemarie looked especially pretty, Phoebe thought, in her short-sleeved, white angora sweater.

Phoebe felt suddenly regretful that she'd organized this meeting. She felt she couldn't be playful, the way she was used to being with Daryl, with someone else there. And she wasn't used to being with Annemarie in person. E-mail had become their way of connecting.

Nobody knew what to say. Phoebe opened her menu. Daryl opened his and studied it. She became aware that Annemarie, to her left, was studying Daryl, everything about him—the faded blue denim shirt he was wearing with its sleeves rolled up to the elbow, his hair, his broad shoulders, his strong forearms, his big square hands.

"So Daryl," said Annemarie—and in those two words, Phoebe heard a tone in Annemarie's voice. Even though

they communicated primarily through e-mail, Phoebe knew with some ancient intuitive wisdom that this was a tone women used to seduce. Annemarie was about to flirt with Daryl; she was already flirting with him.

Daryl looked up from his menu toward Annemarie, waiting for her to continue.

"So—I'll bet you work out," said Annemarie, looking at Daryl's strong forearms.

Annemarie FLIRTED with Daryl! She came on to him!" Phoebe exclaimed the instant Gale had closed the door to her office, even before they were both sitting down.

Gale felt the shock. She knew how important Annemarie had become to Phoebe, as a mentor, a role model, a friend. Gale at once understood the depth of the betrayal, and a part of her felt crushed in sympathy with her courageous young client as she reviewed Phoebe's relationship with Daryl.

Phoebe had been in love with Daryl since he'd befriended her the previous year, when he'd noticed her weight loss and confided to her that the only trouble he was having in his relationship with his girlfriend, Gabby, was that she so often complained about her weight. He'd shown Phoebe Gabby's photo, and Phoebe had been startled to see that Gabby was as big as she herself was. Daryl and Phoebe had been such close friends that when his mother, obese and diabetic, had died of heart failure just before graduation, Phoebe was the first person he'd called after dialing 911.

"What happened between Daryl and Annemarie?" asked Gale.

Phoebe started to cry. Gale waited, breathed deeply and concentrated on staying calm by becoming aware of what was going on in her body. She noticed how tense her jaw was and relaxed it. She focused on her other tense parts and let go. This, she had discovered, was the best thing she could do to support a client in distress. If she could stay calm and present, it seemed to help them do that, too.

Finally, after Phoebe had blotted her eyes and blown her nose, Gale said, "What's going on in your body right now?"

It always annoyed Phoebe when Gale wanted to know about her bodily experience. Phoebe didn't like paying attention to her body. She sighed with resignation and closed her eyes to concentrate better.

"I have a burning feeling," she noted.

"Where?"

"In my stomach. I think it's growing. It's in my chest, too. And in my throat."

"What else?"

"An expanding pressure in my head! As though my ears are going to fly off."

"What would the burning, expanding, pressured feeling say if it could speak?"

"It would speak to Annemarie." She thought for a moment. "It would say, 'How could you betray me like this you, you—'"

"You what?"

"You BITCH!" said Phoebe. "It would say, 'I'm so hurt. Alone. Confused. FURIOUS!'"

Gale said nothing, allowing Phoebe to be with herself.

"She e-mailed me after she got back to L.A. as though everything was completely normal!" said Phoebe with amazement. "Is this who she IS? A man-eater? Am I living in a fantasy world or what? She's like six years OLDER than him, and she KNOWS I'm COMPLETELY CRAZY ABOUT HIM! I'm TOTALLY BUMMED! Even when Daryl and I talked later, he said, 'What's Annemarie's story? Did you notice she was flirting with me. She ACCIDEN-TALLY touched my foot with her foot under the table.' I could tell he thought she was so lame."

She hesitated. "Now I'm even MORE upset because

Daryl must think I'm such a fool to have admired her so much! What do I say to her NOW?" wailed Phoebe.

* * *

The red-and-gold-lettered sign on the glass door read Salvation Army Thrift Shop, and, as Hannah pulled the door open and stepped inside, the familiar smells of mold, dust, Lemon Pledge and old wool engulfed her. She wasn't shopping for anything in particular. The shop was a block away from the bakery, and Hannah had gotten into the habit of stopping there after work. She liked wearing men's plaid sport jackets. Some were too new—made of polyester and not lined. She liked the older ones made of real wool, corduroy or faded cotton madras.

On her way to the back of the large store, Hannah congratulated herself for having worked at the bakery for almost fourteen whole weeks without having binged there once. She had binged elsewhere but not at the bakery where she was surrounded with dozens and dozens of tempting cookies, syrupy glazed pastries filled with sweetened cheese or crushed pineapple, chocolate fudge brownies and rich cakes frosted with buttercream icing.

On her first day of work there, she'd eaten one cookie just

before she was getting ready to go home. She reasoned that once she was out of the store, she would not be inclined to go to the market to buy more cookies of lesser quality than those she'd baked herself. It was a risky move that hadn't worked. She'd gone right to a convenience store and bought enough bakery items to have a binge. She learned from this that when she ate sweet things she became intoxicated, the way alcoholics who had one drink could not choose to stop drinking until they'd had too much.

Hannah couldn't understand how she had been able to resist the attractions of the delectable foods at the bakery that ordinarily seduced her with such overwhelming force.

When she'd expressed her perplexity about this in group, Phoebe had pointed out that Hannah was content when she was at work, that she liked her job and was proud of her talent for baking. Feeling good about herself at work was, Phoebe said, probably what explained Hannah's ability to remain binge-free there.

Hannah didn't know how much longer she would be able to trust herself to remain binge-free on the job, though. She had stopped seeing Pauline. Hannah's feelings about Devie confused her. But Devie's unpredictable mean moments did not make Hannah want to quit her job. Instead, Devie's occasional zingers made Hannah work harder for her complete approval.

As Hannah made her way down the long aisle of the thrift shop on her way to the rack of men's sport jackets, she passed a table full of ceramic items—bowls and figurines and vases and dishes of all sizes. At the corner of the table was a porcelain figurine of a Madonna and child. The Madonna wore a blue robe and had a beautiful face glowing with love as she gazed down into the face of the infant in her arms.

A pressure built in Hannah, rose from the center of her body into her throat and quickly to her eyes where tears gathered. She hastily wiped them away with the back of her hand.

"Are you all right?' said the gray-haired man with the kind eyes who was vacuuming the floor between the racks of clothes. Hannah had seen him in the store before.

"Yeah," she said sniffling, "I'm fine."

She picked up the figurine and brought it to the counter in front.

"How much is this?" asked Hannah, holding up the Madonna and child. "There's no price on it."

"Oh—how about a dollar-fifty?" asked the large woman behind the cash register.

"Good," said Hannah, pulling her navy blue leather wallet out of her bag.

There was a shoebox full of postcards on the counter, and

Hannah riffled through them as the woman put on her glasses in readiness for ringing up the sale. One of the postcards was a picture of a Madonna and child.

"I'll take this, too," said Hannah, handing the woman the card.

"Oh, do you collect Madonnas?" asked the woman.

"I think I do now," said Hannah.

"I collect stuff, too," said the woman, whose eyes looked sad. "I collect pot holders and angels and pictures of Elizabeth Taylor."

Hannah placed the ceramic Madonna and the postcard of the Madonna into the large, red leather tote bag her grandmother had recently given her for her birthday.

Her bedroom would quickly fill with images of the Madonna and child—in the form of ceramic vases that held flowers, in framed prints and postcards, in plastic, and even a Madonna and child night light. Sometimes, the gentle mothers looking lovingly at their infants made Hannah feel better about not having her mother there. Other times, these images only made her feel worse.

Phoebe sat in her newly painted room in front of her computer. That fresh clean smell of latex paint still lingered. The room was a pale, buttery yellow with darker yellow trim. It was such a cheery color that Phoebe wondered if—when her obsession with what to do about Annemarie subsided—she would ever be able to sleep again. She might, she admitted to herself, have chosen the wrong color. At least her father had agreed that she could choose the color.

The computer screen had pink and silver toasters with fluffy white wings flying across it, a screen saver that was becoming tiring to her. She touched the mouse and the toasters flew away. The REPLY TO screen, empty and waiting, was making Phoebe nervous. It seemed to want something from her. She would have to tell Annemarie how she felt about her since she had met and flirted with Daryl.

At the same time, part of Phoebe understood that only a person to whom that sort of flirtation was a natural trait would behave that way, so to that person the behavior would not seem horrible, but normal. Therefore, if she told Annemarie how angry she felt, she would be scolding her for who she, Annemarie, was. Annemarie clearly did not see herself as a shameless flirt to whom no man was ineligible, not even a man who was the center of her friend's entire life.

Having thought all that, another part of Phoebe

questioned whether Annemarie WAS her friend. She closed her eyes tightly for a minute to block out the shrieking intensity of the yellow walls and to consider. She concluded that yes, Annemarie's friendship had been sincere; that, after all, Daryl WAS supernaturally attractive; and that what Phoebe perceived to be treachery was just a part of who Annemarie apparently was—that she would have behaved the way she had with some other friend, too. Phoebe did not feel singled out for shabby treatment; this was more about Annemarie than it was about Phoebe.

Still, Phoebe pondered as she looked at the blank REPLY TO box on her screen, it was painful. It felt dreadful to be run over by a truck even if the truck WASN'T aiming specifically for you. She reflected mournfully about the countless times she had eagerly filled the REPLY TO box, thousands of words flying out through her fingers, connecting her to Annemarie, gathering strength from their friendship.

Because Annemarie was a graduate student in psychology —a subject Phoebe, too, intended to build a career around—Annemarie had been a wonderful resource. Annemarie had once been fat, and had a meddling, controlling mother who, when Annemarie described her, reminded Phoebe of her own father.

Annemarie had never known her father. Maybe, Phoebe

reflected, that was why she needed to collect whatever man happened to cross her path. This idea brought Phoebe a jolt of awareness, followed immediately by a burst of compassion.

Oh wonderful, thought Phoebe. *Now I'm feeling sorry for HER! Poor Annemarie—no daddy! NOW what am I going to say to her?*

When Hannah thought about Devie, about the impossibility that she could ever totally please her, she was overcome with gloom. Sometimes, the gloom was accompanied by shortness of breath, sometimes with an inability to concentrate on anything, sometimes with an ache in her chest and a bitter, metallic taste in her mouth. These were the kinds of feelings Hannah had experienced while her mother was dying.

Hannah wrote fortunes as though she could heal herself with them.

Focus, every day, upon what is most important to you, and good fortune will follow.

If happiness is not yours, it is because you do not believe you deserve it.

To feel good, your energy must be flowing. Breathe.

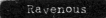

Hannah had begun to think in fortune-cookie language. She was over the edge, she knew. It was a deep edge; it was moving her toward a renewal of her purging. She knew it. She felt that the purging would relieve her of her unendurable grief, loneliness and dread. She was talking with Gale, with Kaneesha, with members of the group about it.

One night, after she'd eaten a box of chocolate-covered doughnuts and a quart of butter-pecan ice cream and purged, she called Gale to confess, to receive absolution.

Hannah said, "I didn't bleed, though."

Gale said, "You need to get another examination from the doctor. But don't be mean to yourself about this. You had to do what you had to do. You're in a 'loop' is all. Never give up! Love yourself no matter what you do!"

From: *PhoebeM@optonline.net*
Date: Mon 6 Nov 2000 11:27:13 EST
Subj: Daryl
To: *Annemarie@ultrasw.com*

Annemarie: It's taken me longer than usual to e you back, I know.

No, thought Phoebe. *Too stilted. Too formal.* She backspaced to delete and started again.

Annemarie: You cannot have failed to notice that

No. DELETE.

Annemarie: This is hard for me to write. I have been puzzling over what happened when the three of us met.

No good, said Phoebe to herself. DELETE.

Annemarie: You may be surprised at what I have to say. You have been what I thought was a friend through hundreds of e-mails for the past couple of months. You became my late-at-night journal, someone I could sort through the inner happenings of my day with.

UGH, thought Phoebe. *I have to start COMPLETELY over.* DELETE.

Annemarie: How many e-mails have I written you in the past few months? It has to be hundreds. I am sure that in at least 95 percent of them, I wrote about Daryl, how madly in love with him I am.

NO! HORRIBLE! DELETE!

Annemarie: Maybe I am expecting too much of you. Maybe you and Daryl were meant for each other, and my feelings are just big clumsy things getting in the way of your destinies.

NO! UGHHHH! Am I CRAZY???? DELETE! DELETE! DELETE!!!!!

Annemarie: Are you aware that when you remarked that Daryl had strong forearms and asked him if he worked out, you were flirting with him?

* * *

Samantha had no idea why, when the ham was passed around at Len's house during his dad's birthday dinner, she took an entire enormous slice for herself. Dinners with Len's family had never gone well for her. The family was small, and sat down to dinner at the table rather than having dinner buffet style, where everyone wouldn't be looking directly across the table at everyone else. What was she going to DO with this huge object on her plate?

More troubling still was what she was going to do with Len. She didn't feel as close to him as she once had, because she no longer felt safe with him.

She had not told him that she and Scott had gone on a couple of dates. Why had she not told him? She supposed she didn't want him to know she was not as timid and devoted and loyal as he thought she was. It crossed her mind that she hadn't told him about the dates because he would assume they were some sort of revenge dates to compensate for his preoccupation with Marika LaRue. She didn't want him to think they were revenge dates.

She felt she needed to break up with Len as much as she needed to break up with the huge slab of ham that was lying on her dinner plate. It was going to be easier to disconnect herself from the ham than it would be to disconnect herself from Len. She didn't like not having a boyfriend.

"Does anyone want this slice of ham?" she asked. "I took it by accident, I can't possibly eat all this."

Samantha was proud to have spoken up; she didn't feel self-conscious about admitting that a big hunk of meat was too much for her to eat. This sort of remark would not have been possible for her only months earlier, when she would have avoided calling attention to herself at the table.

"What the heck, it's my birthday, I'll take it," said Len's dad, and he passed his plate to Len, who passed it to Samantha, who placed the ham slice on it.

She wondered how Len would react when she told him she needed to be free of the worry she felt whenever she thought of him, far away, drawing Marika, thought of how inevitable it was that eventually he WOULD talk to Marika, WOULD invite her to have coffee, and would, of course, show her the drawings he'd made of her. All this was bound to evolve while he was far away.

Whatever had made her believe that she and Len would be able to continue feeling so close to each other when they were so far apart? Wasn't that what Daryl's ex-girlfriend, Gabby, had complained to Daryl about?

Maybe she and Len should be engaged. She'd feel better about their relationship then. But he hadn't asked her; and she, unlike Daryl's ex-girlfriend, would never insist. Anyway, she was too young to be engaged. Being engaged meant getting married, and getting married meant having babies, and having babies meant losing control of your flat stomach and getting fat and all stretched out.

Maybe when she told him she was thinking of ending their relationship Len would beg her to reconsider; maybe he would refuse to eat or get off the couch until she promised to be his forever. Samantha liked this scenario: Len, pining away on the sofa, his forearm flung across his eyes, unwilling to eat or study or play softball or watch *The Simpsons* until she agreed to be his fiancée, then his wife. Maybe he would leap at the chance to transfer to a school closer to home to be near her. She didn't want to be away from home.

"Samantha—do you want something else to eat?" asked Len's mother.

"No, thank you," said Samantha. "I'm fine. I've had lots of everything."

She had had several leaves of lettuce, but had been unable to avoid the bleu-cheese dressing since the salad was already tossed. She had eaten one mouthful of mashed potatoes because Len's mother had placed some on everyone's plate, and it had sort of stuck onto the lettuce leaves that Len's mother had also served everyone. She had squashed and moved one teaspoonful of the potatoes around on her plate until it had disappeared. Her stomach ached with anxiety, but the confusion she felt hurt even more.

Phoebe was thinking about Annemarie. She sat in her room, vague and blunted, staring at her psychology book. Psychology reminded her of Annemarie, and thinking about Annemarie felt like being hit by a truck. She listened to her Fat Barbees CD over and over:

Who needs girlfriends, HUH? HUH?
They borrow your lipstick
They kidnap your soul
And then they want to rock 'n' roll.
Hunting for mascara at the mall
Fishing for compliments not at all
On the treadmill at the gym
Talking only about him.
Who ARE THESE girlfriends, HUH? HUH?
Who ARE these girlfriends, HUH?
They borrow your boyfriend
They crush your soul
And then they want to rock 'n' roll.

Talking late into the night
You trusted her, it just ain't right.
One day she's your greatest friend
And next day she's around the bend.
WHO NEEDS GIRLFRIENDS? HUH? HUH?
Who needs girlfriends! I'm outta here.

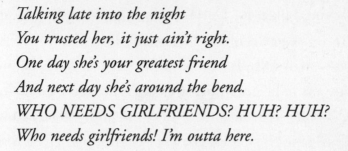

Daryl and Phoebe went walking in the bird sanctuary behind Maple Ridge High School. They strolled on the pier at Port Franklin, admiring the huge yachts moored there. They ate grilled tuna at dockside restaurants and had barbecued tofu at their favorite vegetarian café, Oat Cuisine. Daryl went to a yoga class with Phoebe, and Phoebe went to a Yankee game with him. Daryl hated the yoga class; he was the only guy in the class that day, and because he wasn't very flexible, he didn't feel good about himself. Phoebe loved being at the baseball game with Daryl because she was so happy being near him.

Phoebe memorized every hair that made up Daryl's eyebrows and the exact way his fingernails looked. With her eyes closed, she could picture the shape of his ears. She found the curve of his shoulders irresistibly beautiful.

Phoebe cooked for Daryl in his friend's small apartment where he stayed and studied when he came to be with Phoebe on weekends. She studied with him on Saturday nights, just to be near him. She taught herself to cook, making elaborate stews of lamb with cinnamon, or chicken with white wine in the Crock-Pot Daryl's aunt had given him.

They lay together on the pull-out sofa holding one another for hours, and they made love slowly in soft candlelight, listening to YoYo Ma playing the cello music Daryl loved. Phoebe felt lean and slithery, charged with some new high-voltage sensation when Daryl touched her. Even if he touched only her back, or simply looked at her, or if she was within a foot of him, she felt as though she was having a sexual encounter.

They were inseparable from Friday night at eleven, when Daryl would rush into Phoebe's arms, until Sunday night at ten, when Daryl would kiss her good-bye for the twenty-third time before driving back to school in the dark.

One night, as Daryl was leaving, he looked away from Phoebe when he said, "Gabby called me. She left a message. She wants to talk."

"Are you going to talk to her?"

Phoebe couldn't hide the stricken feeling that had jumped into her throat, making her tone tense and making

her simple words mean so much more than it sounded as though they did.

"How can I not talk to her? Don't you think that would be—cruel?"

Phoebe could not reply, not even to shake her head no.

"Gabby needs therapy," said Daryl, stating the obvious. "She is practically in stalking mode," he observed. "She calls me twice a day and leaves messages on my voice mail, and she's making such a fool of herself I really feel bad for her."

"Therapy would be good," Phoebe agreed. *It would be better than YOU being her therapist,* she thought.

Phoebe didn't exactly know if she felt it was cruel for Daryl to refuse to talk to Gabby. But the very thought of this encounter, whether by phone or e-mail or face-to-face, filled Phoebe with dread, accompanied by images of large quantities of bread.

Phoebe needed the oxygen mask, needed the flotation-device seat cushion. She and Daryl were, however, standing in the municipal parking lot in Port Franklin beside Daryl's car. Phoebe was standing very close to him, and she could feel energy rushing through him like a fast train. She moved closer to him and put her arms around him and could feel his strong back and his body vibrating like a hundred warm cats, purring. She nestled her head into the curve of his neck. There was a biting chill in the air.

※ ※ ※

From: *Annemarie@ultrasw.com*
Date: Mon 13 Nov 2000 2:02:16 PT
Subj: Huh?
To: *PhoebeM@optonline.net*

Phoebe: I'm not sure what you're talking about. I was only noticing that Daryl works out. All I said was, 'I notice you work out.' Is this about your trust issues?

From: *PhoebeM@optonline.net*
Date: Mon 13 Nov 2000 11:39:54 EST
Subj: Huh?
To: *Annemarie@ultrasw.com*

It's not the words you said but your tone, the whole body language thing. Don't talk your grad student 'trust issues' language with me, it brings up all my trust issues.

From: *Annemarie@ultrasw.com*
Date: Mon 13 Nov 2000 8:52:16 PT
Subj: Huh?
To: *PhoebeM@optonline.net*

I'm sorry you're upset but I can't take responsibility for your upset.

From: *PhoebeM@optonline.net*
Date: Tues 14 Nov 2000 00:42:18 EST
Subj: Huh?
To: *Annemarie@ultrasw.com*

Then I can't take responsibility for our friendship. It's done. I'M done.

How could he DO this to me?" complained Phoebe in group. She wore her stretched-out red leggings, baggy at the knees and frayed along the bottom edges, and an old white T-shirt that was misshapen and gray from too many washings. Her hair looked unwashed, and her eyes were red and bleary.

"Exactly," said Samantha. "That's what I've been saying all along about Len."

"It's not something he intended to do TO YOU," suggested Gale. "It's his way of continuing to feel like a hero, something he's doing for himself. He needs to be the savior. You made a good observation, Phoebe, when you said he was rushing in to save Gabby the way he wished he could have saved his mom."

"I thought he was loyal!" said Phoebe. "The GOOD cowboy!"

"He IS loyal," said Billy. "Loyal to Gabby, the needier one."

"He was my best friend," said Phoebe.

"He was everything to you," observed Scott. "That was part of the problem."

"There was a problem?" said Phoebe, looking around at everyone.

Billy and Faye exchanged looks and rolled their eyes, and Scott threw his head back dramatically to look at the ceiling.

Phoebe's laughter burst out of her while her tears continued.

"Really!" she said, as she took a tissue Hannah offered. "I didn't see it."

"Didn't you notice you got the first B in your entire school career?" said Billy, who, because he had a crush on Phoebe, was not displeased with how things had developed between her and Daryl.

"Didn't you see how you've been using buttered (cough) rolls as a form a Prozac?" asked Faye.

"Didn't you notice it was taking you almost a week to return phone calls?" observed Samantha.

"DIDN'T YOU NOTICE YOU WERE THINKING OF THROWING UP?" said Hannah.

"That bad?" said Phoebe.

"DUH!" said Hannah and Scott and Faye.

* * *

Gale handed Hannah a new box of tissues. Hannah, exhausted from having made two wedding cakes in one week in addition to keeping the bakery going since Devie had moved to Vermont, had used a whole box of tissues to absorb her tears.

Gale noticed that in spite of her youth, Hannah looked almost as faded as her worn jeans. Her face looked drawn above the high neck of her rust-colored sweater. Hannah looked thinner, and she had purged twice that month.

Hannah blew her nose, now red with irritation, and pushed her hair away from her face. She sighed deeply. She missed her mother. She missed Pauline. She missed Devie, even though she did not miss the zingers. She missed having her father to herself. She missed being four years old and feeling what it was like to run, to feel so strong and fast and happy, missed living comfortably in her little four-year-old body. She missed being so small she could curl herself up and be enfolded in her mother's arms.

She missed feeling as though she existed all over and not just in her head. The only way she could get herself to feel embodied now, she'd told Gale, was to stuff herself until her stomach hurt. Then, she'd notice she was in her body.

She missed everything that was no longer possible, and she missed everything that she'd never have.

"You must grieve your losses," said Gale. "Every day."

❋ ❋ ❋

Phoebe looked at the plump, golden sweet rolls in the pastry case at the Moonstone Café and smelled their sweet, yeasty fragrance. Eating several of these rolls would, she knew, insulate her, put what would feel like a wall of Styrofoam between her and her terror of Gabriella and her terror of what she knew about Daryl. Eating several of the rolls with butter would feel so soothing, make her eyelids feel heavy, make her body feel thick and solid and safe. Eating the rolls would help her forget what she felt and what she knew.

What she knew about Daryl was that he was loyal and steadfast and kind. What she knew about him also was that he was powerfully attracted to wounded animals. *Eating several of those rolls,* she thought, *will make me forget how like a wounded animal Gabby must sound to Daryl right now, and how Daryl will always go to where he thinks he's needed most.*

Phoebe decided she would need at least three of the rolls. She could get them "to go" so that the woman behind the counter with the turquoise eyeglass frames and the little white cap would not think Phoebe was going to eat all of the large rolls herself.

If she ate the rolls, she would have to deal with the possibility that she would not be able to fit into her jeans in the morning. Then again, she was used to that. It was not a big deal to not be able to fit into jeans. She'd been not fitting into jeans for most of her life. On second thought, she'd order five of the sweet rolls.

Daryl had not called her yet to let her know what had happened, whether he had decided to talk with Gabby, and, if he HAD decided to talk to her, if they had already talked, and if they HAD already talked, whether they had done so in person or on the phone, and if they had talked in person OR on the phone, what they'd said.

Phoebe had used every iota of strength in every rational cell of her body to resist calling Daryl to say, "Have you decided yet?" She knew she had to resist doing that because if she did it, she would be guilty of the same invasive, controlling tactics which had gotten Gabby fired from the relationship in the first place. She could see why Gabby had been unable to resist calling and checking up on Daryl every ten minutes.

Phoebe noticed an old woman in the café, looking into the pastry case closer to the back of the shop. She was emaciated, frail and stooped, and her skin was papery thin and white. Her hands shook as she indicated to the clerk which cheesecake she wanted. Phoebe felt suddenly guilty to be making such a big deal about her boyfriend problems. At least she HAD a boyfriend; at least she was young and healthy.

"Are you ready to order?" said the woman behind the counter.

* * *

Phoebe ate two of the rolls as she drove back to her house. She finished the fourth one sitting on her bed. Now, as she licked sweet, sticky crumbs off her fingers, she felt as though she'd swallowed poison. She did NOT feel as though there was a wall of Styrofoam between herself and her terror. She did NOT feel distracted by guilt or by the bloated feeling in the middle of her body.

It crossed her mind to throw up. Why couldn't she get her digestive tract to reverse its peristaltic direction? She'd actually tried this before, but it hadn't worked after she'd finished the leftover apple pie at a shoot at the studio (her father had already gone for the day), taking just one more bite at a time until there was no pie left at all.

Now there was one roll left. The idea of eating it made her queasy. She did not throw it away, however. She left it where it was, on her bedside table wrapped in butter-spotted tissue paper and stuffed into the small white waxed paper bag with Moonstone Café printed hundreds of times in tiny letters all over it among yellow stars and blue crescent moons.

She surveyed her options. She could eat the roll. She could eat other stuff. There was chocolate-fudge brownie ice cream, and there was blueberry pie, and there was crunchy granola and rice pudding. Wouldn't all those things be delicious together? She could sprinkle the crunchy granola all over the ice cream and rice pudding and put those things on top of the blueberry pie.

She could make a call to Billy or Hannah or Samantha or someone else from group. She could call Pearly. She could go down to the basement and climb stairs to nowhere on the StairMaster. She estimated that it would take over seven hours to burn off the calories it had taken her less than fifteen minutes to take in. She could go shopping. She could go online and chat with a kindred soul. She could write in her journal.

She could call Daryl. He was probably back in his dorm by now after his late-afternoon lab.

* * *

As Hannah finished her day at the bakery, she reflected that one of the things she liked about working there was the orderliness of her time there, the logical sequence of tasks that was dependable and unvarying. There was no decision making; one action had to follow another in a reliable pattern. While the bread dough was rising, she cleaned the bowls and mixers and started the batters for the cakes, muffins and cookies. While the bread was baking, she'd put the batters into the designated pans; and while the cakes and muffins were baking, she would clean the bowls and mixers again. She felt securely held in this world, safe in her duties, which, once started, carried her along.

The only decision she had to make that afternoon had been which messages to place into her fortune cookies. Her favorite one that day, which she'd found earlier in the week, was:

**To those who have fought for it, freedom
has a flavor that the protected will never know.**

Some days, she liked to listen to the fragrant silence of bread baking; some days she listened to her own thoughts, which primarily revolved around Devie. Today, she was thinking of her dad and his fast-approaching wedding, and she decided to listen to music. She popped her Fat Barbees CD into the machine and heard Rosetta Stone singing:

Let's put the funk back in dysfunctional! Let's put the funk back in dysfunctional!
Scapegoat's smokin' too much dope,
It's just her way of having hope.
She's the one that tells the truth
Then goes and eats a Baby Ruth.
Let's put the funk back in dysfunctional! Let's put the funk back in dysfunctional!
While Dad is drunk and Mom is crying
The family clown just won't stop trying.
She's the one that tells the jokes
Trying to cheer up the folks.
Let's put the funk back! Let's put the funk back! Let's put the funk back in dysfunctional!
The hero has to get an A
Because she has to save the day.
But being good just drives her wild
Because she's never been a child.
So let's put the funk back! Let's put the funk back! Let's put the funk back in dysfunctional!

A child who's lost is hard to know
You've got to take it really slow.
She hides away to save her soul
She will not rock she will not roll,
SO LET'S PUT THE FUNK BACK IN
    DYSFUNCTIONAL!

Hannah left through the bakery's front door and walked toward the bus stop through a driving wind. It had begun to snow. It was only a few weeks until Christmas, when she'd be able to afford a down payment on a car.

*　＊　＊　＊*

"Well—is she SUICIDAL?" Phoebe demanded, when Daryl told her how distraught Gabby had been when they'd met at his school cafeteria for lunch after she'd driven all the way up to his school to see him.

"She didn't say that word. But she's tried suicide before— once. Before I knew her."

You're getting back together with a suicidal person? Phoebe said to herself.

"She's lost so much weight," Daryl continued, "that I almost didn't recognize her."

SHE'S LOST SO MUCH WEIGHT?!?!?! Phoebe thought, horrified.

Phoebe felt so furious and afraid that she couldn't feel anything. She felt as though she was watching herself on TV or a movie screen. She watched herself and thought, this character is so stricken she's numb. She will feel the fear and outrage and hurt and loss of trust in Daryl later in the movie. She will surround herself now with as many of Hannah's lemon poppy-seed cakes and pound cakes and marble cakes and chocolate fudge brownies as she can get her hands on, and she'll eat all of them. Then, probably, she will subside into a comatose state while sad music plays over the image of her tangled in her sheets, drooling onto her pillow as dawn brightens her miserable room to once again awaken her to her fat, miserable life.

"So, what have you decided to do then?" demanded Phoebe.

"Phoeb—she's SO MISERABLE!" said Daryl by way of explanation of what he had decided to do.

"So does that mean it's up to you to make her better?" said Phoebe in a tone she hated.

"She needs me right now. She's going through hell with her mom's cancer and—"

"You're reliving your mom's illness through her, you know you are," interrupted Phoebe. "You feel if you can somehow save Gabby, intervene in her misery, it will make up for not being able to have saved your mom."

"Do you have to psychologize everything?" said Daryl curtly.

* * *

I hate school," said Samantha as she and Lacey walked through the snow from Samantha's car to the side door of Lacey's house. "I just hate being in school. I have no idea what I'm doing there."

"What will you do?" asked Lacey, pushing open the door and stomping the snow off her boots in the little foyer off the kitchen.

"I don't know. I just want to be married, that's all," said Samantha, unwinding her long green muffler from around her neck and shaking snow out of her hair.

"But what will you DO married?" persisted Lacey.

"I don't know," Samantha answered. "Vacuum?"

Lacey laughed. "Does Len want to get married?" she asked as the girls climbed the stairs to Lacey's bedroom. She loved the tropics and had a huge fake palm tree in one corner and a scene of a beach painted on one wall at the edge of the sand-colored carpet. The other walls were teal blue and hot pink and the bedspread was printed with palm fronds and parrots. She had three tattoos: a Hawaiian lei around her left ankle, a palm tree on her right shoulder and a starfish over her heart.

"Len? Married?" said Samantha. "I don't know. We used to talk about it. But we were in high school then. Anyway, I can't be with Len anymore. I mean, I want him to love me so badly that I stopped noticing how tense it is to be with someone you keep thinking doesn't love you."

"Wow!" said Lacey. "I've never heard you sound so sane. Your therapy's really working!" she said with admiration.

"I know," said Samantha. "Now if I could only eat."

Lacey looked at her as though she didn't know who she was. "Really?" said Lacey, awed.

"NO!" said Samantha. "Cancel! Delete! I'm not ready for THAT yet. No way!"

Lacey put on The Fat Barbees CD that Samantha had given her for her birthday.

Rosetta Stone sang, with the familiar musical mix of reggae and rap with Latin rhythms:

> *Daddy Oh, Daddy No*
> *I don't want you to leave me.*
> *Daddy Oh, Daddy No*
> *I don't want you to grieve me.*

Don't want you to flirt me
Don't want you to hurt me
Just want you to give me what I need.
Don't need your desertin'
I'm absolutely certain,
I just want your respect in word and deed.
Daddy Oh, Daddy No
Your money isn't how to show you care.
Daddy, why? Daddy I
Really truly am someone quite rare.
Have you ever seen me—Seen the precious queen me?
Daddy Oh, Daddy No
I need for you to hold me like a daddy.

"How's your dad doing?" asked Lacey, whose own father had left the family when Lacey was almost three and had never been seen since.

"I haven't seen him," Samantha replied. "I can't right now."

Then she felt stupid to not be seeing her dad when Lacey didn't even have a dad she could choose not to see. Samantha suddenly felt how luxurious it was to have a dad to be mad at. It confused her.

Lo?" answered Daryl sleepily when the phone woke him at 3:00 A.M.

"Oh no! I woke you!" said Phoebe.

"Yeah," said Daryl groggily.

She couldn't analyze his mood. Was he annoyed to have been awakened? Was he glad to hear from her? They had talked at three o'clock in the morning plenty of times. Phoebe ached to know whether Daryl and Gabby were spending the night together.

"What's up?" asked Daryl.

"I just miss you," Phoebe said.

"Yes," said Daryl, as though Phoebe had asked a question.

"Yes," said Phoebe, senselessly.

"Can I call you tomorrow?" Daryl asked.

"Sure," answered Phoebe, applying to the word a tone of cheer she did not feel.

Phoebe crept quietly out of the house and risked starting her Land Cruiser, hoping her parents wouldn't wake up. She drove the car to Port Franklin playing The Fat Barbees CD, the track entitled, "Lovesong, Not" at high volume.

> *I cannot canNOT go on*
> *Since since since since you've been gone.*
> *Why do I keep doing this?*
> *Can't I see how nuts it is?*

You do not do NOT see me,
I'm just the sugar in your tea,
For I dissolve right into you,
Dissolve! Dissolve! It's all too true!
This is this is this is NOT love
Not with so much friction.
This is a bond of another kind
THIS IS AN ADDICTION!
Addict! Addict! Addict! Me!
I am just despairing
That I will ever EVER find
A really healthy pairing.
Do not do not do NOT call me
You're not you're not my lover!
For I am done with such as you
And I'm starting starting over.

❋ ❋ ❋

"Billy?" said Phoebe shyly the following evening. "Is that you?"

She had not called Daryl the next day, and he had not called her.

"The one and the only," answered Billy, cheerfully. "Do I detect a tone of distress in your fair damsel voice?"

"Yes," said Phoebe, sniffing away her tears. She was sitting cross-legged on her bed speaking into the mouthpiece of the new headset she'd gotten for her phone.

It was 7:00 P.M. Her mother had gone to visit her parents, both of whom had been diagnosed with Parkinson's disease. Phoebe felt so sad when she pictured her grandparents shaking the last time she'd seen them, which had been at her high school graduation five months before. Her father was downstairs where he had shifted from being hypnotized by *MacNeil-Lehrer* to being hypnotized by commercials. He was placed into an altered state by TV.

"What can I do for you, lovely maiden?" asked Billy, in his courtly way.

"Well—I—need something," said Phoebe.

"Good," replied Billy. "Welcome to the human race."

Gale had encouraged the members of the group to be aware of needing. Then they could figure out what it was they needed. For the time being, Phoebe knew she needed something. She didn't know how to put into words what it was she needed. The need felt like emptiness, a hollow ache that buttered rolls had until now filled very nicely—that is, until she'd wake up the next morning and discover that the hollow ache had been replaced (courtesy of the buttered rolls) by a hard, solid lump which was even more uncomfortable than the emptiness.

"I don't know what it is that I need though," Phoebe reflected. "Except to have Daryl back."

"And what would having Daryl back give you?" asked Billy. He had learned this questioning procedure from Gale. She would keep asking, "And what would THAT give you?" until the person figured out, by systematically answering that same question over and over, what it would feel like to be whole, to be okay.

"My—self-respect," Phoebe replied, after a hesitation. "My best buddy. My hugging partner, my—"

"WHOA," said Billy. "Do you need HIM, specifically, to have self-respect?"

"Well, I guess not," answered Phoebe.

"Do you need Daryl specifically to have self-respect, a best buddy, a hugging partner?"

"Well, I guess someone else COULD be those things," Phoebe conceded.

"So why does it have to be him specifically?"

"Because I'm so—attracted to him," confessed Phoebe. "That high-voltage thing about him."

"So, is Daryl the only one with that high-voltage thing?" asked Billy.

"I don't know," admitted Phoebe. "I've never been that close to another guy. You know that."

"Would you like to be?" asked Billy. He kept his voice strong, neutral, and consistent with the rest of their conversation so far, but he knew a tone of hopefulness had crept in.

Phoebe pictured Billy holding his phone to his round pink ear. She pictured his round belly, his kind blue eyes, his long brown hair that he wore in a pony tail, his pudgy, short-fingered, unDarylesque hands, his good-natured voice, and wanted at that moment to say yes, she would like to be that close to someone else—to Billy, in fact—but she just couldn't say it. It wasn't anything about how Billy looked or sounded. It was just that he wasn't Daryl. But she wanted a friend—a guy friend.

"Could you come over to keep me company?" asked Phoebe.

"At your service, fair lady," Billy replied.

* * *

Hannah made an altar to commemorate everything she had lost and everything she would never have. Every object placed on her altar was symbolic. She bought a small table at the Salvation Army Thrift Shop and a green tablecloth with gold threads woven through it and placed the table under the window in her room.

She placed her Madonna-and-child figurines on the table to signify her lost mother. She placed a bottle of her mother's favorite shade of bright red nail polish among the figurines, along with her mother's wedding ring. Her mother had smoked, and Hannah placed a pack of Marlboro Lights on the altar, and a page out of *TV Guide*, with the listings from 3:00 to 5:00 P.M., the hours she'd usually spend with her mother on the cream-colored satin bedspread. Among the Madonnas, she placed some delicate pink shells and a piece of coral from their walk on a west Florida beach when she was eight.

To signify her loss of Pauline, she placed on the altar a brochure from the Morgan Library describing the exhibition of Freud's original manuscripts.

Hannah still had the little purple plush teddy bear her father had won for her at a carnival when she was ten. This she placed on the altar to commemorate the loss of her centrality in his life.

A photo of Devie in Vermont with her sons reminded Hannah that she was hundreds of miles away.

Hannah placed a wedding-cake bride and groom on her

altar to remind her that while her father would marry, she would not, not in the conventional sense. She placed a small plastic baby doll on the altar, too. She did not know if she wanted to have a child who would grow up to die, and spend much of its secret life fearing death.

She placed on the altar a photo of herself at four, running, her legs a blur of motion.

After Phoebe had been sitting on her bed crying, this time in Billy's arms, for an hour and ten minutes (they had been listening to The Fat Barbees sing "I'm Allergic to Home" over and over again, and then to Phoebe's Nefarious Potato CD), Phoebe dried her eyes and felt no better.

She wanted to DO something. She felt as though she needed to stretch, but not her body. She needed to stretch some other part of herself.

"I need something," said Phoebe with an authority she barely recognized.

"Tell all!" said Billy, sitting propped against pillows on Phoebe's bed with a stuffed green plush alligator in his lap.

"I need you first of all to get rid of little Allie here," Phoebe said, feeling suddenly giddy now that she had decided to seduce Billy. That was the word that had sprung into her mind to describe what she was going to do— seduce. The word had glamour and slinky white satin nightgowns and movie stars from the 1940s embedded in it, Phoebe thought.

Billy threw the soft stuffed alligator onto the carpeted floor with a sweeping gesture.

"Done!" he said gallantly.

"Now—make love to me," commanded Phoebe imperiously. *Was this how Queen Elizabeth spoke to Prince Philip in their royal bedroom?* wondered Phoebe when she heard herself.

"Seriously?" Billy said, wide-eyed, pulling himself upright, away from the soft nest of the pillows behind him.

"Now," ordered Phoebe, amazing herself.

"Now?" Billy repeated.

"Are you a parrot, or are you a friend?" demanded Phoebe, surprised at how aroused she felt by her new, take-charge attitude.

Billy, uncharacteristically at a loss for words, began to unbutton his shirt. Phoebe pulled down the blinds in her room and locked the door. She loved this new feeling of power she had discovered, the feeling of how much Billy wanted her. She trusted him because he wanted her more than she wanted him. She witnessed herself having these

thoughts in the few seconds it had taken to walk the four
steps to the door of her room, turn the lock and walk back.

* * *

Scott popped his Suicidal Clones CD into his player and
collapsed on his bed. His work today, teaching people
how to use computers, had been particularly exhausting
because he was trying not to think of Samantha while he
pointed and clicked and sat patiently beside people who
were afraid they were going to do something wrong and
break the equipment.

He realized that this was the way he lived his life—afraid
to take a step because he was certain he was going to do it
wrong and break something that could never ever be fixed.
That was the way he was handling his relationship with
Samantha: he was taking no steps at all to let her know how
he felt about her. He felt he could never get it right, whatever "it" was. He felt completely different from other people,
"normal" people who had girlfriends and took chances.

He selected the third track on the CD and listened to
Suicidal Clones' lead singer, Claudia Claudia:

Two eyes, a nose and the usual lips
And two overdeveloped hips,
One heart beating its sad sad song
Why do I feel I don't belong?
I'm not like other people.
I don't belong with them.
I can't be normal like everyone else.
I don't fit in.
Don't trust me, don't trust me
I'm not from this place.
I can't even trust myself 'cause I'm from outer space.
I look normal but I'm in disguise
There's an alien behind my eyes.
Who could love such a crazy freak?
If you x-rayed me, you'd just say "eeeeeek!"
Don't trust me, don't trust me
I can't trust myself.
I can't trust myself
I CAN'T TRUST MYSELF.
I'm not like you.

❊ ❊ ❊

Gale had on dark green leather boots with flat heels.
They were not new, Samantha could see that by the

scuffs around the toes where the green color looked fainter. It occurred to Samantha that she spent a lot of time looking at Gale's shoes and legs. It also occurred to her that here she was in a therapy session, and she was thinking about footwear. At least she was IN a therapy session. And she was here willingly, that was a miracle. It was true that her mother had originally leveraged her into therapy by letting Samantha know that if she chose not to get some therapy during her senior year of high school, she would have to be hospitalized. Samantha had come to see Gale, but had refused to talk for several sessions.

"What's going on, Samantha?" Gale asked. "You're off somewhere. Far away, it looks like."

"I'm thinking about last year when my mom made me come here. And about your boots."

"What else?"

Gale waited.

Samantha did not want to talk about what else. She assumed that was why she had been interested in the boots. She felt awful. It seemed to her that she did not have a single joint or muscle that did not ache. Even her ankles hurt, and her back felt as though it had been broken. Sitting was uncomfortable. Even when she leaned against the padded back of the big upholstered armchair, each vertebra of her spine felt exposed, irritated and raw. Her throat felt sore, too, and her eyes burned. But her stomach felt flat and empty. That was the prize, the compensation for all the rest of what she had endured.

Samantha stayed quiet. She'd reached some threshold, she realized, and had regressed to using silence as a way to feel safe from change. She had lots of awarenesses now that she did admit to finding interesting. But that was all they were—interesting. Identifying her coping strategies had not, thus far, resulted in change. She had become expert at analyzing her own psychology. She realized she was not completely sane. Sometimes, she even glimpsed the delusional nature of her condition—that she felt so fat, and even LOOKED fat to herself sometimes.

Emptiness was what she longed for yet also complained about. She struggled to achieve a feeling of emptiness by starving herself. Then she suffered because she felt so empty.

"I'm going to have to eat something besides lettuce and apples," Samantha said finally.

Gale said nothing.

"Eventually," said Samantha, staring ahead of her with unfocused eyes.

"Samantha," said Gale. "Look at me."

Samantha blinked and focused her gaze on Gale's boots.

"Make eye contact with me."

Samantha looked at Gale's face, into her kind eyes that were full of concern.

"Say what you just said about eating."

"I am going to have to eat something besides lettuce and apples. Eventually," Samantha repeated.

"You said that like an automaton, like a recorded announcement," Gale observed. "Say it like you mean it."

"I'm going to have to eat something besides lettuce and apples, eventually."

"I don't know if I believe in what you said yet," reflected Gale. "Do you believe yourself?"

"I don't know," said Samantha.

"When IS eventually?" Gale asked.

"I don't know," said Samantha. "I'll tell you this, though."

"What?"

"I'm terrified."

* * *

So, where's Daryl's call tonight?" asked Michael McIntyre. He had become accustomed to the phone ringing each night at six while he watched *The MacNeil-Lehrer Report* until dinnertime.

"Uh—we broke up," Phoebe replied. *This is going to be trouble,* she thought.

"Your weight?" asked her father predictably.

"No. Her suicidalness," said Phoebe flatly, too tired of her dad's harping on her weight to explain any further.

"Gabriella?" asked her dad as he flipped channels. He always said how much he liked the news on public television, but he loved watching commercials because sometimes they were commercials he'd shot. He liked watching other people's commercials, too, because he could see how other photographers shot them.

"Yeah," said Phoebe glumly. She sat across the room from her father giving herself a pedicure. She wished she'd stayed in her room. It was too late now to move to her room without smearing the polish. She was confused about why she'd chosen to sit downstairs with her father. She supposed the group was right about the need to stick with something until you got what you needed from it, even though the idea of getting approval from her father was becoming ludicrous.

She had decided to give herself a pedicure as a way to engage her hands (and feet!) so that she would not be able to use buttered rolls, or large chunks of cold leftover meat loaf, or pints of pistachio ice cream as anesthetics. She would not have been able to eat her way through the evening, anyway, with her father at home. But she was practicing what the group called "better coping strategies" for dealing with the overwhelming anxiety she felt now.

"Gabriella's a beautiful name," said her father. He ALWAYS said that when he heard Gabriella's name, thought Phoebe furiously.

Phoebe, suddenly enraged, said, "Why don't you give me a break!"

"Take it easy, sweetheart!" said her father.

"NO! YOU take it easy. Be easy on ME for a change! I'm in pain here, and you're like a beauty-pageant judge, and you treat me more like a disqualified contestant than a daughter, YOUR daughter!"

Michael McIntyre stopped changing channels.

"And could you PUT DOWN THE REMOTE CONTROL WHILE I'M TALKING TO YOU!" shouted Phoebe. "I feel like you're trying to control ME with that thing, and not remotely enough, either!"

Michael McIntyre put down the remote control device. He opened his arms to her.

"I'm sorry, sweetheart."

Phoebe's father held her through fifteen entire minutes of the news (suicide bombings in Jerusalem, air attacks on Iraq, AIDS epidemic in China, global warming threat, human cloning imminent, baby in Dumpster) without changing the channel even once, but he didn't turn off the TV.

* * *

Dear Journal:

Group was sad tonight. Or rather, I felt sad in group. Hannah is so afraid of everything, and Gale said every-thing she's afraid of is really her fear of dying like her mom did. Hannah said she's afraid of getting a cold because the cold might kill her, and she's afraid of enjoy-ing things because they will eventually be taken away, so, when she's enjoying something like shopping or taking a bath, she gets panicky because she knows it will be taken away when she dies, so she doesn't enjoy enjoying things. I feel sorry for her. I feel lucky to have parents who are both alive. One of them is pretty crazy, but at least is alive; though, sometimes, I want to kill him.

At least I want to kill him and not myself. Gale says that is healthier, at least.

Coed Kills Father Instead of Self. Shrink Congratulates!!!!!

Differences between Hannah and me: Hannah is obsessed with death and disease; I am obsessed with Daryl.

Hannah is afraid of germs, dirty shoelaces, fat grams, fatness; I don't have the sense to be afraid of those things.

I don't know how Hannah gets through the day. She is always thinking she is about to die. She told us in group tonight that she notices how beautiful everything is at times like that, when she's sure she's about to die. She notices the color of the sky and how the bubbles in the bathtub feel on her skin.

Scott is definitely interested in Samantha. It's so obvious to everyone but Samantha. She is all messed up over this Len thing. I know how she feels. Maybe Len shouldn't have been so honest. It's not the best policy, not always, because look how hurt she is. Still, I can understand why he would want to tell her stuff about himself. How do people maintain their sanity in relationships without feeling shredded? I don't know if they do. Look how many times Liz Taylor got married and divorced. Samantha's parents are divorced. I don't know how my mom can stand my dad. Maybe she's on Prozac.

* * *

Phoebe and Billy spent many nights locked in Phoebe's bedroom. Billy's tenderness and funny, courtly way of speaking to Phoebe helped her to forget that 6:00 P.M. had come and gone without a call from Daryl for almost a week. Daryl had been right, Phoebe reflected, about how having a romance might one day spoil their friendship. He was probably feeling so guilty about getting back together with Gabby that he didn't even call anymore.

Once, when Billy was late coming to Phoebe's house, she noticed the longing for Billy she felt. It was his admiration, his complete devotion to her, that she loved.

Billy wrote e-love letters to Phoebe:

"You are my Phoebe of the night, my moonlight-bright angel who takes my heart and flies away to the stars."

Billy had spent seven consecutive nights locked with Phoebe in her room. (Miraculously, Phoebe's father had not commented on this nightly routine. Phoebe realized it was because he automatically did not see fat people. Billy was invisible to him. He must have assumed, Phoebe thought, that she and Billy were studying or listening to music together.) Then, Daryl called.

Billy and Phoebe had just locked the door and were removing their clothes. Phoebe discovered, to her own surprise, that she didn't mind undressing with Billy in a lit room. This was partially because she had been reading *Mode* magazine so she didn't feel as out of place in the world after looking at the pictures of the normal-sized women in there, and because Billy was more overweight than she was, and because he seemed so crazy about her, and because she loved the feeling of power that came with watching Billy watch her.

When Billy had removed all his clothes (the khaki Dockers, the gray crew neck sweater, the white T-shirt that said "Neptune" in red across the front) except for his left sock, and Phoebe was unhooking her chartreuse bra, the phone rang. Phoebe and Billy heard Daryl's voice say, "Phoeb—it's me. Please call me as soon as you can. I'm sorry."

Phoebe felt a curious lack of feeling upon hearing these words, that voice. Billy froze, his hand gripping his white athletic sock. Phoebe rehooked her bra and sat down beside him on the bed.

"Are you going to call him?" asked Billy, sounding tense.

"It seems cruel not to," Phoebe replied.

***

From: *NewzakfromLen@aol.com*
Date: Wed 22 Nov 2000 10:28:16 EST
Subj: Doc?
To: *Slamantha@optonline.net*

Sam—How did your doctor appointment turn out? I miss u. Len

From: *Slamantha@optonline.net*
Time: Wed 22 Nov 2000 11:39:56 EST
Subj: Doc?
To: *NewzakfromLen@aol.com*

I had to have a bone scan to test my bone density. I am REALLY scared because they said I have osteoporosis. Maybe that's why my back hurts so much all the time. I didn't get my period again this month. I miss u 2. Sam

***

envy everybody!" said Scott. "I feel like it's shameful to be so envious, like it's—not manly. I feel like I just want to be anyone but myself. I see guys driving Porsches and guys with bigger muscles and guys who are taller and who don't think about their bodies, and I want to be any one of them."

"How do you know what other guys are thinking?" asked Phoebe as she sat with Scott, Sam, Lacey and Hannah at the Moonstone Café.

"I don't know," said Scott. "I just assume."

"Don't make assumptions," said Lacey. "It will make you unhappy to make assumptions. It will make you just miserable. I read a book about that. You can see what cars other people drive, but you can't know what they're thinking or feeling."

"I just want to be anyone but myself," said Scott.

"COMPUTER GENIUS IN FLIGHT FROM HIMSELF!" said Phoebe.

"I AM in flight from myself," said Scott earnestly. "And the flights leave every ten minutes!"

"I identify so much with you," said Hannah. "I figured out that I'd rather be other people. When I look at other women, there are very few of them I'd rather not be. I'd trade my hair for their breasts, or my eyes for their legs. I find myself getting completely into looking at body parts and comparing them to mine and always thinking everybody else's are better and just WISHING I could have what they have, be who they are."

"I envy Phoebe," said Samantha, surprising everybody.

"YOU? ENVY ME?"

"I do," repeated Samantha, "because you can eat pizza and be normal. And you can LAUGH while you're eating pizza! When I even THINK about eating pizza I feel so starved and terrified at the same time that it's impossible to even IMAGINE myself doing that."

"Why do you want to be able to eat pizza so badly?" asked Phoebe, to whom eating pizza came as naturally as breathing.

"Because eating pizza is NORMAL!" said Samantha. "I want to be normal."

She listened to what she'd said. Then she added, "Well— a PART of me wants to be normal. But another part of me is TERRIFIED to be normal, hates the idea, thinks it's disgusting to be normal."

She sighed. "No. I don't want to be normal at all. See how crazy I am?"

Samantha answered the phone after it had barely rung. Only the hint of a ring, the merest vibration of the device alerted her that the phone was ringing.

"You haven't gotten your period in over a year and a half!" said Len. "Not since I've known you. Not since even before that. Should we be worried that you haven't gotten your period recently, in the past couple of months?" he wanted to know.

"I guess not," said Samantha, who, though she hadn't gotten her period in so long, had begun to worry that she was pregnant. After all, when she hadn't been getting her period before, she hadn't been having sex with anyone.

"So what about the osteoporosis?" asked Len.

Samantha could hardly hear him. He was calling her from his cell phone and there was an intermittent crackling noise, as though the phone was on fire, and Samantha's sister, Patti, was in her bedroom with some friends and they were playing music, Patti's latest favorite band, The Redheaded Deviants. Samantha took her phone into her bathroom.

"Gale said she was afraid of this exact thing happening with my bones, because I don't have enough body fat to create enough estrogen to help my bones suck in the calcium from what I'm eating."

"From what you're not eating," said Len.

"I know, I know. I'm scared," admitted Samantha.

"So what are you going to do?"

"I'm going to eat more."

"Great!" said Len. "Can you?"

"I don't know," Samantha said, looking at herself in the full-length mirror on the back of the bathroom door and liking what she saw there: a petite blonde with a tiny waist and a perfectly flat abdomen. Of course, she would always like to lose five more pounds as insurance against possible weight gain from breathing, from just taking in air.

"I'm mad at myself. But it's too late now, because I can't get the bone back even if I CAN get myself to eat."

"There MUST be some medicine that can help you get the bone back, Sam."

"I don't know! I don't know! I don't know if I even WANT there to be a medicine that could help me get the bone back, because then I'd have to eat. Don't you think I'm completely insane? I feel completely insane right now."

"I do think you're crazy, but for some reason, it doesn't make me love you any less," Len said.

"Are you still drawing her?" Samantha asked timidly.

"I sent her the drawings, anonymously, through a friend of a friend," said Len. "It's over, whatever 'it' was."

Samantha didn't know if she felt better or worse.

* * *

When Phoebe and Daryl recoupled, it took all Billy's will to get himself to speak to her. Confronting Phoebe, just being in her presence, just THINKING of being in her presence, made him short of breath.

Billy knew Daryl had told Gabby, again, that it was time to move on. Phoebe patiently explained everything to Billy after Daryl had called, as she and Billy sat locked in her room for the last time.

"So, I'm like a toy you got tired of playing with," Billy said sadly.

Phoebe had no reply. She was so ashamed, knowing Billy was right.

"Oh Billy!" Phoebe cried. "How can I make it up to you? What can I do to take away the hurt?"

"You can tell Daryl to take a walk," said Billy, flatly.

"What ELSE can I do?" asked Phoebe. She just wanted to be near Daryl. Just looking at him, memorizing the freckles on his shoulders, felt like food to her.

At the first group meeting after Billy and Phoebe had stopped seeing each other, Billy arrived late. Phoebe felt uneasy as she looked at the clock every minute and a half waiting for him to come. The group members seemed equally uneasy, silently commiserating with Phoebe's discomfort and imagining Billy's. Gale looked at her watch, quickly deliberated, and decided not to make assumptions about Billy's late arrival. She could see how unsettled Phoebe was, the strain on her face. She was wearing jeans and clogs and her sage green turtleneck from J. Crew, the one she'd bought at the outlet store when she and Billy had been together every night.

When Billy arrived and saw her in the sweater, he felt queasy, loss and anger joining in his belly as though the sweater was a flag symbolizing the loss of everything Phoebe and he had shared, and she was waving it in his face. As soon as he saw her in the sweater, he thought he might have to skip group that night and try it again the following week. Then he thought he might ask Gale if she was leading another group he could be in.

Phoebe was sitting next to Samantha, who, when Billy came in, had been talking about how hungry she was all the time but could not get herself to eat, and Gale had suggested that Samantha ask someone to help her eat by sitting with her to get her through it. As Samantha had finished speaking, Phoebe turned away from her and smiled at Billy.

Looking at Phoebe, her heavy, curly hair falling onto her shoulders, her smooth, rose-petal skin, and her small white hands that had touched him so tantalizingly that he could not hate himself at those times, Billy was reminded that she had taken herself away, reminded him of everything about himself he loathed, of how he worked too hard to be accepted, devised a funny way of expressing himself, and offered favors and gifts to become a memorable, indispensable person to make up for all the "guy" things he wasn't: lean, muscular, athletic, tall.

It's no shock she chose Daryl, thought Billy. *I'd pick Daryl, too, if I were her.*

Billy's own hatred of himself expanded so suddenly that he felt as though he had been hit in the solar plexus, and he had to close his eyes tightly to keep from crying out.

"What's going on, Billy?" asked Gale, with concern. "Is something wrong?" *Naturally something is wrong,* she thought. But she wasn't going to speak for him.

Samantha had finished describing her confused feelings about Len and how lettuce and apples were still the only foods with which she felt safe, even though she could endure a quarter of a bagel with nothing on it.

"Yeah," said Billy, opening his eyes. "I'm having trouble breathing when I look at Phoebe."

Phoebe looked at her lap, horrified at the speed with which she had abandoned Billy. Though Phoebe's father had been encouraging her, all her life, to dislike herself based on the size and shape of her body, he had never completely succeeded in convincing her to do so. Instead, in defiance of her father, Phoebe had resolutely clung to her positive assessment of herself. She'd respected her many outstanding qualities: loyalty, kindness and sensitivity to the feelings of others were among the traits she was proud of possessing.

These admirable qualities, she thought, were now nowhere to be found since she had abandoned steadfast, sweet, smart, funny, adoring Billy, who had comforted her and accompanied her through her darkest hours.

Phoebe looked up from her lap, not at Billy specifically, but at the whole group, and said, "I am a horrible, disgusting person."

Billy was the first to speak. "You're not horrible and disgusting just because you hurt me," he said. "Maybe you hurt me because I'M horrible and disgusting."

"YOU'RE NOT horrible and disgusting!" Phoebe protested. "What did YOU do that was horrible and disgusting! All you did was comfort and be sweet to me. I'M horrible and disgusting because I pushed you away!"

"You're not horrible," said Billy sadly. "You just picked the better man."

❋ ❋ ❋

Gusts swirled around her as Hannah walked across the parking area toward the diner. She held the fake-fur collar of her gray coat close around her neck as she made her way across the large lot, wind tossing her hair across her face.

When she came into the bright restaurant, Samantha was already sitting in a booth, the huge menu closed on the table in front of her. The image of a frail baby bird flashed through Hannah's mind again: Samantha seemed so small and so afraid.

"I'm scared of menus," said Samantha. "Especially these HUGE menus. How pathetic is that—to be menuphobic?"

Hannah pushed her hair away from her face and flung off her coat, letting it bunch into the corner of the booth and sliding in after it.

"It's not pathetic. It's just that you're struggling with doing something new. Welcome to the human race!" Hannah, now a veteran of many changes, said encouragingly.

"What are you going to have?" asked Hannah. "Have you decided?"

"No. I can't even look at this big menu by myself. Would you look at the menu with me?"

"Sure," said Hannah, as the waitress, seeming to read their minds, handed Hannah another of the large menus, twelve oversized laminated pages edged with dark red plastic.

"I don't even know which SECTION to start in," said Samantha. "There are so many! Should I look at salads, or burgers, or 'diet platters' or 'from the grill' or should I look in 'breakfast all day' or 'eggs and things' or 'fisherman specials' or what? This is impossible. I can't DO this!"

"I know what you mean," said Hannah evenly, turning the plastic encased pages. "Well—you wanted to add protein to your lettuce, right?"

"I guess so. I guess that's what I SAID I wanted to do," said Samantha.

"So, just look at the protein foods," suggested Hannah. "Do you want something hot or cold?"

"Does one have more calories than another?" said Samantha, who was perfectly serious.

"You're acting blonde again!" Hannah teased.

"Well," said Samantha, looking at the menu again and sighing. "I could have a small piece of chicken. But they're going to bring me HALF a chicken, I just know it."

"You don't have to eat the whole thing," said Hannah patiently. "There is no such thing as the diner police."

"Yeah," said Samantha. "Good thing, huh?"

"Yeah," said Hannah. "Why don't you order the chicken, and I'll help you by having a bite or two."

"That's all right with you?" said Samantha gratefully.

"It's absolutely fine," said Hannah.

* * *

Hannah started worrying after twenty-five minutes, when Samantha had not even picked up her fork, hadn't touched the chicken or poked disdainfully at the blob of buttered mashed potatoes.

While Samantha was not eating, the girls talked about how afraid Samantha was to have the chicken inside her body, how she would imagine her stomach (really her abdomen, Hannah pointed out) rounding out, imagine solid substance forming all around her, encasing her in what would feel like an imprisoning cage. Samantha told Hannah she wanted to be lighter than air and just as invisible, she wanted to feel wispy, transparent as an angel, the wind, a breath.

After forty-five minutes of Samantha staring at the chicken (the beige gravy congealing all around it and the mashed potatoes forming a slightly hardened crust as they cooled), Hannah said, "You're going to have to take at least one bite."

Samantha looked at her pleadingly.

"You're going to have to take at least one bite," Hannah repeated. "Otherwise, we are not leaving here."

"Help me with this!" wailed Samantha. "You said you'd take a few bites."

"All right," said Hannah. "I will."

Hannah reached across the table and plunged her fork into the breast of the chicken. It was so dry that no juices squirted out where the prongs of her fork pressed into it. Reaching across the table, she maneuvered with her knife and fork to cut off a piece of the chicken and popped it into her mouth, chewing in an exaggerated way to demonstrate to Samantha that this COULD be done.

"I can't do this," said Samantha sadly. "I don't want to disappoint you. You came all the way here and . . ."

"Sam," said Hannah, in a tone that made Samantha afraid of what was coming next. "I am not leaving here unless you take one bite of that chicken."

"I don't think I can do it," said Samantha with conviction.

With equal resolve, Hannah said, "I watched my mother starve herself to death and didn't say ANYTHING. I'm not going to let the same thing happen to you. You have OSTEOPOROSIS! You aren't even TWENTY YEARS OLD, and you have the bones of an old woman! I'm not going to watch anything else horrible happen to you. I'm just not." She folded her arms across her chest to emphasize that her position was nonnegotiable.

The waitress appeared. She stood beside their table with her hands on her hips, her long, midnight blue nails with little gold moons painted on them forming a stark contrast with her white apron.

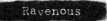

"Is everything all right?" said the waitress. A pin on the strap of her apron bore the name Michelle.

"Uh—yeah," said Samantha. "Fine."

"Can I get you anything to drink?"

"No. Thank you," Samantha said, wishing Michelle would go away so she could pursue her agonizing struggle with the roast chicken in silence.

When Michelle had moved away from the table, Samantha lifted her fork. She held it awkwardly, fearfully, as though it were too big, or alive. She pressed the edge of the fork against the chicken breast. The fork slipped and the chicken slid partially off the plate, pushing some of the mashed potatoes along with it.

Suddenly, Hannah had an image of a sulky four-year-old at the dinner table. She resisted saying, "Oh stop playing with your food, Sam! Eat like a grown-up!" She realized that in the presence of food, Samantha probably did feel like a four-year-old. Look at the way she was holding her fork! Hannah tried to remember the experience at the steakhouse when Sam had come along with her to meet Abbey, The Girlfriend, for the first time. Samantha seemed to use her fork normally then. Maybe that was because she'd had only salad and did not feel threatened, thought Hannah. Or maybe she's self-conscious because I'm staring at her.

"I'm feeling self-conscious because you're staring at me," said Samantha. She wiped gravy and mashed potatoes off the table with her napkin. Then she folded the wet, sticky gravy into the center of the napkin and wiped off the rest of the table.

"Why don't you clean off all the other tables while you're at it," said Hannah.

"I'm postponing," Samantha confessed.

"DUH!" said Hannah.

Samantha put the crumpled napkin near the little ceramic cup that held packets of sugar and artificial sweeteners, beside the salt-and-pepper shakers, out of sight. If she was going to eat a mouthful of chicken, she would need orderliness more than ever.

It was 3:35 on Monday morning, and Phoebe couldn't get to sleep. Daryl had driven away hours earlier, and Phoebe had been pretending to herself she was asleep. Watching her thoughts move through her mind, she noticed that all of them were about Billy, what he'd said about her having picked the better man.

She reflected now (at 3:46) about Daryl. He was certainly less attentive than Billy was. Whenever she and Billy had been together, Billy was so focused on her it was as though they were the last two people on earth, or at least on Long Island. Billy looked into her eyes so deeply and with such probing intensity, she felt undiscovered places in her penetrated, parts she'd kept hidden even from herself.

And the way he touched her told her she was precious. Though Billy was not beautiful himself, he showed her how to experience her own beauty. She seldom felt like eating large quantities of bread every ten minutes when she and Billy were together.

With Daryl, she was anxious most of the time, worried that she'd do or say something wrong, or look unattractive. Though Daryl seemed to enjoy watching her eat, she didn't enjoy eating when he was watching her. He would encourage her to have more food than she felt comfortable taking in while he was watching.

Maybe he wants me fat, thought Phoebe looking at the clock again (3:52 now). Maybe he needs the fatness so that he can feel he is with someone who reminds him of his mom. Maybe he wants me fat so that he feels secure that no one else will want me. That was what Faye had suggested in group.

Now, Phoebe began to imagine large quantities of bread. Bread of all kinds, fresh and fragrant, a whole catalog of breads filled the pages of her imagination: braided golden challah bread, eggy and sweet; bagels with generous smears of rich cream cheese; thickly buttered slices of whole-grain cinnamon toast, the kind with chewy pieces of sunflower seeds scattered throughout; dark wedges of date nut loaf.

Boy, I must REALLY be anxious and confused, thought Phoebe, looking at the red illuminated numbers on her digital alarm clock (4:10 now) as she witnessed the images of bread marching through her mind. *If I were a character in a movie right now*, she thought, *this would be where the song would play. I'd be at the waterfront in Port Franklin in a soft misty fog, and the seagulls would be swooping around in the pale white sky, and while the song played I would be walking by the pier in close-up so that you could see the worry and confusion in my face as I tried to choose between Daryl and Billy.*

* * *

S amantha ate six bites of roast chicken at the diner last night," Hannah announced at group.

Scott looked at Samantha with admiration. Billy, sitting beside him, looked at Scott expectantly, knowing Scott would be relieved that Samantha had kept her word to herself and to the group, that she had done the hard thing.

Billy had been spending more time at his job, working overtime and on weekends now when there was indoor construction to do. Construction work was limited during the winter; he could do more varied sorts of jobs when it warmed up. It pleased his boss that Billy was willing to work more, and it helped Billy's self-esteem, which had suffered such a blow since Phoebe had taken herself away.

They were still friends, sort of. There was so much hurt; it was painful for Billy to even think about Phoebe, and being in group together was still hard. Maybe it would be hard for a while and then let up. Maybe it would always be hard; maybe he'd have to find another group. This made him resentful because he'd started in this group before Phoebe had.

"I did," agreed Sam proudly. "They were small bites. But it was terrifying."

She had suffered for an hour after the sixth bite of chicken had been chewed and swallowed. Hannah had taken two bites for each one of Samantha's. Michelle, the waitress, watching from an appropriate distance, was mystified by how long it had taken for this meal to be eaten.

"How was it?" asked Faye.

"The chicken?" said Samantha.

"Everything," said Faye, to whom eating was also an exotic endeavor.

"Well—the chicken—it was like eating flannel pajamas, and I felt the whole time like the flannel was going to either choke me or make me blow up into an unrecognizable shapeless ooze, like every time I swallowed it was killing off more of me."

"So then what happened?" asked Faye, who had not eaten any form of animal, even milk, in over eight years.

"Then I told Hannah I couldn't eat any more."

"And I said she didn't have to, she did great," said Hannah, beaming with pride at what her friend had accomplished, and pleased with herself at having been of use.

"The waitress was kind of freaked-out, though," added Hannah. "She couldn't figure out WHAT was going on with us."

"Why did you eat six bites and not three or four or five?" Faye asked.

"Because Hannah spent two hours with me!" said Samantha. "I had to make it worth her time."

"Do you want to do that routine again?" asked Gale. "Have someone sit with you while you eat?"

"Never! Not ever again!" said Sam, laughing but meaning every word.

✳ ✳ ✳

Billy parked his blue Ford pickup in front of the deli and stepped out onto Oldtown Lane. His dog, a black Lab named Karma, jumped out of the truck to accompany him into the store where Billy went every day to get his lunch. He always used to order a veal-and-pepper hero there. Mrs. Millefiore made great heroes with extra olive oil drizzled onto the thick roll, and the store was always packed at lunchtime. The hero sandwiches were pretty bready, though, so Billy had been ordering turkey on rye. He figured the two slim slices of rye added up to less bread than the thick hero did.

He noticed a new person behind the counter today, a young woman of about his age with long, straight, brown hair she wore pulled back into a green scrunchy and a fringe of bangs. She was busy making sandwiches for the long line of people, many of them also in the building trades. But when she glanced up to see who was next and saw Billy, she smiled and her smile—maybe it was her teeth—reminded him of Phoebe's.

His feelings about Phoebe were confusing, as thinking about her made him hungrier and made him lose his appetite all at the same time. He would notice an emptiness inside but was repelled by the thought of filling it. The loss of appetite was a new experience for him; the emptiness was not.

"What can I get you?" asked the new counterwoman, smiling at him.

"I'll have a turkey sandwich on rye toast with lettuce, tomatoes and mayonnaise, please," he said, leaning down to pet Karma who was panting beside him.

"Anything to drink with that?" she asked. Her teeth were really white, like Phoebe's, and her lips, without lipstick, were beautifully shaped, also reminding him of Phoebe. She did not actually resemble Phoebe physically, aside from these few similarities. But, then, everything, and everyone, had been reminding him of Phoebe, lately. That was because he started the day thinking of Phoebe in the first place, he supposed. The lack of appetite intensified and so did the empty feeling in the center of him.

"Yeah," he said. "I'll have a decaf with that, with just milk. Where's Mrs. Millefiore today?"

"She's on vacation," said the girl as she busied herself making the sandwich. "You must come in here often."

She had her back to Billy now, cutting the turkey for his sandwich on the big slicer. She was wearing a white apron over her jeans and white T-shirt and had a trim but curvy figure, he noticed.

"Every day," he replied.

"Even on weekends?" she asked as she took sliced tomatoes from a big mound of them and added them to the sandwich.

"Yeah, well I've been working on weekends," he said. "Lately."

"Oh—so I'll see you here tomorrow then," she said smiling, handing him the sandwich, which she'd neatly folded into waxed paper. The sandwich had more heft than Mrs. Millefiore's, as though there was more turkey in it. She saw him weighing the sandwich in his hand.

"I put extra turkey in it," she said. "For the dog."

"What's your name?" Billy asked.

"Marcia," said the young woman, who was wiping off her cutting board, getting ready for the next sandwich.

"I'm Billy."

"Hey," she said to him as she nodded to the next customer in line.

Billy walked to the cashier with Karma, who was wagging his tail.

Marcia likes me, Billy thought. *She likes ME. Why?*

I feel as though I've lost two mothers," said Hannah to Devie mournfully. "Pauline was like a mother to me, too." She didn't say, "You're like a mother to me—sometimes sweet, sometimes mean . . . like my mother was."

They sat at the white enamel table in Devie's big kitchen in Montpelier. It was the first time Hannah had been to see Devie in Vermont since she'd moved there. Hannah was crying quietly. Devie stood, walked across the kitchen, and tore a paper towel from the roll above the sink. She came back to the table and handed the towel to Hannah.

"I was so glad when that 'Literature of Death' class was over," said Hannah, accepting the paper towel gratefully.

"You must have been," said Devie, resetting herself into her red chair and lighting a cigarette, turning away from Hannah to exhale the smoke. She had taken up smoking again after having separated from her husband just before moving to Vermont.

"I had to see Pauline twice a week in class even after we had stopped dating," said Hannah. "But I'm glad I took the class," she said, sniffling and blowing her nose into the paper towel. "I'm not so afraid of dying anymore for some reason."

She took a deep breath suddenly, involuntarily, as though she'd been under water and was coming up for air.

"I'm making a list of all the things I'm not going to mind leaving behind when I die," said Hannah.

"Uh-huh," said Devie, exhaling smoke. Devie was more accustomed to talking with Hannah about buttercream icing and muffin recipes than about death. She was getting to know her young friend better. "Like what things will you not mind leaving behind?"

Hannah couldn't tell Devie the truth. If she could have felt safe being honest, she would have said she felt that bulimia and lesbianism would have been good things to leave behind. Instead, she said, "Oh, like a world where everyone thinks they're not good enough unless they look like a Barbie doll. I'll be happy to leave behind a world where children die of starvation, a world that elects Princess Di the most important woman of the last century when Mother Teresa was also a candidate."

"Uh-huh," said Devie, who didn't know what else to say. She hardly thought at all about death. It was all she could do to get everything done each day between running the bakery and raising two boys.

"It's going to be such a relief to leave all that behind," said Hannah. She started crying again suddenly. Devie got up and brought her the entire roll of paper towels.

"What can I do for you?" asked Devie softly.

Hannah took a big risk. She'd seen how Samantha had asked for help, and it had worked.

"I need someone to hold me," said Hannah.

Devie stood, moved her chair closer to Hannah's, and sat down in it again. She leaned sideways and held Hannah, awkwardly, stroking her hair.

* * *

Phoebe quit everything that made her doubt her own inner and outer loveliness. She quit working for her father at his studio. Instead, she got a job at the mall as a Christmas elf. And, because she felt jumpy when she thought about Daryl and his need to save the most vulnerable person of the moment, she stopped seeing him.

At the mall, Phoebe wept on Daryl's broad shoulder, her arms around his strong back, her tears falling on the navy blue cashmere sweater she'd given him last Christmas, their bodies twisted clumsily toward each other. They were at the end of the long, wide corridor of shops where even in the bustle of mid-December shoppers, there was not much traffic. They sat on the edge of a huge planter from the center of which spread a jungly profusion of plants with large, glossy dark green leaves the size and shape of surfboards. Phoebe, on a break, was dressed in green felt as an elf.

She was crying so hard her body shook as she struggled to take in one complete breath between sobs, the aching deep and cold in her chest.

"I'm sorry!" she cried. "I love you so (sob) much, but I just can't trust you anymore because whoever's in the most (gasp) need will get you, at least for a while, and (sob) I can't just always BE HERE for you whenever (sob) you are in the mood to (sob) come home because . . ."

Here she stopped talking and stopped sobbing and took a slow, complete in-and-out breath. She withdrew herself from Daryl, from his handsomeness, his enigmatic power, and, looking at him as much as at the inside of her own heart, said, ". . . because I'm not your mother."

Later, after she had changed out of the pointy green felt slippers she had to wear all day, and peeled off the green tights, she came home and wrote of her agony in her journal.

Despairing Christmas Elf Weeps Beneath Mistletoe!

McIntyre Wraps It Up As Pre-Med Student Pines

Phoebe McIntyre cited lack of trust as the reason she gave the dashing Daryl M. his walking papers only days before Christmas. The beleaguered coed has also quit her glamorous job as a photographer's assistant at her famous father's prestigious studio to pursue yuletide jolliness as an elf at the mall.

"It's all an act," she told sources close to her. "I'm brokenhearted. I've lost my lover and my best friend."

✳ ✳ ✳

Samantha, Scott, Hannah and Kaneesha dragged themselves through the mall, exhausted from Christmas-shopping decision making. The group members chose a lavender-scented candle for Gale. They'd stopped by to see Phoebe at her post as an elf and each of them had given her a hug when they heard that she'd said good-bye to Daryl.

"Really?" said Scott, incredulous. "You broke up with HIM?"

"What do you mean by that?" Phoebe wanted to know. "You think he's the only one who can do the breaking up?"

"I'm just so—amazed," said Scott, fumbling for words. "Surprised, that's all."

"You think it was wrong?" said Phoebe, anxiously.

"NO!" said Scott reassuringly. "You had to do what you had to do. The whole relationship was driving you crazy after a while. I'm just surprised that you were . . ."

"So strong?" said Phoebe. "I know. I'm psyched. I'm not insulted because I surprised even myself. I'm not living with feeling 'less than' anymore. I'm just not going to do it."

Hannah said, "Wow!"

Samantha felt inspired. She wanted to feel more at ease with Len. She puzzled about how it was possible to think you were in love with someone with whom you felt anxious all the time. WAS it really love she felt when she was with Len? She had no idea, and that Phoebe could break up with Daryl, who she had been so crazy about for so long, put her in awe of Phoebe.

When Phoebe was done with her break and had to go back to being an elf, the rest of them had some coffee at the food court and talked about how they felt lonelier at Christmastime than at any other time. Kaneesha said she couldn't understand loneliness. Her father was from a family of fourteen children. She had forty-seven cousins, most of whom lived close enough for family gatherings, though it was hard to find a big enough place to meet. Scott had said that loneliness had nothing to do with cousins, it had to do with whether you felt you belonged, whether you matched with other people.

They were browsing in the record shop when the first cut on the new CD from The Suicidal Clones (*My Faded Genes*) started playing in the store. The lead singer, Claudia Claudia, sang:

I'm a clone and I'm all alone
None of my friends is a clone.
I'm a clone alone, a clone alone, nobody else is one.
How can I disagree with my mother

When I'm her identical twin?
Exactly her in every detail
Obeying HER every whim!
I look in her high school yearbook
And I see my face in there.
There's my slightly goofy smile,
And my long black wavy hair.
I'm a lonely clone, the only clone, nobody else is one!
Who is gonna hang out with me when the day is finally done?
How can I ever differ from my mom
To lead my very own life?
Will I marry the same kind of man she did
And become my father's wife?
I have only my mother's thoughts
Because I have her genes!
What's the point of having a life
That she's already lived?

* * *

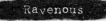

Phoebe wrote:

Lonely Phoebe Has Her Cake and Eats It, Too!!!!!!!!!!

Handsome, heartbroken hunk Daryl Morgenstern confided to sources close to the Tufts pre-med student that his galpal was not with him when he visited his twin sisters in Pennsylvania at Christmas vacation.

"Daryl looked really depressed," said one friend who wished to remain unnamed. "He poured out his sadness and cried. He feels so guilty about breaking up with Gabby and completely crushed about Phoebe breaking up with him," said a schoolmate who accompanied him to the secluded home where Daryl's gorgeous twin teenage sisters now live with their aunt since the tragic and untimely death of their mother from heart disease last year.

"Phoebe misses Daryl horribly," said Hannah Bonanti, a source close to the chubby college freshwoman who has loved Daryl forever. "She's eating tremendous amounts of cake."

P hoeb? It's Han. Do you have a minute?"

"Yeah, I was just writing in my journal. I was writing about me and Daryl, and then I was writing about group the other night. About you, in fact," said Phoebe. "About all your death stuff."

"Yeah, well I just watched an amazing, sad movie," said Hannah. "It was all about death, about total nuclear destruction."

"Sounds like a laugh riot," replied Phoebe. "But I know you probably felt like somebody understood you, huh."

"Exactly!" said Hannah. "It was about how America pushed the atomic bomb button to protect Taiwan against an invasion or something."

"Probably America wanted to protect its factories over there," said Phoebe.

"Anyway," Hannah continued, "everybody gets these little blue pills that will kill them painlessly within five minutes once they are sure the radiation is moving in on them, which is better than dying while throwing up and developing these ugly red sores on their faces and being in agony. And I realized while watching the movie that what is the POINT of being thin and pretty or ANYTHING if we are all going to die anyway? I mean, we ARE dying, just more slowly than in the movie."

"And more painfully than in the movie," Phoebe reflected. "But I try not to think about it."

"Well, I can't help thinking about it," said Hannah. "I just want to sink into a box of Mallomars right now. I feel so lonely. As though the radiation is moving in on me. I don't have a little blue pill."

"Do you want me to come over?" asked Phoebe. "You haven't gotten your car yet, right?"

"Right," said Hannah.

"So, do you want me to come over?" said Phoebe.

"I'm afraid to ask you," confessed Hannah.

"Ask me," urged Phoebe.

"I can't."

"Ask me. I won't come unless you ask me. You have to practice asking."

"Will you come over?"

"I'd love to. Then you'll be keeping me company, too. I'm feeling pretty radioactive myself right now," said Phoebe.

"Could you bring the poodles?" Hannah said. Hannah loved to have Phoebe's poodles sitting in her lap.

"I'll bring the poodles," said Phoebe.

Phoebe was planning on spending New Year's Eve baby-sitting Matthew Blaine, who would be in town for the weekend visiting his grandparents while his mother was away in St. Bart's. And she was planning on spending New Year's Day with the members of the Tuesday night group. They were going to meet for a late lunch at The Wharf Café in Port Franklin, and then, bundled in sweaters and parkas and mufflers and hats, take a walk in the bird sanctuary behind the high school in Maple Ridge.

On Christmas day, as Phoebe was putting her new red sweater into a dresser drawer, Daryl called.

"Phoeb? Are you there? If you're there, please pick up. Please!"

Phoebe felt sick with confusion as anxiety rumbled through her. She hesitated, her heart racing.

"Phoeb—please! I think you're there. I drove by less than an hour ago on my way out of town. I saw your car. Please, Phoeb!"

Phoebe could not find her phone. She looked under a pile of unpaired socks recently out of the laundry, smelling soapy. She pushed aside a stack of magazines, *Mode,* and *Big Beautiful Woman.* The phone was beside her computer, partially obscured by the monitor.

"Hello." She wanted to punish him with her voice, its flat neutral inflectionlessness. She tried to affect a scolding

tone—a thousand-word run-on sentence of denunciation, condemnation and despair distilled into one simple five-letter "hello."

She thought she might have succeeded when he said nothing, as though he'd heard the entire meaning of her thousand words in one word, with all the harmonic parts resonating richly with her disappointment, confusion and grief.

Finally he said, "I'm so sorry. I'm begging here. I'm pleading. I know I have work to do on myself. I'm in my car, otherwise I'd be on my knees."

Phoebe collapsed figuratively into his distant arms. How could she ever resist him?

* * *

I need someone who, if he is going to be obsessed by someone, is going to be obsessed by me!" said Samantha. She was trying out the "N" word. It wasn't so bad, she decided.

"I'm obsessed. I'm totally obsessed with you!" Len declared.

She and Len were sprawled on her bed, torn wrapping paper and tangled ribbons and mangled boxes all around them, some on the bed, some on the floor, one on her night table, a small red velvet box, open, but empty.

Samantha started to sit up. "I need to get up and organize."

"I need you to stay here and let me admire your ring," said Len, reaching for her left hand.

Reluctantly, she lay back down, smiling. "Thanks," she said. "I needed that."

"I need to kiss you," said Len.

"I need you to kiss me," Samantha agreed.

She was hungry, but she was happy, right down to her bones, the bones of a sixty-three-year-old woman, the doctor had said.

Tomorrow, after she'd shown her beautiful opal ring to everyone she knew, she needed to eat again. She needed help with that, needed to overcome the pride which, she'd learned, was a hiding place for her shame. She was always scared of finding it.

Hannah sat in the bakery's little back office, staring at the laptop on the desk, reviewing the day's receipts. Deep in concentration, she squinted at the small, illuminated screen. The fortune cookies were the best-selling items the bakery offered, and Devie was going to introduce them at Botticelli Due in Vermont.

When Hannah thought of Devie—which she did, every day—she thought of her small, darkly intense eyes that had sometimes been so hard. Even though Devie's unkindnesses had been few, it was these that Hannah replayed in her mind over and over again. She hardly thought of what Devie was like the majority of the time—good-natured and appreciative. And when she did think of the many times Devie had shown her kindness, these images lacked substance, seemed less real. It was the pain that came first when she thought of Devie.

She had not told Devie the two things about her that troubled her most. Hannah could hear Gale's voice in her mind: "You don't have to tell everyone everything about yourself to give yourself high scores for honesty. You have to have boundaries. Be discriminating. Trust takes time. With Devie, you still don't have that. It's all right, Hannah. YOU'RE all right."

Hannah was hearing Gale's voice now along with the ones that told her she was bad.

"It's all right, Hannah. YOU'RE all right," would sometimes replace the voice that told her how hopeless she was. She didn't know which voice to believe, but she did trust Gale.

She looked at her watch—only three hours before she'd be standing beside Abbey as her maid of honor at the wedding.

Hannah had made the cake, of course—white, with three tiers edged in candied violets—and had, as a surprise to the bride and groom, placed fortunes inside it. There were 122 fortunes inside the cake, one for each of the slices that would be served to each guest, and all of the fortunes were the same:

If you bring forth what is within you, it will save you.
If you do not bring forth what is within you,
it will destroy you.

* * *

Phoebe, bent forward from the waist (or what, she observed ruefully, would have been her waist had she had less of a meaty midsection), saw Hannah behind her, also folded in half, Hannah's long wild hair hanging onto the pale polished wood floor. The girls often attended yoga class together late on Monday afternoons, and today they were going to visit Samantha at Little Pisa, the restaurant where she worked, afterwards.

They weren't going to actually eat at Little Pisa; they were going to hang out there until Samantha got off and then take a drive to The Wharf in Port Franklin in Hannah's new used black Honda.

Phoebe reflected on how odd it was that, though Samantha had worked at the restaurant, which was noted for its wide variety of interesting pizzas ("Pizza for the Particular" was their motto) since her junior year in high school, she had never once tasted a single morsel of their most popular offerings. Samantha had passed up broccoli and red pepper pizza with bacon, Caesar salad pizza, cheddar cheeseburger pizza, and pineapple coconut chicken pizza, thought Phoebe as she unfolded, took a breath, stood up straight, and then even straighter for mountain pose.

Phoebe was glad Hannah had agreed to come to yoga this afternoon, especially since she'd had a binge at the bakery the day before. Though Hannah had been bingeing a couple of times a week for a while, she'd never, until yesterday, done so at the bakery. Now, virtually overnight, thought Phoebe as she perched on her lavender yoga mat on all fours to prepare for downward dog, Hannah had become afraid of being at the bakery, which had formerly been her sanctuary.

Phoebe glanced briefly in Hannah's direction as she moved from downward dog into cobra pose, and saw the strain in Hannah's face, the sadness and defeat in her eyes. Phoebe knew it was Hannah's dad's wedding on Sunday that had unsettled her. She told Phoebe she'd eaten so much that she was afraid if she didn't throw up, something inside her would burst. But she hadn't purged. That, she told

Phoebe, would have been too awful. She couldn't let herself go there, slide so far down again.

Phoebe noticed how swollen Hannah's belly looked, and how puffy her face was. Hannah said carbohydrates in the quantity she'd eaten them made every inch of her bloat. She'd eaten an entire bowl of chocolate-chip cookie dough, emphasizing to Phoebe that "an entire bowl" in a bakery was far bigger than a bowl a normal home kitchen might have. She'd eaten two loaves of bread (rosemary herb and Tuscan olive) with butter, and five iced-chocolate cupcakes.

Hannah, along with the rest of the class, turned over onto her back for wheel pose. Phoebe could see that Hannah was not moving with her usual fluid grace, the weight of her worry and of the cookie dough making her move more slowly and more clumsily.

Before the class had begun, Hannah told Phoebe she didn't know if she could work at the bakery anymore now that she had betrayed herself there.

Phoebe tasted the minty toothpaste flavor of Daryl's tongue and the sweetness of his breath. Daryl's breath, she reflected, was as fresh and milky as a baby's. His skin was creamy and taut, and the volumes and contours of his muscles were proportioned like those of the marble statues of gods.

Were these the qualities that defined Daryl? Did his beauty make him who he was? Or was it something about Daryl the person, his warmth, his sincere interest in people, for example, that made him so attractive? Daryl's personal qualities were certainly admirable. It was confusing.

Phoebe tried to imagine Daryl BEING Daryl, but looking some other way. She found that she could not. She could not separate Daryl the person from his handsomeness, and it made her uneasy.

Daryl held Phoebe close, so close she could feel his breath on her neck, but she was thinking about Billy. Billy brought her bouquets of fragrant peonies and made her laugh. He drew cartoons for her depicting the two of them in mock peril: the two of them, waiting on an endless line at the Moonstone Café with everyone else dressed in J. Crew and L.L. Bean, but with Phoebe dressed as Wonder Woman and Billy dressed as Batman, except that the letters across Billy's chest spelled "Fatman."

Phoebe let herself be held by the man of her dreams, but her heart was full of longing.

T

o All My Readers:

I wish I could talk to each one of you individually, but I cannot. However, at times when I have talked to young people in distress, most of them have expressed the feeling that there is no one for them to talk to who they think would understand.

I encourage you to talk to your parents. Even if you think they will not hear you or not understand what you're going through; even if you have talked to them before, wanting to share the secrets of your heart but not receiving the response you had hoped for: *Talk to them again, now.* Then, if they cannot listen the way you need them to, talk to your guidance counselor, your family doctor or a teacher whom you trust. *It is extremely important that you not suffer in silence any longer.* The sooner you get help, the sooner you will feel better and the easier it will be to change the direction of your life.

If you try all the above and still can find no one who can help you, I recommend you contact one of the following organizations:

American Anorexia/Bulimia Association, Inc.
www.aabainc.org

National Association of Anorexia Nervosa and Associated Disorders
P.O. Box 5112
Eugene, OR 97405
503-344-1144
www.anad.org

The National Anorexia Aid Society
5796 Karl Road
Columbus, OH 43229
614-436-1112
www.eatingdisorderinfo.org

S.A.F.E. Alternatives
7115 West North Avenue, Suite 319
Oak Park, IL 60302
1-800-DONTCUT
www.selfinjury.com

Eve Eliot has had a private psychotherapy practice for eleven years and is cofounder of the popular Menu for Living Weekend Workshops for compulsive eaters, currently offered in Manhattan and East Hampton, New York.

Eve appeared on *The Sally Jessy Raphael Show* twice this year, the first time on March 22 on a show featuring three fifteen-year-old girls entitled, "I Hate Everything About Myself." She was invited to return a second time for a show aired on July 10 entitled, "Pro-Anorexic Web Sites." She has been interviewed on radio numerous times in the past year in connection with her first book, *Insatiable,* and has been interviewed for more than a dozen newspapers, including *The*

Boston Globe. Since the publication of *Insatiable,* she has received daily e-mails from grateful readers expressing the hope that there will be another book.

She will be a presenter at HCI's fourth annual Anger, Rage, Trauma and Addiction: The Connection conference in Las Vegas, scheduled for March 14–16, 2002. Her presentation is entitled, "Insatiable: When Too Much Is Not Enough."

She is a sought-after expert in the field of eating and body image disorders and is a consultant to both The Caron Foundation's ACOA Treatment Week and their Compulsive Eating Treatment Program. Eve is in recovery from all the major eating disorders and finds personal experience to be her most powerful tool for helping others change.

Also from
Eve Eliot

Code #8180 • $12.95

Insatiable, the precursor to *Ravenous,* is the compelling story of four teens, food and its power.

Code #942X • $14.95

Let's face it—the pressures of life can be overwhelming.
Now, for the first time ever, *Chicken Soup* tackles some
of your biggest and most difficult issues.

A **Taste-Berry™ Teen's Guide to Managing the Stress and Pressures of Life**

With contributions
from teens for teens
Bettie B. Youngs,
Ph.D., Ed.D.
Jennifer Leigh Youngs
**Authors of the national bestseller
Taste Berries™ for Teens**

Code #9322 • $12.95

Conquer your stress the Taste-Berry way! On the days when stress sets in, pressures mount and anxiety lingers—this book will help.

Written entirely by teens, this third volume in the *Teen Ink* series focuses on the highs and lows of relationships with friends and family.

Code #9314 • $12.95

Code #9136 • $12.95

Code #8164 • $12.95

Telephone (800) 441-5569 • Online www.hcibooks.com
Prices do not include shipping and handling. Your response code is BKS.